Praise for James Luger's Prev

"I peeked at page one and stayed up all night. I couldn't put the damn thing down!"
— Larry Stoller (Minnesota USA)

"Wow, what a novel! Lots of surprises, twists and turns, and unexpected mysteries."
— Janine Nu Huynh (San Jose, California)

"Your written words took me there. I enjoyed reading it so much."
— Marjorie Vincenti (Perth, Australia)

To Katie

Jim Luger

Return to Iquitos

Suspense and Romance on the Amazon River

A Novel

James Luger

HIGH FLIGHT
PUBLISHING

Published by High Flight Publishing LLC™
Minneapolis, Minnesota

Copyright © 2021 by James Luger, Minnesota USA. All rights reserved.

ISBN: 978-1-7330982-6-7

This book is also available as an e-book, ISBN: 978-1-7330982-7-4

A CIP catalogue record for this title is available from the Library of Congress.

This High Flight Publishing paperback edition published 2021

Printed in the United States of America

Edited by Hollis Willeford
Map illustrations by BMR Williams
Interior design by Lin White
Cover design by Jessica Bell

For author information, comments or questions, and forthcoming book announcements, please visit www.JamesLuger.com

With love to Judy, my supportive wife and best friend.

Previous suspense romance novel by James Luger

Lost in Dalat

A woman's father was reported MIA just a few days before she was born. While growing up fatherless, she always felt an empty place in her heart. When her adult life eventually unravels beyond hope, she travels to Vietnam to search for her father's last battleground, hoping that a spiritual connection with him will heal her emotional turmoil. While in Vietnam, she falls in love—but deadly forces are soon unleashed against her.

RETURN TO IQUITOS is a fictional story very loosely based on an expedition my friend Hollis Willeford and I organized into the wilds of the Peruvian Amazon Forest. We journeyed hundreds of miles upriver in a wooden thatched-roof boat to the powerful clash of two Andean Mountain rivers that converge to form the mighty Amazon River. On another trip, we trekked through the foothills of snow-capped Andean Mountains. These two explorations formed the backdrop of this story.

The characters in this novel, however, are purely fictional and the locations were chosen arbitrarily, without any reference or comparison to actual individuals, places, or events. Any likeness to a real person, either living or deceased, is unintended and purely coincidental.

—James Luger

Return to Iquitos

COLOMBIA

ECUADOR

AMAZON
JUNGLE

Iquitos·

·Tamshiyaco

Amazon River

Genaro Herrera·

Marañon River

Ucayali River

Contamana·

BRAZIL

Pucallpa·

·Tingo Maria

·Huaraz

Andes Mountains

PERU

N
W   E
S

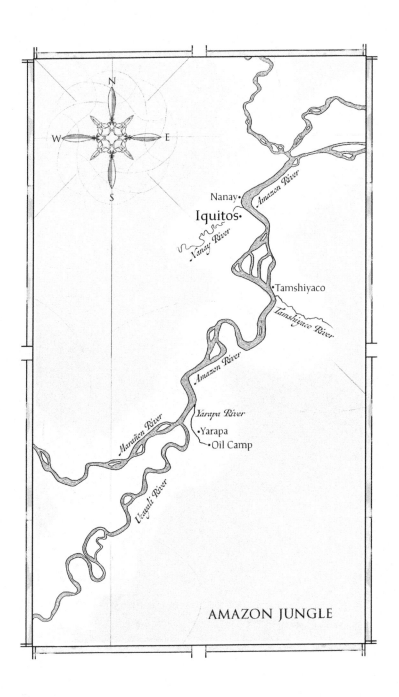

AMAZON JUNGLE

Chapter 1

Early Friday evening a few Peruvian policemen drifted into the bar for their weekly gathering at Iquitos's *Restaurante del Selva*. But their usual bluster and grumbling slipped into something more sober this time—hushed rumors about the American sitting alone with a beer in the adjoining dining room.

The gossip livened when the officers started one-upping each other about what they claimed to know about the shadowy American named Mitch Winslow. And they spoke of grave concerns about what they did *not* know about him.

They all agreed that Mitch must be involved in something illegal or immoral—or both—and it was obviously making him rich. Their only complaint was that he never shared his good luck with those who could help him, or could leave him alone. They never heard of him tipping officials or policemen with gifts of money or liquor—not even cigarettes. You can't trust a man like that.

Mitch knew they were talking about him, but tonight he was more distracted by Darla Peters' lateness. He always counted on her being late, but the usual wait time had become longer with the passing of days, as if the tedious pace in Iquitos had slowly entangled her like a strangle vine. But it was more likely just the laziness, he decided. And that was inexcusable, in Mitch's view. Sloth was not a virtue.

When his mental lecture quieted down, he had to admit that his own energy had become sluggish over time. The sweltering equatorial heat eventually weighs on a person, especially midday when the overhead sun almost baked the city into a stuporous standstill. And there was no relief from a breeze in the jungle, except from one's own making while walking through the heavy air. And after the sun set for the day, it left behind enough heat to last through the night.

But Mitch always found relief when he cruised up the Amazon River, with his boat full of trade goods. He would be leaving again tomorrow, and that prospect buoyed his spirits while he took a swallow of his barely-cool beer.

Marcel DuPreise, owner of the restaurant, lumbered over to Mitch's table while dabbing his baggy cheeks with a yellowed handkerchief. "Where's Darla tonight?"

"She's supposed to be sitting right here with me," Mitch said.

"She might be with a secret lover, Mitch, someone more interesting than you."

Mitch sniffed a relaxed laugh. "In that case, Marcel, you can be my date tonight."

Marcel dragged a wood chair out from the table. He sat heavily across from Mitch and set his highball glass on the table. "Maybe she had trouble with her fishes again."

"Yeah, her save-the-earth fish farm. I keep reminding her that the rivers are already full of fish."

"I'm sure she appreciates your reminders."

"Fish don't need farmers, Marcel. They do just fine with freedom."

"Yes, but freedom makes them harder to catch."

"Don't tell me you like her stupid fish farm idea."

Marcel took a sip of his rum-and-cola highball and set the almost-empty glass back on the table. "No, but someone must like her idea. Someone with money, I think."

"And maybe someone who wants more than her fish."

Marcel smiled and shrugged. He knew about the failings of good-intentioned newcomers like Darla. North Americans, especially, have brought their ideas about taming resources and people in perhaps the most untamed place on earth. Some came to prospect for gold in the rivers, others paid local men to harvest rubber in the jungle. A few misguided gringos have tried to teach local people how to alter their traditional lives in some idealistic way. But the rivers and the jungle and the people remained as always, long after the fortune hunters and zealots gave in, gave up, and went home.

Marcel had seen this progression back when he piloted cargo boats up and down the Amazon River from Peru to Brazil, hauling exotic lumber or plywood processed in Iquitos. When those opportunities temporarily thinned, he would pack a chartered boat's hold with gunnysacks of coca leaves, which had been trucked down treacherous roads and trails from the Andes Mountains. He sold the coca at the port of Leticia, Columbia, a short trip downriver from Iquitos, Peru. The coca would then find its way to makeshift mountain camps, to be processed into cocaine.

Working in any link of the narcotraffic chain was dangerous business, though, and Marcel had reluctantly risked that trade only a few times.

But now those adventures were behind Marcel DuPreise. He had settled permanently in Iquitos ten years ago after falling in love with a pretty but tough-minded local woman. He spoke very little Spanish at the time, and she didn't a speak word of English or French. But they both understood the language of love. Now he spends his nights in the restaurant his wife inherited from her parents. He and his wife grew it from a neighborhood eatery to one of the most popular restaurants in Iquitos, with white linen table cloths and waiters in white shirts and black pants. Every evening, you would find Marcel sipping rum-and-cola highballs and smoking American cigarettes from his private bistro table in the dining room's back corner, making sure the food and service were flawless, and trouble-makers were promptly dispatched.

***

When Mitch Winslow arrived in Iquitos two years ago, rumors trailed him like hungry dogs. He arrived as a deck hand on a rusting Turkish ship that had docked at Iquitos for plywood. Mitch became deliriously sick while in port, and the ship's captain left him behind with a few hundred dollars of back pay.

Mitch rented a bed from a family who lived in a floating riverside raft shack. He recovered a few weeks later, thanks to their care, and after paying them, he bought a derelict boat that had been tied up and for sale for years at the Iquitos wharf. It was a grand old steal-hulled river trawler that had been out of service for a few years because of repairs that never happened and parts that never arrived, and an owner who stopped caring. But Mitch cared when he saw it. He visualized beauty behind the scaly hull and sun-bleached woodwork.

He hired the family that had nursed him back to health. The husband and wife, and their two children—a young girl and a younger boy—went to work sanding the teak woodwork, then restored it with rubbed palm oil. The children then polished all the metal brightwork they could reach, including all copper and brass fixtures, while the parents sanded and painted the hull glossy midnight black with glacier white trim. Mitch bought marine-quality enamel cheaply from a sailor who stole it from the merchant ship he worked on.

While the family restored the boat's beauty, Mitch worked on the mechanicals below. He freed the two engines' seized cylinders with machine oil. After that he cleaned the gas lines and filters, he overhauled the diesel injectors on both engines. His last task was to overhaul the generator and recharge the batteries.

When the renovation was done, Mitch summoned the family and bestowed on them the honor of being his first crew members. For the initial launch celebration, Mitch spent almost ten dollars to buy rubber sandals for the children, a yellow cotton dress for the wife, and for the husband, a green baseball cap with a Peruvian flag patch sewn onto the front.

The next morning, Mitch showed the children how to coil the tiedown ropes at the bow and the stern. Then he invited the parents to join him in the wheelhouse. He turned the ignition switch for the first time, and the electric starter shrieked for several revolutions before the engines coughed and wheezed and sputtered their way back to smoky life. Mitch carefully engaged the gears, and the driveshafts spun freely after some initial grumbling. The boy and girl held the guardrail and waved at onlookers who gathered to see the old boat proudly waddle away from the pier, and make its way onto open water. The children crewmembers cheered when Mitch gave a long victory blast with the horn. The exhaust from the rear stacks sent gray plumes of smoke into the still air, and when Mitch sounded his horn again, heads turned all along the riverfront quay.

Later that evening, Mitch rummaged through the ship's old logs over a beer in Marcel's bar. The boat had been named *Paraiso,* which is Spanish for Paradise—a name that would prove ironic in the months to come.

Mitch soon hired a local out-of-work boat pilot named Luis Riva, who also worked as a guide, interpreter, and sometimes prospector. Marcel had enthusiastically recommended Luis for his resourcefulness, honesty, and guts. Initially, Mitch compensated Luis by letting him give local residents hour-long rides aboard Paraiso on Sundays. After paying for the fuel, Mitch let Luis keep any extra money or trade goods he was able to negotiate from the passengers.

More rumors about Mitch had drifted through town when he and Luis started taking Paraiso on long trading expeditions far up the Amazon River. He mysteriously passed by mestizo villages on the way, not stopping to trade goods with the mixed-blood residents. Rumor had it that Mitch found a more a profitable destination far upriver in uncharted territory. And he had always returned to Iquitos, amazingly, with American dollars.

***

Darla Peters finally strode into the dining room with a woven bag over her shoulder and a ready smile for Mitch and Marcel. Darla might have adopted the Peruvians' lack of punctuality, but she still carried the brisk gait of a North American.

Marcel got up and offered the chair to her. She dropped her bag next to the table and sat down, then nodded a thanks to Marcel. She refreshed her smile for Mitch, hoping to offset his scolding look.

"Did your farm fish get sick again, *ma cherie?*" Marcel asked.

Darla dropped her smile. "More than half of them belly-up this morning." She glanced at Mitch and waited for a sarcastic remark.

"That sucks," he said with a bit of sincerity.

Marcel waved for a waiter's attention and ordered a glass of Darla's favorite Chilian white wine. "Try a little rum in your fish tanks. I've heard that some tropical fish traders do that to calm their catch."

"I don't think the fish need calming. But I do think the workers had something to do with this. The three of them asked for higher wages again last week. As usual, I told them I didn't have enough money yet, but they just stared at me and waited as if that shouldn't matter."

"It's because they don't understand how free enterprise works," Mitch said, perking up to the discussion now. "Remind them that dead fish, especially when poisoned, can't be sold, and without sales, there is no money to pay them."

"They're not stupid, Mitch. They just think all American gringas come from rich families or have rich husbands somewhere. I once mentioned that many American women own businesses and earn their own money. They just smiled, too polite to call me a damn liar."

Mitch leaned back in his chair. "How about this. Tell them you get lots of money from the U.S. government, but most of it is pocketed by officials in Lima, and the rest skimmed by Iquitos's mayor and the police. They'll believe that."

"But it's not true."

"So what? They already think you're a liar. They'd believe this story, and it would give you some credibility, maybe even sympathy."

A waiter set Darla's glass of wine on the table, and she took a quick sip. "They should at least give me credit for trying to help Peruvians. A fish farm like mine could feed a lot of hungry people."

Mitch sat back in his chair. "Sure, then they'll depend on you instead of the river. Listen, Darla, no one's starving in Iquitos. They might lack a lot of things, but the Amazon River hasn't run out of fish yet."

Marcel realized the conversation no longer included him. He got up and said "I must check my waiters before they steal too much from me. Enjoy your dinners. I recommend the paiche tonight. It was caught this afternoon."

Marcel stopped at the bar to buy the policemen a round of pisco—Peru's traditional white grape brandy—before they left. They appreciated his personal gesture, even though Marcel never charges them for their drinks. This arrangement was profitable for Marcel, because it afforded him special favors, both official and unofficial. For example, officials looked the other way when he spliced into an electric wire on a nearby cement power pole, giving him unmetered electricity. The police would rough up any airport ground crewman who was caught pilfering Marcel's weekly liquor shipment from Lima, and when drug traffickers were in town, no one bothered them while in Marcel's restaurant.

Shortly after the policemen left, a waiter brought Darla and Mitch plates filled with grilled paiche fish steaks with a side of tangy chimichurri sauce, mashed manioc, and steamed onions. Marcel's restaurant was the only place in Iquitos where you could always count on fresh paiche, the area's most prized river fish. Whenever he needed another of the hundred-pound or so fish, he would tell one of his waiters to take his speedboat to nearby villages to find a paiche that had been trapped and kept alive. After the local fish monger beat it senseless, the waiter would speed it back to Iquitos to fillet it and store the meat in the designated refrigerator in the kitchen.

Darla said "I didn't have time to buy your favorite beer, Mitch. Can I substitute wine tonight?"

"Fine." But Mitch was preoccupied with something going on behind her at the bar.

She glanced over her shoulder. "What?"

Two men had walked in and were pulling up stools at the far end of the now-vacant long bar. They both wore American-style straw cowboy hats and baggy Patagonian rancher pants. Their outfits looked comical this close to the equator—the best of horses would die of disease or heat exhaustion in the jungle, or get nibbled to death by clouds of insects.

The men looked Darla over with whispers and menacing grins.

"They're just some trafficker's bag men," Mitch said, his jaw flexing. "I'd like to smash the smile off their faces."

"Don't smash anybody tonight, okay? You're leaving early tomorrow morning, so let's just enjoy the evening."

"Okay, but these guys are looking for trouble."

"Maybe, but just let the jungle cowboys flirt with me if they want to. They're probably just passing through Iquitos trying to get rich. Like you."

"I'm not rich, Darla, and I'm not trying to be rich. I just want to earn a certain amount of money, then I'll sell my boat and clear out."

"Where to?"

"Costa Rica."

"For fun in the sun? That doesn't seem like you."

"I want to buy a flower farm there."

"You want to be a flower farmer? And you think my fish farm is nuts?"

"I think I'd like the flower business. I worked for the owner for almost a year, and he told me he's ready to sell and retire. He said if I raise five thousand dollars for a down payment, I can gradually pay the balance off from profits, which would give him enough to live on and reduce his taxes on the sale. I thought I could earn the money working as an ocean ship deckhand. That's how I worked my way to Brazil, then up the Amazon River to Iquitos."

"You've never said anything about this dream of yours. Are you sure you know enough about growing flowers?"

"Enough to get started, and I'll get guidance from the owner. You should see that place, Darla. There's a small white house on a hill, where you can see acres of waving fields, and each one a different color. Beyond the fields you can see the dark blue Pacific Ocean. The house catches cool sea breezes all day. I sometimes daydream about that place to forget how hard it is to live here."

One of the men at the bar walked nonchalantly across the dining room toward Mitch and Darla, pausing halfway to pull a sip from his beer bottle.

"You have a cigarette?" he asked.

"No," said Mitch. "Go buy your own cigarettes."

The man forced a grin and turned to his companion, who nodded.

"Maybe señorita have," the man said, still grinning. He nudged Darla's bag with his toe, all the while with an eye on Mitch.

"No *cigarillos*," Darla said.

Mitch rose to his feet and stepped away from the table. "The lady said no cigarettes, shit head."

Darla said, "Leave it alone, Mitch."

The man tried to hold his grin. "You should listen to

your woman."

Mitch clenched his teeth. "And you should listen to me."

The man huffed contemptuously and started to walk past Mitch—but he spun around and punched Mitch in side of his face.

Darla jumped out of her chair. "Hey!"

Before Mitch could regain his balance, the man landed another punch into Mitch's stomach. The few other diners pretended not to notice.

The other man slid off his barstool and rushed toward the fight, but Marcel spun him around by his arm and with his huge fist, bashed the side of the man's head, sending him to the floor. Marcel jumped over him to grab the other man, but Mitch connected a lightening jab that cracked the man's nose. The man reflexively made a wild swing at Mitch but missed, and Marcel caught him in a choke hold while the man twisted and gasped against Marcel's unforgiving death-grip.

Mitch squared off at the man. "Let him go, Marcel. I'll put his lights out."

"Leave his lights alone, my friend." The booming voice came from the restaurant's entrance.

Mitch saw Rafael Domingo standing at the door. His two bulky bodyguards wore expressions somewhere between amused and ready.

Rafael was the most powerful drug lord in the area. He trafficked between coca growers in the Andes Mountains and the cartel-controlled cocaine processers in nearby Columbia. But the Columbians were becoming wary of Rafael. Recent reports from their spies, which they call *falcons,* confirmed rumors that Rafael was setting up his own processing camps in the Andes. Even more alarming to the cartels, he was secretly experimenting with his own lines of distribution directly into European markets—bypassing the traditional Caribbean routes—and from Europe to the United States. Rafael knew the Columbians were on to him. He has his own falcons. And his own bodyguards.

***

The man who Marcel had dropped to the floor staggered to his feet and froze when he saw Rafael. The other man pinched his bleeding nose and gave Rafael a puzzled look, as if he had been an innocent bystander in the middle of some kind of scrape.

Mitch picked up Darla's bag and handed it to her. "Let's get out of here."

"No need to leave," Rafael said. "Please, sit, enjoy your dinners."

Rafael's two body guards stepped toward the fake cowboys with menacing looks, but the beat-up men were already up and rushing toward the exit.

Before they got to the door, Rafael said, "When you make trouble in Iquitos, you make trouble with me. You're both finished here. I'm sending you back to the mountains and you can go back to digging potatoes."

The man with the bleeding nose paused. "But, Señor Domingo, I—"

"Get out before I stop being so friendly."

One of Rafael's body guards grabbed the back of the man's collar and shoved him toward the exit, while the other man rushed past his stumbling companion.

Marcel didn't mind the fracas because his customers applauded when the men were gone. Amused waiters had collected at the kitchen door, and now scurried back to their duties while Mitch settled back down at their table.

Marcel turned to Rafael. "Those are your men? I've never seen them around here."

"They used to collect taxes for me near my mountain compound near Huarez. They came here for a short vacation, but I'll make sure they never return. I'm learning that mountain people can never understand jungle people. They come here thinking they are more important—maybe because they live higher and closer to God. But they have no right to mistreat local people who are my friends and neighbors."

Rafael turned to Mitch. "You are an outsider, too, but you understand and accept life here. I think you should work for me. I will pay you well."

"No thanks. I already have a business."

"Yes, but I will pay you more than you earn on the river. And I will buy your boat for a high price, more than it's worth, and with American dollars."

"I don't need your money, and you don't need my boat."

"If I only had what I needed, I would have to live in the jungle like the Indians. I don't see you doing that."

"I'm not interested in your line of work, Rafael, so let's leave it at that."

"You sound noble, but I have heard some things about you. I heard you can never return to your own country, and you are hiding here."

"Do you believe rumors?"

"Not always. But if you are running from something, Mitch, you might be running out of time. And when your time runs out, who else would buy your boat? I'm your best buyer, Mitch. I can make good use of your boat. But the longer you make me wait, the less I will pay."

Darla cut him off. "This has been a difficult evening for all of us, Rafael. Can this business wait for another time?"

"Of course. I have plenty of time." He gave Mitch a condescending grin and strolled out of the restaurant with his body guards in tow.

Darla sat back in her chair and watched Mitch touch his red cheek.

"Does it hurt bad?"

"Not as much as my ribs. How well do you know that gangster?"

"Rafael? Just a little. He contributed to my fish farm research."

"You accepted his dirty money?"

"Dirty or not, it helps. Rafael helps a lot a people around here."

"What does he get in return?"

"I don't like the tone of that question." Darla got up and pushed her chair in. "If you're finished scolding me, I'm going home." When Mitch started to get up, she added, "Alone."

Chapter 2

Tessa Cortina tearfully considered each item of clothing before stuffing it into her flower-print canvas bag. Anything not absolutely necessary would have to be left behind. She had to travel light.

Her father would be angry about her sneaking away like this. He might even disown her—the way he had publicly disowned her older brother, Estevan. People in her small town of Tamshiyaco would consider it a disgrace for her to turn her back on her father this way, it might even be a mortal sin. As the town's teacher, her father was a highly respected man—even more so than the mayor—and people would pity him for his misfortune, a widower who has been abandoned by both of his disrespectful children.

This morning a long double-deck passenger boat, called a *collectivo,* was scheduled to arrive in Tamshiyaco, the town where Tessa had lived all her life. It was named after the nearby Tamshiyaco River, one of the many tributaries that flowed into the nearby Amazon River. After departing Tamshiyaco, the typically-overloaded collectivo would travel a few miles to its final stop in Iquitos, the largest Peruvian city on the Amazon River.

Tessa could see the Amazon River from her bedroom

window. She would have to hurry to the collectivo with her bag when it arrived, before her father noticed her missing. The letter to him on her bed explained why she had to travel to Lima, to fulfill her dream of attending university to become a nurse. Then, if he permitted her to return home, she might be able to help in the town's medical clinic. If not, she would at least try to get a job at the hospital in nearby Iquitos. But she knew it would be hard for him to understand her dream. He would wonder why a naïve young Tamshiyaco woman would foolishly travel all the way to Lima, live alone in that coastal desert city, surrounded by millions of strangers, some cunning and dangerous. Worse, she would no doubt be helped by her misguided brother. That would be her ultimate disgrace.

Tessa hoped her carefully drafted letter would help her father understand. Whenever she tried to bring up nursing, her father tried to dissuade her. He became angry if she didn't agree with his hope for her, to get married and have children and live in Tamshiyaco for the rest of her life, the way her late mother did—the way all women in Tamshiyaco did.

Ever since Tessa's mother died, her father had groomed plans for her and her brother. He wanted his children to live respectable lives in Tamshiyaco, until they finally joined him and their mother in heaven. But Tessa's brother had disappointed and shamed their father by leaving the village for an immoral life. Now her father's only hope was to at least make sure his daughter lived like a proper Tamshiyaco woman. But today she would disappoint him.

Tessa could tell by the sun's position that it was almost midday. The collectivo should have been in Tamshiyaco long before now. When it finally did come, it would be behind schedule and the captain might be pressed to leave immediately after a hasty stop.

She glanced at the letter to her father on her bed, and hated the vision of him reading it, filling his heart with contempt. She grabbed her bag and ran out of the house, praying that he might understand at least a little, and maybe a little more with the passing of time. She hoped that she could someday return to Tamshiyaco to fulfill her calling as a nurse, to have her own identity instead of the shame of being her notorious brother's younger sister.

She strode toward the river's pier, but not fast enough to attract attention. She looked straight ahead so her eyes would not meet anyone else's. But when she got to the concrete stairway leading down to the riverside pier, she skipped a breath and stopped. Her father stood on the landing below, talking to a local fisherman. She had told only her best friend about her plan, and that friend apparently betrayed her. But now that wasn't important. Now she had to confront her father.

Tessa stepped carefully and quietly down the stairs. When she got to river's edge landing, she stopped, glancing again upriver for the collectivo. The man with her father stopped talking when he saw Tessa. He left when her father turned around and took a step toward Tessa, his eyes wild with emotion. "Do you have to sneak away? Like a thief? Like your dead brother?"

Tessa gasped. "Estevan is dead?"

"He is to me."

"I left a letter for you on my bed."

"A letter? You don't have the respect to talk to your father?"

"We've talked many times about this, Father."

"Yes, and you always refused to respect my advice. So now

you are going to humiliate me and shame the soul of your poor mother."

Tears collected in her eyes. "It's not fair to say that. I'm only going to Iquitos for now. Maybe I'll be afraid and come back home."

"Come home with me now, Tessa, and we'll leave this mistake behind us."

"I'm sorry, Father."

"You should be."

"Even if I go all the way to Lima, I will come home to visit when I can."

Her father walked up to her and slapped her face. "No, you won't. You no longer have a home here. You no longer have a father or a family."

He strode toward the stairway, but paused and turned to his forsaken daughter. "That fisherman told me the collectivo sank upriver early this morning. Almost everyone aboard drowned. I hope your sin did not cause that."

Tessa felt lightheaded and almost lost her balance. Tears streamed down her eyes and she hid her face in both hands while she cried. When she looked up and sniffed, her father was already gone. Alone now, she faced the river and sobbed. If anyone knew she was there, they were staying away to spare her embarrassment. Or to shun her. She had felt this lonely and helpless only two other times in her life—when she was lost in the jungle overnight, and the day her mother died.

She sat on the hot concrete landing and unzipped her canvas bag, then felt for the gold necklace her mother had given to her. She clasped it around her neck and held the tiny crucifix against her heart, praying to the Virgin Maria for help.

Chapter 3

Hazy morning sunlight saturated Iquitos like an over-exposed photograph. Heavy still air slowed the pace of workers loading Mitch's boat for his journey up the Amazon River. Paraiso's glossy black hull, set off by white trim, gleamed against the silty brown river water. Its brass fittings glistened in the intense sunlight, and a limp Peruvian flag drooped from a flagpole on the stern guardrail.

As always, Luis Riva supervised the loading. Mitch watched from his table at the Gran Maloca, a riverside cafe named for its huge conical thatched roof. The cafe overlooked the entire pier area, and its shade allowed Mitch some relief from the morning heat. He sliced a peeled mango into little smiles on his plate, then chewed them slowly to savor their syrupy perfumed juice. That little ritual helped distract him from his usual edginess before these monthly expeditions to an Australian oil camp, located almost to the Amazon River's turbulent source.

He also found comfort in Luis's ability to properly oversee the loading. The local vendors knew better than to try cheating Luis with provisions that were low grade and high priced.

Mitch had already made a thorough pre-departure inspection of the boat's engines, fuel and oil levels, electric lights and control systems. Still, there was always much that could go wrong on an expedition like this. Except for a few mestizo towns and Indian villages along the way, he and Luis would be on their own through the remotest section of the Amazon River, one of Earth's wildest stretches.

They would make their last stop just short of the Amazon's headwaters, where two roaring rivers from the Andes Mountains—the Marañon and the Ucayali—collide into a roiling fight for direction, then conjoin to create the wide, placid Amazon River. Because of differing origins, the two rivers arrive tainted by a unique blend of silts and tannins. This gives the Amazon River's opposing shorelines different tints of brown for a few miles before gradually blending into a light shade of tan that reflects the brilliant sky's deep blue.

***

The morning of departure, Luis Riva supervised barefoot boys carrying boxes and baskets on their shoulders, each containing beer, plastic bottles of water, and food like canned butter from New Zealand and canned bread from Canada. The boys followed each other from pickup trucks along the wharf area, then down to the pier to where Paraiso was tied. A bony old iceman wearing nothing but dark green shorts followed behind the younger porters, balancing a massive slab of dripping ice on his leathery brown shoulder.

Luis had arrived at the waterfront at dawn to supervise the early loading of delivered trading goods. Two vans arrived and kept porters busy hauling crates containing radios, flashlights, batteries of various sizes, kerosene lanterns, cans of kerosene, and boxes of 16-gauge shotgun shells. The oil camp workers kept shotguns to hunt for fresh meat, usually monkeys, waterbirds, and crocodiles, and to discourage attacks from unfriendly Indians.

Porters rolled four ten-gallon tanks of gasoline onto the boat, and brought two small gasoline generators. A long-shaft outboard riverboat motor was added, with six chain saws, and spare chains. Luis always ordered bags of colorfully wrapped Brazilian hard candy to treat mestizo children along the way. Any gifts to Indians, usually a handful of cigarettes, could only be given to the chief, who would then share puffs with members of his tribe.

The mestizos—people with a mix of Spanish and indigenous blood—typically had little or no money for trade goods, but in some villages, men made trips deep into the forest where they tapped sap from scattered wild rubber trees. They cured the sap by slowly rotating poles over camp fires while oozing fresh rubber sap over the growing ball at one end. They hid the basketball-sized balls near their village, and sold them to the raw rubber dealers who came from Iquitos two or three times a year. When the Paraiso arrived, they were ready to spend their earnings on fishhooks, casting nets, cigarettes, antibiotic ointment, tee shirts, fabric to sew into dresses, sneakers, and baseball caps with American logo patches that no one understood. Once a village man asked who John Deere was. Mitch tried to explain about tractors, but there are no farms in the western Amazonian forest, so this led to even more confusion. Luis finally intervened and said John Deere was a famous saint.

Sometimes men would ask Mitch for a job as a deck hand, to work their way up or down the river. But he and Luis could handle Paraiso alone. He also declined offers of fruits and dried meats in exchange for passage to other villages. Hauling passengers would be much more troublesome and less profitable than hauling trade goods.

The last item to be loaded that morning was brought directly from the hospital, a re-supplied backcountry first aid case with malaria medicine, antibiotics, syringes and fresh vials of snakebite antivenom.

After the porters left, Luis joined Mitch in the Gran Maloca Cafe.

"We have almost everything," Luis said, "The fruit was too ripe, and the baker stayed home today. He's sick with worms again and his healer is treating him with poison berries."

"Maybe we can stop along the way," Mitch said, stretching his arms. "Sit down, Luis. Have a coffee."

"No coffee. I already have enough strength this morning." Luis sat down and took off his New York Yankees baseball cap. He treasured this American hat because Mitch had given it to him. He heard that New York was bigger than Iquitos, but smaller than Lima, and a friend told him that Yankees are some kind of revolutionaries.

Luis said "Is Darla coming to see you off?"

"We had dinner together at Marcel's last night. It didn't go well."

"She will love you again when we get back."

"There's never been any real love between us. When I leave Iquitos for good, she won't be with me and she won't miss me."

Luis leaned forward with his elbows on the table. "When are you planning to leave Iquitos?"

"Someday."

"Is someday very soon?"

"When I get enough money, I want to buy a flower plantation. I know about one in Costa Rica."

"I heard Costa Rica is beautiful, like America. There is no fever there, and no mud or crocodiles. You can eat anything that grows there—even flowers, I think. Luis put his hat back on and gazed across the river. "I sometimes forget that we have been working hard so you can leave."

"I was planning to talk to you about that, Luis. I want you to come with me. I'll need help managing the plantation, and when we make enough money, we'll bribe government officials to let your wife and children join you."

"That is a good plan, Mitch. I have never had a friend as good as you. But Iquitos will always be my home. And what would we do if fungus kills the flowers, or communist revolutionaries take your plantation? My family would starve, and it would be my fault for leaving Iquitos."

"Let's keep it simple. When I have enough money saved, I'll sell Paraiso, and split the profit with you. We'll run her downriver to Brazil and sell her for a good price at Belém. That way you can come back to Iquitos a rich man."

Luis's expression grew solemn. "You are very generous, my friend."

"There's something else I wanted to tell you. I plan to sign papers at the bank authorizing you to take the money from our checking account if I die."

"What about your family in America?"

"I don't have a family."

"That is very sad, Mitch, but I will make sure you do not die. I like you better than money."

A short, muscular man wearing a red Hawaiian shirt and a conspicuous Panama straw hat strolled into the Gran Maloca. Eddy Whisp, an American who lives in Iquitos, carefully scanned the dining room. He always seemed suspicious about something. The prevailing gossip—which, of course, was never reliable but always believed—is that Eddy was an American spy. This was conclusive because he seemed to have nothing better to do than to go around asking people strange questions, especially about newcomers who obviously were not tourists, but hung around Iquitos when they didn't have to.

Rumors also confirmed that Mitch was a spy. In his case, the prevailing logic was that an American gringo wouldn't move to Iquitos unless he was either a CIA or DEA agent— or was crazy, which Mitch didn't seem to be.

After looking over the pier area, Eddy moseyed over to Mitch and Luis's table.

"I was hoping to find you here," Eddy said. He ordered coffee, then pulled up a chair to join them. After removing his hat, Eddy pushed back his sweaty blond hair with his fingers. "Is it getting hotter around here, or is it just me?"

"It's always hot in town," Luis said. "When you move to your farm land, the jungle's canopy will shade you."

Eddy exhaled and nodded. "That move could take a while, I'm afraid. I'm still entangled in legal problems over title to the land."

"You've been tangled since I've known you," Mitch said. "At this rate, you'll go nuts proving you can grow veggies in the jungle."

Eddy said, "I've learned to be patient, and it'll be worth the wait. That particular acreage is valuable because of its black topsoil. An archeologist told me that prehistoric people must have successfully farmed that area after bringing top soil down from the Andean foothills."

"I hope it pans out for you, Eddy. You're patient all right. Some say *unbelievably* patient."

"People say all kinds of things about me—and about you. By the way, I heard you got into a tiff with a couple of Rafael's goons last night."

Luis cut the conversation short by getting up from the table. "I must check how our supplies were stowed by the porters. We can leave whenever you want, Mitch."

Eddy said, "Say, Luis, there's a Cuban ship docked downriver at the plywood plant. Isn't that unusual when the river is this low?"

Luis pondered for a moment, as if wanting to offer Eddy something of value. "I haven't heard anything, but maybe they're just loading plywood."

"Yeah, it could be that simple."

After Luis left, the waiter set a steaming cup of water on the table. Eddy looked up at him. "Where's the coffee powder?"

The waiter said with a blank expression, "One moment please," and strolled back to the kitchen.

Eddy shook his head at Mitch. "Peruvians, man. They can screw up a steel ball."

Mitch bristled at the putdown, but said nothing. He had known Eddy for almost a year, and although Eddy apparently hated Peru, Mitch never cornered him about his flimsy reason for staying. As if returning the courtesy, Eddy never questioned Mitch's past. Mitch reasoned that if Eddy was an American intelligence agent, as everyone seemed to believe, he'd know all about any American who settled in Iquitos.

The waiter soon returned with a jar of instant coffee and a spoon, and then left. Eddy wiped the spoon with his shirt and stirred a spoonful of the black coffee crystals into his cup. He glanced over his shoulders, then looked gravely at Mitch. "You should leave Iquitos as soon as you can, Mitch. A friend told me Captain Santos plans to arrest you."

"What for?"

"Oh, he'll make up some ridiculous charge, and then fine

you or jail you, maybe both."

"I haven't broken any laws."

"He'll break one for you. For example, if Santos produced a bag of coke and said it came from your boat, he could arrest you for drug trafficking. He can then legally confiscate your boat when—and not *if*—a local judge finds you guilty."

"Without a trial?"

"Oh, you'd get a trial. But the judge and jury will be taken care of, and you could end up in a stinking Peruvian prison—and I mean for a *long* time."

"All this so Santos can take my boat? It doesn't make sense."

Eddy scooted his chair closer to Mitch. "Santos doesn't want your boat. I'm told Rafael is behind this. And Rafael has something Santos *does* want—lots of money. Rafael also has political connections in Lima—people who could make life either rough or rosy for Santos."

Mitch spotted two uniformed policemen walk onto the pier where Paraiso was tied up. "Damn, I think I'm already in trouble."

One of the policemen appeared to be hassling Luis, while the other officer stepped aboard Paraiso and went below. Within a minute or two he emerged with a small plastic bag in his hand. The two policemen brushed by Luis and strode off the pier and up the concrete stairs to the riverside road.

"You better run for it, Mitch, and I wouldn't come back to Iquitos for a while if I were you."

Mitch threw a few Peruvian soles on the table to pay for his breakfast, and ran toward the pier. Eddy tried to keep up with him.

"I can't afford to clear out of Iquitos yet." Mitch said.

"Maybe you could haul cargo downriver for a while."

"Without my oil camp deal, I'd have nothing to start with.

Besides, I don't think Luis would leave Iquitos."

Luis stepped out of the boat's wheelhouse when he saw Mitch run down the pier.

"Two policemen—"

"I saw the whole lousy thing, Luis. Let's get out of here."

While Luis fired up both engines, Mitch cast off the bow and stern lines, and pulled the short wooden gangplank aboard. When he got to the wheelhouse, Luis pushed the two throttles forward and reversed one of the propellers to squirm sideways away from the pier, narrowly squeezing by two rusty fishing vessels.

Luis said "One of the policemen said he found a bag of cocaine below, and asked where you were. I said you were at the Tip Top bar."

A police cruiser made a hasty stop above the wharf stairway.

Mitch said "I think they figured out your trick."

Luis said, "I wondered when Chief Santos would want a bribe."

"Eddy said he wants to arrest me and confiscate Paraiso, then sell it to Rafael."

Luis nodded. "That way he'll get paid by Rafael instead of you. He is a very clever police chief."

Two police officers stood by their cruiser and watched helplessly while Paraiso slowly backed out of the crowded wharf area. Luis turned and cruised full speed ahead toward the deep middle of the Amazon River, which would put them over a mile away from either riverbank.

Mitch peered through the binoculars always kept in the wheelhouse. "We shook 'em off, Luis. I think we can forget about cops for now." He continued to scan the Iquitos waterfront. "The river seems to be getting a little higher."

Luis throttled back to cruise speed. "The rainy season should be starting in the mountains, especially in the eastside foothills. The new water will be bringing some of the uprooted jungle with it."

"What I'm more worried about right now is Santos. He'll be waiting for us when we return."

"Yes, he is greedy, and greedy people are always waiting for something."

"So, I might have to buy my way out of this mess."

"Not if Rafael is behind it. If he's the one who really wants Paraiso, he will outspend you. A boat like this would help him haul more coca to the Columbians in Leticia."

"I'll sink Paraiso before I let any of that happen."

After mulling that over for a moment, Luis said, "Maybe you'll think of a better idea."

Luis and Mitch both studied the river for partially-submerged tree trunks. If they ran dead-on into one big enough, it could rupture Paraiso's steel hull. If that happened, their only hope would be to beach the boat before it sank, and then try to survive in the jungle until another vessel came by—which could take weeks, maybe even months this time of year.

Luis headed Paraiso at an angle toward the far bank.

After a few silent minutes, Mitch gave him a puzzled glance. "Where are you going?"

"Tamshiyaco. It will be our last chance to get fresh bread, fruits, and vegetables. We'll be there very soon."

"It's important that we reach San Fernando before dark."

"We still can. The current against will still be lazy for a few days."

Chapter 4

They could soon see Tamshiyaco, and arrived at the nearby tributary's namesake village late that morning. While two men watched from the village's floating pier, Luis maneuvered the boat toward the wood pier. Mitch was ready to toss tiedown lines to the men when the boat nudged against the pier, and Luis shut the engines off while the men tied the lines.

Mitch had already stepped onto the pier. "Let's hurry."

"Of course."

Luis climbed the cement stairs and smiled at the people starting to collect above the wharf. Paraiso had never been docked at Tamshiyaco before, so residents were especially curious about the stunning boat with such an unusual design. They talked among themselves about where it might have come from and where it was going.

Most of the town's elderly residents remained at a distance. They had their own suspicions about Paraiso's presence, and concluded that the two crew members must be fortune seekers who came to drill into the jungle for oil. There was a frightening rumor that gringo oil men will eventually kill the entire Amazon forest when they have sucked all the black blood out of it. No one in Tamshiyaco had ever seen an oil driller, and no one wanted to.

One of the men said Paraiso was likely a drug trafficker's personal boat. He had been warned about such extravagance from the Catholic priest who came every Sunday in his speedboat to say Mass. The priest said he was told by another priest about a Columbian drug lord who drove a car made from solid gold. This stunning boat could be another example of such sinful excess.

A more ominous, though doubted, suspicion arose during the discussion. The friendly Yagua Indians who lived upriver told one of the villagers that their shaman had seen evil spirits dwelling in black smoke that followed a gigantic canoe wherever it went. This story had been dismissed as fantasy by the mestizo villagers of Tamshiyaco, but now some of them deemed it worth considering.

One of the men reminded them that the Yaguas also believe that when pink dolphins swam close to a monstrous canoe they died. This was particularly troubling to the Indians because they believed the pink freshwater dolphins' spirits were closely related to those of humans. They also believed that a male dolphin could impregnate a human female if she was foolish enough to bathe in the river, and the baby would be born with fins.

The people of Tamshiyaco always agreed these tales were outrageous, and no one admitted to believing them. Still, Tamshiyaco women never swam in the river.

Luis came back aboard the Paraiso carrying clear plastic bags full of bread rolls in his woven bag. He slung the bag up onto the boat deck.

"A man will soon come with vegetables and fruit," Luis said. "I will have to bargain for them."

Mitch waited a couple of minutes, but no vendors

came. "Let's go, Luis. Maybe we can buy fresh foods in San Fernando."

"The bargaining will be quick if I start with our final offer."

"Okay, we'll give it a couple more minutes."

The man soon arrived with a plastic bag full of various fruits and manioc roots. Luis offered a few Peruvian soles, and the man took them, apparently sensing there would be no time for bartering this late in the morning. Luis climbed up onto the deck and Mitch handed the bag to him. While Luis stowed the food below in the galley, Mitch went to the wheelhouse and waited. He unfolded a map of the upper Amazon River, trying to estimate how much distance and time they'd have to make up before nightfall.

It wasn't long before Luis appeared at the wheelhouse door. "A woman needs our help."

It wasn't the first time Luis brought aboard someone in dire need during a stop. One time a teenage mestizo boy was bitten by a snake and needed antivenom. Another time a woman with a problem pregnancy needed passage to Iquitos for a medical doctor. Once they gave an Indian a ride upriver to his village because an injured arm made it impossible to paddle his dugout canoe. They gave him antibiotics and towed his canoe behind with a rope. Luis knew that people living along the river would never ask for help unless they had no other choice. In those cases, Luis would make a convincing plea to Mitch on their behalf, and Mitch always gave in.

"What's her problem?" Mitch said.

"Her problem is very difficult. She needs to reach Lima for nursing school, but her flight leaves Iquitos within the next few days.

"Can't she take a collectivo?"

"The collectivo sank this morning. The next one will be

here too late."

"We might not be able to go back to Iquitos. Did you tell her that?"

"Yes, I told her. But she said we are the answer to her prayers."

"Luis, untie us and let's get going. Someone else can answer her prayers."

"She already came aboard."

"Then tell her to un-board."

"I did but she cannot go back home. Her father disowned her. She won't leave the boat until she speaks to you."

"Oh, yeah? Then drag her off the boat if you have to."

"I have never had to drag a woman."

Mitch got up and tossed his map onto the chair. "Okay, I'll try to reason with her."

Mitch went to the foredeck and saw a woman leaning against the steel rail with both hands, looking down at the river. Her face was partial obscured by wavy black hair, but he could see the profile of a young, attractive woman. She wore white sneakers and a green-and-yellow floral print dress. A colorful woven travel bag lay on the deck next to her feet. When she lifted her head and turned, Mitch could see that her brown eyes were reddened.

"Do you speak English?" Mitch asked.

"Yes, I learned it in school."

"We don't take passengers and we just left Iquitos."

"I will stay out of your way until you return. I have a friend in Iquitos who can pay you when we arrive."

"It looks like you're prepared to leave. How did you know we would stop here?"

"I didn't know. I prayed for help, and you came."

When she absently pulled her hair back over a shoulder,

Mitch saw a red blush on one cheek.

"Did someone hit you?"

"Will you take me?"

"You didn't answer me."

"You asked a private question, Capitán."

"Sorry…but I can't take you anyway. We're going upriver to an oil camp, and it'll be at least a week before we get back to Iquitos. Maybe we can pick you up on the way back."

"I cannot go back to my father's house." With a quick swipe of her hand, she stopped a tear from rolling down her cheek, and then stood rigidly. "I won't be an idle passenger. I will work for you while I'm on your boat. I can cook and wash clothes."

Luis asked, "What is your name, Señorita?"

"Tessa Cortina."

"Tessa, if we take you alone to the oil camp, it might soil your reputation. I already told the baker where we are going and he said some people think the oil camp is inhabited by men who are like wild devils."

Tessa considered this for a moment. "Couldn't I hide somewhere on your boat when we get there?"

"Yes, but we can't control what the people of your village will say, and they will say whatever they can imagine. We would never again be welcome in Tamshiyaco if we were accused of disgracing your reputation."

"My father already feels disgraced by me."

"How? Or is that another private question?"

She looked down at the deck floor "Yes, it is."

Mitch said "Well, Tessa, I wish we could help you, but I'm already brimming over with trouble, and we've got to get underway."

Mitch went back to the wheelhouse alone and started

the engines. He saw Tessa saying something to Luis, and he nodded when she was done talking. Luis went back up the stairs to the wheel house.

"She will even clean the boat," Luis said, "plus cooking and washing laundry. She is desperate, Mitch."

"So, she changed your mind."

"Yes, her mind is strong."

"Maybe she's just more stubborn than you."

"She has to be because her problem is worse than we thought. She cannot go home now because her father has disowned her. He is the respected school teacher here, even more important here than the village governor. Her brother has somehow brought shame to their community, so no man in Tamshiyaco would marry her. She is alone now, Mitch, and without hope. That must be hard for a brave man like you to understand."

"I do understand."

"She said that until her friend in Iquitos pays for her passage, you can keep the gold crucifix necklace her dying mother gave her as a guarantee. She has nothing more valuable."

"I don't want her necklace, or her friend's money."

"Then helping her will especially bring honor and good luck."

Mitch looked out the wheelhouse window and saw Tessa gripping her flowered duffle bag in both arms. He shut the engines down and went back to her.

"All right, miss, you can come with us. But we might have a problem returning to Iquitos. I left behind some trouble there this morning."

A smile blossomed on her face. "I know about leaving trouble behind. I will pray that yours will heal."

Mitch turned to Luis, who gave him a satisfied grin.

"Okay, Luis. I guess everyone's happy now. Let's get the hell out of here."

Luis restarted the engines and opened the throttles. Paraiso eased away from the dock, and Luis resumed their journey up the Amazon River.

***

While standing on the foredeck alone, Tessa dabbed her eyes with her sleeve and carried her bag to the boat's stern. She watched two little barefoot boys from her village run to the end of the pier and wave as if they'd never see her again. Tessa waved back until the boat rounded a bend and the village where she had lived all her life gradually disappeared from sight.

Chapter 5

A few minutes after leaving Tamshiyaco, Tessa sat on the deck, wondering if she would have to stay outside during the entire trip. She heard footsteps on the metal deck and turned to see Luis walking toward her. She picked up her bag and stood up.

"Mitch is at the helm now. Are you feeling better?"

"Yes." She spoke English out of respect for the Anglo captain. "Thank you for helping me."

"I just helped Mitch understand your problem. It was his decision."

"Thank you anyway. How long will it take to get to the oil workers' camp?"

"Just a few days, señorita."

"Does the captain of this boat work for the oil company?"

"No. Mitch doesn't work for anyone but himself. His boat is like a floating *mercado* that shows up a day or two after the oil workers have received a cash draw on their monthly pay."

"Who brings their money to them?"

"Most of it is deposited in a bank in Lima. A small amount, with their mail and basic camp supplies, are brought by a small airplane from Lima. It comes down through a pass in the mountains."

"How does the airplane land in the jungle?"

"It lands on the river. It uses floating tanks instead of wheels."

"I would like to see such a strange airplane someday. Will I sleep outside at night?"

"Oh, no. There is a comfortable bunk in a cabin downstairs. Come with me and I'll show you."

Tessa followed Luis to the companionway door, which was located behind the wheelhouse, then stepped down the stairway to the lower steps. They walked through the narrow passageway toward the stern of the boat. Along the way Luis pointed out where the bathroom and galley were, then he opened the door to her compact quarters.

"You can move any of these cargo boxes to make more room. The sheets are clean and the insect netting is always tucked into the mattress. Those noisy motors below are turned off at night, and you can use a flashlight from the galley cabinet. If you need water or something to eat, take whatever you want from the galley."

"I saw a little stove in there. I can cook meals for you and Captain Mitch."

"You don't have to. You are a passenger, not a crewmember."

"I would like to be both."

"Fine, then I'll show you how to light the alcohol stove when we stop for the night. Mitch has been steering the boat, but now I should take my turn."

After Luis went topside, Tessa pulled the netting free from one side of her mattress and set her bag on the bed. After scooting a few heavy wood boxes closer to the curved hull wall, she sat on the bunk to test its thin but dense mattress. The white sheets were neatly foldeed at the foot of the bed, but there was no pillow. She tried lying on the bed with her bulky bag under her head, and made it more comfortable by removing a few clothes.

She lay on her back and closed her eyes, but the growling engines and her living nightmare prevented any sleep. She couldn't escape the image of her angry her father, and the searing pain from his open hand across her cheek. When he chastised her at the river landing, it was loud enough for curious bystanders to hear, and they would tell others and soon everyone in Tamshiyaco would know about her humiliation. It was as if evil had poisoned her father's soul. He had yelled at her before, but he never slapped her. And he had never rejected her. She had gotten used to living without a mother for so many years, and now she would have to live without a father. She sat up and tried to hold back her tears, but she was alone now, so she let them come.

Her thoughts turned to Luis and Captain Mitch, and she wondered if they might try to harm her. Would they sell her to the oil camp devils? Fear quickened her breathing for a moment and she stopped sobbing. She recomposed herself by grasping the small crucifix on her gold necklace, the one that once belonged to her mother.

After she felt collected, she unrolled a brimmed cloth hat from her bag and put it on, then returned topside. Mitch was sitting in a folding canvas deck chair near the boat's bow, staring ahead. She wondered if he heard her clumsy footsteps up the steel companionway. If so, he was deliberately ignoring her. If not, she might startle him if she said something. She wanted to thank him for letting her come aboard, but it might be too soon for that.

Tessa had seen the same kind of folding chair in her room, so she went below for it. When she got back to the bow,

Mitch's chair was empty. She looked up at the wheelhouse and saw him talking to Luis.

She set up her chair a few feet from his and sat in it. She soon noticed that this stretch of the Amazon River was wider than it was at Tamshiyaco. The Amazon was a deep tan on the shady riverbank, but it reflected blue sky in sunlight. She wondered if the Amazon's massiveness made it appear to be moving slower than it really was. She watched how the thick jungle changed while they moved past it, with varying tree types and hues of green. The trees were similar to those around Tamshiyaco, but taller and with thicker canopies.

She wondered if Mitch was going to return. She wanted to look up at the wide-windowed steering room that she heard the men call a *wheelhouse,* but she didn't want to distract them now. The boat was big, but not big enough to avoid each other for several days. She pulled the visor of her cloth brim hat down to better shade her eyes, and rested with her eyes closed and her head against the tall chair back.

Tessa's head bobbed sideways and woke her from a dreamless sleep. The sun was lower now and Mitch's chair was gone.

Pastel clouds washed over the early evening treetops, and the riverbank shadow on her right had spread its reach. Darkness would soon creep in and replace the fading light. Twilight was always brief in the jungle, and nighttime arrived with barely a warning. Tessa saw the pale moon peek over the river's east treetops, trying to reflect off the darkening water. Soon, fat fireflies blinked and bobbed along the western riverbank.

Luis began to scan the river ahead with a search light fastened to the wheelhouse roof, and controllable inside. He looked for floating jungle debris that might bend the two propellers or get tangled around them, or uprooted trees that could damage the hull.

He slowly guided the boat closer to shore with the engines near idle. As he got closer, he could hear the nocturnal racket alive in the jungle. Giant rats chattered their shrieks, howler monkeys screamed warnings about their territorial claims, and swarming insects buzzed and chirped and clicked in the background. A faint growl interrupted most of the din for a second or two.

When Luis flashed his beam along the river's edge, red crocodile eyes shone from the waterline grasses like bright rubies, and small green eyes of spiders reflected the spotlight's intrusion from the bushes. His light beam found a glistening snake that hung from a branch like a mottled vine. It waited for creatures that didn't notice.

Mitch came down from the wheelhouse stairs with a flashlight, and strode past Tessa as if she wasn't there. He stood at the bow while Luis maneuvered Paraiso with little more than idled power.

Mitch hollered "Three o'clock close!" Tessa stood and saw Luis spin the wheel in the opposite direction to veer clear of whatever Mitch had spotted.

The suspense brought Tessa to the bow rail. "Can I help you watch?"

"Let me know if you see anything floating. Anything at all. Even something small can be big under the water."

Mitch continued to scan the water ahead with his flashlight. Tessa pointed to a twig, and then a turtle's head peering out of the water. She and Mitch both spotted a submerged uprooted tree ahead, and Mitch hollered to Luis, "Dead ahead! Close!"

After Tessa successfully spotted another tangled-vegetation cluster, Mitch handed her the flashlight. "Keep watching and call out what you see. I'll be right back."

Mitch joined Luis in the wheelhouse and said "Where in hell *are* we?"

"We are not in hell, but I think we are near Tambo Yarapa."

"Do you really think so, or are you trying to make me feel good?"

"You can feel good because I think I am right. I've noticed those giant ceiba trees to the left on other trips. Here, I'll show you on the map." Luis pointed to the Yarapa River tributary and slid his finger down to show their estimated location.

Mitch knew that Luis had an uncanny sense of their position, like a taxi driver who knows his city. Luis kept track of the time underway, he recognized foliage changes and the river's width, unusual bends, and their compass heading. After mentally braiding all that together, he might confirm his location with a paper map.

Tessa's beam of light landed on a fallen tree hanging into the river. She looked up and saw Luis showing something to Mitch. "You're heading for a dead tree near the shore."

Luis looked up and spun the wheel hard right. They were almost on top of the deadfall tree, but before he could shift the propellers into reverse, the boat crushed against it. The sudden stop slammed Luis against the steering wheel and Mitch stumbled to his hands and knees. They heard Tessa scream.

Luis cut the engines while Mitch grabbed his flashlight and ran to the bow. The two empty deck chairs had slid up against the bow's guard rail, and Mitch yanked them aside to train his flashlight on the water below. "Tessa! Talk to me!"

He turned to Luis, who was running toward him. "She doesn't answer. I can't see her."

Luis yelled her name, but with no response.

Mitch flashed his light across two uprooted trees, mostly submerged into a dense jumble of interlocked branches. He couldn't see any trace of Tessa, on or below the black water's surface. He handed his flashlight to Luis, then in one move he threw his leg over the rail and jumped into the river. His head bobbed up between two large branches. He gasped for air, then immediately sunk back under. Luis trained his flashlight beam onto that spot. He soon heard Mitch say, "Here..." Luis desperately ran his light across the shoreline and around the fallen trees. The light finally found Mitch, who had his arm around Tessa's back, and the other around a small branch. She hung limply over his shoulder, but with her face out of the water.

"Luis, throw me a rope!"

"Your arms are already too busy. I will bring it."

Luis ran to the steel equipment chest in back of the wheelhouse and pulled out a folding hook ladder and a coil of rope. He ran back to the bow and hung the ladder on the guardrail, then tied the rope to the guardrail. He tied the other end to his waist and jumped in clear of the branches. Hand over hand, he pulled himself through stiff branches that snagged and scraped him like tentacles of a water monster.

Tessa moaned something, but she was barely conscious.

Luis grabbed Tessa with one arm and clung to a branch with the other. Mitch grabbed the rope from him and tied a non-slipping bowline knot under her arms.

"Hurry," Luis yelled. "Water snakes never sleep."

Mitch clutched the rope and pulled Tessa through the water while he swam on his back with one-arm strokes. Luis followed and pulled aside as much debris as he could.

When they reached the boat, Mitch scrambled up the ladder and pulled on the rope to keep Tessa's upper body out of the water. Luis hiked one of his knees up onto the bottom rung of the ladder and lifted Tessa with all his strength. When they got her to the rail, Mitch grabbed under her arms and pulled her across the top of the rail and onto the deck. He knelt and rolled her to her side and cradled her head. Her breaths were labored and shallow. She coughed a couple of times and her eyes squinted open. They squeezed shut again when she coughed harder and gagged and vomited river water onto the deck.

Luis cried, "Help me, Mitch. Something is biting my legs!"

"Hang on. I'm coming."

"Piranhas! Hurry!"

Luis flailed helplessly to keep his head out of the water, while Mitch scurried onto the ladder and reached down.

"Luis, give me your hand."

Luis disappeared under the water for a few seconds, then resurfaced and gasped.

Mitch stepped down to the last rung and grabbed Luis's belt. He pulled most of Luis's body free from the water and struggled to the next rung while Luis floundered wildly with his arms and legs to find a handhold or foothold. His foot found the bottom step, then he grabbed the ladder and pulled himself free of the river. Mitch bent down and grasped Luis's arm to help him to the next step.

They struggled together awkwardly, desperately, until Luis could finally droop his body over the deck rail. He fell onto the deck exhausted. His trouser legs were in shreds and small wounds oozed blood. Whenever he moved, his legs smeared the deck with blood.

Mitch knelt next to Tessa. "Will you be all right for a few minutes while I take care of Luis."

She used all her strength to get up on one elbow, but when

she tried to talk, she coughed and gagged. "I am fine…" She stared at him and whispered, "What happened to Luis?"

"Something in the water bit his legs."

"It looks like many things bit him. Piranhas, I think."

"Luis thought so too."

While Mitch helped him to a sitting position, Luis winced, then mumbled, "I'm afraid we are beached, and maybe worse."

Tessa strained to sit up, her eyes wide now. "Will we sink?"

Mitch said "I don't think so. We're probably just stuck on a mudbank. I'll check everything after I bandage Luis's wounds."

Luis said, "Don't worry, I'll be fine. If we're taking water, that's a bigger problem."

"You're not fine yet," Mitch said.

"At least check the engine hold. If there is a leak, it will show there first."

"All right, but first let's get you below." He looked back at Tessa. "I'll be right back."

She nodded, then looked at the morass that had almost drowned all of them.

Mitch lifted Luis from his sitting position and got him to his feet. He wrapped Luis's arm around his neck to take weight off his legs. They slowly shuffled together that way to the companionway door. It was difficult for them to climb down the steep stairs. Each step was a struggle that forced Luis to pull a deep, hissing breath through clenched teeth. When they got to Luis's room, Mitch helped him roll sideways onto his bed, then lifted his legs onto the mattress.

Luis said "You must leave me now to check the engine hold."

Mitch took a flashlight from the galley and yanked up

the floor hatch, located in the hallway near Tessa's cabin. A quick scan along the riveted seams showed no evidence of water. He closed the hatch and hurried back to the galley, then returned to Luis's cabin with a first aid kit, cloth towels, and two liter bottles of water.

"I hate to hurt you more, Luis, but I have to disinfect those bites."

"You don't have to worry. The pain cannot be any worse."

Mitch pulled off Luis's sneakers, and unbuckled and unzipped his tattered trousers. He carefully pulled one pant leg down a few inches, and then the other until the trousers were free. The bleeding had slowed, but Luis' legs were pocked with small gouges. Piranhas are no bigger than North American sunfish, but their jaws are longer, and are filled with small sharp scissor teeth.

The deepest of Luis's wounds still bled slowly, and some of them were loosely covered with a flap of skin. Mitch unscrewed the cap off a bottle of water and helped Luis take a long drink. That left enough room in the bottle to add pink antiseptic soap from the first aid kit. Mitch put his thumb over the opening and shook the bottle, and then daubed the mixture onto Luis' wounds with a folded washcloth. Luis's entire body tensed up when Mitch patted his legs dry with a fresh towel.

"I have to roll you onto your stomach, Luis. I need to treat the wounds on the back of your legs."

Luis rolled himself over, and Mitch was glad to see Luis's resolve. He refolded the washcloth and drenched it with the treated water. Luis gasped while Mitch gently bathed each bite.

After loosely wrapping Luis's legs with a roll of sterilized gauze, Mitch said, "Will you be all right if I take a minute to check Tessa?"

"Of course. I am fixed now, so don't worry about me."

"I'll leave the other bottle of water on the bed for you. Your body needs water to make more blood."

When Mitch returned to the main deck with a clean towel, he found Tessa sitting cross-legged, propped up with her hands against the deck. Her head drooped and matted black hair concealed some of her face.

Mitch knelt next to her with a towel. "How are you feeling?"

Her eyes opened and her head jerked up with a startled expression. "Better." She sat forward and took the towel and dabbed her face, then tried to blot her soaked hair. "I'm sorry, but my stomach emptied again onto your boat floor."

"That's where it belongs, not in your stomach."

"I must have twisted my neck after I hit the water. I don't remember. I don't remember anything after I fell in the water."

"Do you think you can walk?"

"Yes. I think so."

Mitch put out his hand, but Tessa ignored the offer. He backed away to give her room while she struggled up on wobbly legs.

"Thank you for rescuing me," she said while looking at Luis's blood on the deck.

"Luis is the one to thank. The piranhas caught him before they found you and me."

"Can I see him?"

"Of course, but he might be sleeping now. He has very little strength."

"I will pray for him."

Tessa started toward the companionway door with Mitch following close. When she faltered on one leg, he caught her by an arm. She drew back. "I need to find my own strength."

"A little help won't hurt you."

"You let me ride on your boat, and then you and Luis saved my life. I can't ask for any more help."

He followed from farther back while she tested her footing on each step of the companionway, and clutched the steel handrail. She looked up at him with a thin smile when she reached the last step, as if to reassure him all was well—and then she dropped to the floor.

Mitch rushed down the steps and helped her up.

She said "The boat must have moved."

"You were the only thing that moved. Maybe you got a little dizzy."

"Dizzy? I don't know that word."

"It means trouble keeping your balance."

"I think my legs were dizzy. Should we see if Luis is awake?"

Mitch led her to Luis's room, but she waited by the doorway while he felt Luis's head. Tessa could see that he was sleeping, and she went in and touched the gauze with her palm. Mitch head-motioned for them to leave.

She followed Mitch to the galley. "There is already fever in his legs."

"I treated the wounds with antiseptic."

"Do you have antibiotic pills?"

"Yes. You know about medicine."

"I used to help the visiting nurse at our village's clinic."

"I have to turn out the lights now. If they drain the battery, we won't be able to start the engines in the morning. We'll use flashlights the rest of the night."

"Is there someplace to wash the river water off? I want to get into clean clothes."

"There's a shower in the toilet room, which we call a *head*. But use only enough water to get wet, then again to quickly rinse off the soap."

Mitch got a flashlight for each of them from the galley cabinet, and Tessa followed him while he looked for water seepage in every room and storage space. When he was satisfied the hull was sound, he went topside to assess their predicament, and to give Tessa privacy while she showered.

The night's crisp moon cast a bluish soft glow on the white deck. When he got to the boat's stern, he scanned the shoreline with his flashlight. The river had nudged Paraiso against a shallow mud bar, and the relentless current captured it there. The bow was entrapped from a combination of shallow mud and the tangle of underwater tree branches.

Mitch considered trying to power Paraiso off the mud bank, but if the propellers buried themselves in the dense clay, the sudden stop could bend the props and damage the engines' crankshafts. He guessed that Luis would use only the engine in the deepest water. Or he might use both with opposing thrust to twist Paraiso off the shore. But these were risky guesses. He had learned many piloting tricks from Luis, but they had never before beached Paraiso. And even if he could wrestle the boat free with the engines, he didn't want to navigate single-handed in the dark with two injured people below. He felt somewhat relieved with that non-decision.

But then he worried that the river might push more mud around the boat, something that could make them indefinite prisoners. There was almost no boat traffic this far up the Amazon, especially during the low-river season. A mistake might force them to survive for weeks until the flood season eventually lifted the boat free. But the batteries could lose their charge over time, making it impossible to start the engines. Now might be the best time to escape.

He started down the companionway stairs to wake Luis for advice, but then dismissed the idea. It would have to wait. Luis would be delirious at best, and his advice unreliable.

Mitch went to the wheelhouse and stared at the power switches. He put his hands on the wheel and squeezed it. Without thinking anymore about it, he turned on the electrical system and pushed his thumb against the first engine's starter. It fired. A belch of black smoke rose and cast an ominous moon shadow across the bow. He made the other engine roar to life just as easily. But then came the risky part. He held his breath and eased the propellers into gear with the power setting low. He heard the water churn and burble furiously— the props were at least turning freely, even if somewhat above the waterline. The back of the boat started to squirm side to side and the bow tugged against the stubborn deadfall branches. When he pushed the throttle an inch or so, the hull rocked back and forth. The props continued spinning, but the boat remained stuck. Mitch put both propellers into reverse, grit his teeth and pushed the throttles to full speed, turning the rudders one way and then the other. The hull began to list eerily to the right and the stern seemed to move off the shore, but the bow held fast. Mitch desperately tried other combinations of reversing and pushing to wiggle loose, but nothing worked. He stopped the engines and shut off the electric master switch, then leaned against the wheel feeling defeated. His mind raced for another idea.

***

Tessa had to brace herself during her hasty shower. Violent rocking and the roaring engines made her wonder if the boat was coming apart. She wrapped herself in the towel she had found in one of the passageway cabinets, then scrambled out of the shower to her room, holding the towel shut with one hand, and keeping the other hand on the wall to keep from falling. She dried off quickly and slipped into jeans and a red tee shirt. By the time she got to the deck, the commotion had stopped.

The dark jungle stood unusually quiet, especially for nighttime, and the steady river moved silently, without a ripple. The stillness suddenly scared her, like the way she felt on that horrible childhood night when she became hopelessly lost in solid darkness.

She used her flashlight to go topside, and went to the side rail, where pale moonglow reflect on the river, looking cool in the windless heat.

Mitch called down to her from the wheelhouse's open door. "Sorry for rocking so much."

"Did it help?"

"No, we're still stuck. I need daylight to see what's going on. Maybe the river will loosen us by morning."

He watched Tessa amble barefoot across the deck to the bow, moving with the grace of a small-town Peruvian woman. She held the guardrail with both hands and looked down at the water, as if confronting the horror that almost killed her. When her wavy black hair spilled forward, she stood to toss her hair back over her shoulders. As if sensing Mitch's gaze, she turned to face him.

Mitch thought she looked more self-assured than when he met her in Tamshiyaco that morning. But then, she was forced to part with her father and her community, probably for the first time in her life, and maybe forever. He knew how that must have felt for her. It had happened to him.

She broke her gaze on Mitch and started to run toward

the companionway. "Luis! Where are you going?"

Mitch turned to see Luis wearing only his undershorts and the gauze that covered his legs. Luis tried to grab the wheelhouse door frame when Mitch caught him from tripping on the step.

"Luis, for God's sake!" Mitch steadied him with an arm around his waist. He saw crimson blots that had soaked through Luis's bandages.

"You don't help your legs by walking on them so soon. Stay in bed, my friend. "

Luis leaned his weight against Mitch's arms. "Of course, you are right—as soon as I set Paraiso free."

"The boat will be fine here tonight. Let's get you to bed, and then you can tell me how to free us in the morning."

"It's not something I can tell you. It's a problem that I must put my hands on."

"All right, but put your hands on it in the morning."

"The river's current might push us harder into the mud by morning. We would have to survive here until the river flooded enough."

"I know, but we'd eventually get help from another boat passing by."

"Mitch, how often do we see vessels other than dugout canoes or log rafts this far upriver?"

"It's still possible."

"Not this time of year."

"Let's talk about this later. You should rest or you won't heal. After you are in bed, I'll get an antibiotic pill for you."

He put one of Luis's arms around his neck and started him toward the companionway. Tessa came to Luis's other side, and pulled his other arm around her neck. She and Mitch paced their steps with Luis's slow, painful shuffle, and they worked together to get him down the companionway steps. Tessa helped Mitch ease Luis into bed. While he went for the medicine, she carefully lifted Luis's head with one hand to slide the pillow under.

Luis looked up at her. "I'm sorry you had to hear about our problem. I think you must feel sorry that you came with us."

"No, I was leaving a worse problem."

"Mitch might be right," Luis said. "Paraiso and I will rest tonight and the river might be kind enough to let us loose."

Tessa felt his forehead with her palm. "I will pray it does."

"And forgive me for making you fall in the river."

"I fell in by myself. There is nothing to forgive."

Mitch came back with the antibiotic pill and a bottle of water. "Luis, do you how how safe it is here?"

"I think the only Indians in this area are Yaguas. They are peaceful if we don't look like a threat. What do you think, Tessa?"

"I have never been this far up the Amazon, but I have never heard about any unfriendly Indians here."

Mitch helped Luis's sit up to swallow the pill with a wash of water. He said "Sleep well and dream about your happy wife and children."

"I will."

Mitch waited a moment and saw Luis close his sleepy eyes. When he left the cabin, Tessa was waiting for him in the passageway.

"He is very sick," she whispered. "I could feel fever in his neck and forehead. I think you should take him back to Iquitos tomorrow."

"The antibiotics will keep him safe. We'll return in just a few days."

"Each day adds to his danger. He needs a doctor."

"Let's see how he's doing in the morning, all right?"

Tessa lingered with an accusing look, then went to her cabin.

Mitch followed her to the door before she closed it. "Are you still angry because I didn't want you to come with us?"

"I was never angry. I was sad…and afraid. I am still sad and afraid, but for other reasons."

"It must have been terrible when you almost drowned. It was scary for all of us."

"I'm not afraid about that anymore. It's over and I'm safe. I'm worried about Luis now. You tell me he doesn't need a doctor, but we both know he does. And I'm afraid that we might be stranded here. It's true that I have never been this far up the Amazon River, but I know there are headhunters in this region. I'm sure Luis knows too, but we lied to each other to hide the danger."

"I'll have my shotgun loaded and handy if they bother us."

"You would never see a tribe of Jivaros until it's too late. You would be helpless."

"I might be outnumbered, but I'll never be helpless."

"I believe you. You saved my life today, and I will always remember that. I should rest now."

"Do you want something to eat. I have canned ham spread and the fresh bread we bought in Tamshiyaco."

"No, thank you. My stomach needs to rest from so much river water."

Tessa closed the door and slid under the bed's insect netting. She put her face into the pillow to muffle a little cry. After tucking the netting under the mattress, she rolled onto her side, with eyes closed but feeling wide awake. She wondered if Paraiso's arrival at Tamshiyaco had really been an answer to her prayers, or was it sent to punish her for dishonoring her father. Either way, Capitán Mitch doesn't deserve to have two helpless people to worry about. And why should Luis be injured for her sin? It wouldn't be just, and it couldn't be God's wish. But fatigue and sickness diluted her ability to think clearly about such things, so she gave up for the night. She kissed her necklace's tiny gold crucifix and prayed for forgiveness if she had been the cause of all this terrible trouble.

***

Mitch loaded the double-barreled shotgun he kept in his cabin closet, and stuffed extra shells in his pockets. He opened an iced bottle of Crystal beer in the galley, then walked up to the wheelhouse. After resting the shotgun against the instrument panel, he sat on a wood stool and took a long drink of the cold beer. When his eyes dilated for night vision, he got up and scanned the still jungle under stingy moonglow. There was enough light to see dark smears left by Luis's wounds on the white deck. He wondered if Tessa was right about immediately returning to Iquitos for Luis's sake, or was she just being overly careful—or did she just want to get to Lima as soon as she could?

But if he couldn't free his beached boat in the morning, there would be much more to worry about.

Chapter 6

When the morning's first pale light glistened against the wheelhouse windows, Mitch blinked and got up from sleeping on the hard steel floor. He checked the morning sky and instead of seeing billowy white cumulous clouds that typically float overhead most of the year, he saw wind-driven cloud fragments scattering in from the west, telling of rain in the Andes foothills, and that new rush of water would eventually make the rivers wilder.

He rushed to Luis's cabin. Mitch saw that he was asleep, and was relieved to see him breathing freely. It was early, so he let Luis sleep in before tackling the painful ordeal of treating his wounds and rewrapping them in fresh gauze.

Mitch went back to the main deck and assessed the boat's condition. The hull formed an eddy in the current that swirled in against it. That gentle, relentless disturbance all night might have been enough to wash mud away from the props and loosen the mudbank's grip. The bow appeared to be loosely bobbing against the deadfall tangle, but if he could get the stern free, he might be able to simply back away. He readied himself behind the wheel, then decided to get Luis's advice before starting the engines.

He knocked lightly on Luis's door, then let himself in.

Luis's eyes were barely open, his mouth slightly agape. Beads of sweat dotted his forehead.

Luis said hoarsely, "I could use a little pisco. My legs are angry with pain."

Mitch blotted Luis's face with a towel, and felt his forehead. "You still have a temperature. An aspirin might be better than pisco brandy. "

"I'm wet with sweat." Luis said. "The heat must have been worse during the night. I don't think I slept. Did the boat move?"

"A little. Maybe enough to pull loose."

"You must dance Paraiso into the deep water. Keep changing each prop's speed and direction to make the boat find its way free."

"All right, I will. Then we're heading back to Iquitos. We could arrive before nightfall."

"No, Mitch. Do not give up this trip. I know Tessa has compassion for me, but I have survived worse curses. I will feel better during the day, and we are almost to the oil camp."

Luis tried to raise his head off the pillow, then gave up.

"We need a doctor to look at you."

"If the police are waiting for us, my fever will not be our worst problem. Let's go on to the oil camp, Mitch. When we return to Iquitos, you can leave me with Tessa. She can go with me to the hospital, and you can take Paraiso up the Nanay River. I have been thinking about this all night. You can tie up at Tambo Nanay, and when my legs heal a little, I'll come for you in a friend's speedboat. After that, you can take Paraiso to Brazil."

Mitch said, "That might work…"

"It will if you make it work. We can't return to Iquitos without selling the cargo we've already paid for."

"I guess you'd be safe with the antibiotic pills for a couple of days."

When Mitch started to tug at the cotton gauze, Tessa came in and felt Luis's forehead with her palm, then she timed the pulse in his wrist. "He still needs a doctor."

Luis crinkled his forehead to pry his tired eyes wider. "Señorita, the medicine we have here will heal me."

Mitch looked at her. "I think we should give the antibiotics a chance. Wouldn't that be what a doctor would do?"

She sensed he didn't want her answer, so she didn't give him one.

While Mitch rummaged through the medicine chest for antiseptic and bandages, she delicately lifted away Luis's stained gauze.

"The piranhas left the stain of their evil behind," she said.

"It's infection, not something evil," Mitch said.

"I understand the difference, but you don't understand the similarity."

"I was just being a smartass. Sorry. I didn't sleep well last night."

"No need to apologize because I don't know what a smartass is. I also don't know why you can't take Luis to a doctor in Iquitos."

"There's a couple of reasons. First, we're loaded with expensive cargo that I'm stuck with if we don't sell it."

"Can't you sell your things on the next trip?"

"There won't be a next trip if I lose my boat. That's the second reason."

"Señorita," Luis interrupted weakly. "I think the storm of my fever is over, so I will heal now."

Mitch went back to dabbing Luis's wounds with a cotton ball saturated with antiseptic, but his mind was elsewhere now. Luis winced with some of the dabs and tried to smile occasionally to reassure Tessa.

She turned to Mitch. "You still haven't told me why you would lose your boat in Iquitos."

"I'm on the wrong side of a corrupt police captain. I've done nothing wrong, but a policeman did something to make me look guilty of a crime."

"May I ask what the bad policeman did?"

"He had a bag of cocaine that he said was aboard my boat. But he is lying."

Tessa cocked her head, as if trying to understand this. "I believe you, not the policeman. Could you sell your boat, then use the money to leave Peru?"

"There's only one person in Iquitos who could, or would, buy it. And I won't sell it to him."

"Why not?"

"Because he's the one who wants my boat, and I think he's paying the police captain to help him get it."

"Who is this terrible person?"

"A narcotrafficker named Rafael Domingo."

"I know about Rafael. Not everyone thinks he's evil."

"Rafael must have a fan club in Tamshiyaco."

"I don't know what a fan club is, but Rafael is known in Tamshiyaco, if that's what you mean. I think he has done some bad things, but he has done good things. If you must judge someone, you should do it fairly."

Mitch turned from her and started wrapping Luis's legs with fresh gauze.

She walked to the door. "I shouldn't have said that. I am sorry. My father always says I am too stubborn and outspoken."

"No need to be sorry. I won't judge you. I can be a little

bit stubborn and outspoken, too"

She left the room while he finished applying the gauze.

Luis whispered with a grin, "She likes you, Mitch,"

"Why do you think that?"

"Because she argues with you like you are a friend, not just a boat Capitán."

Chapter 7

While Luis rested, Mitch went topside to check the boat's position. There was no change, and he still worried that the river's current could make things worse. He had to risk either damaging the props or burying them deeper in the muck now, or letting matters worsen on their own overnight. Letting their situation deteriorate from doing nothing didn't appeal to him, so he decided to take the first risk.

When he got to the wheel house, he immediately started both engines. He allowed no pause to reconsider it. As soon as the engines idled a few seconds, he engaged the props and pushed the power levers forward. When the boat lunged forward into the deadfall's morass, he reduced power and shifted into reverse, then added more power. The props churned freely in the water, but the hull clung to the mud. He could almost feel its steel belly wallowing against the shallow mud bar's grip. He hesitated to add more power because it could bend or crack a propeller if it struck something solid. But he had seen nothing solid behind the boat, and he couldn't stay like this. Either risk wringing all possible power from Paraiso's engines, or sit there and hope for good luck. Neither risk was good, but the best one seemed obvious to him.

He held the steering wheel with one hand and with the

other he pushed the throttles to full power. He changed the power settings from one engine to the other, while Paraiso's heavy hull rocked back and forth. His sweaty shirt clung to him while he idled to reverse the props again, then pushed the throttles back to full power. The hull fought for freedom, then leaned hard to one side, listing at an alarmingly steep angle toward the shore—suddenly, it jerked free from captivity.

Mitch throttled back to let the boat bob freely in the open water, and settle into the placid buoyancy she was designed for. He nudged both throttles to low power and listened. no vibrating, so the propellers held. The engines hummed their usual throaty growl. He went to a cruise setting and steered her out to the Amazon's deep middle.

When he looked out the wheelhouse's side window, he saw Tessa clutching the wheelhouse handrail with fear in her eyes. Mitch smiled at her, and trimmed the boat's speed and direction before going to the doorway.

"I'm sorry for the wild ride," he said.

"I thought the boat was breaking apart."

"No. The boat and the mud bar fought for control, and the boat won. We'll be all right now."

She looked at the river. "I thought we were going back to Iquitos."

"I forgot that the oil camp has a medic, and we're almost there. We can let him treat Luis without losing much time. Do you approve of that?"

Her answer was a bashful smile.

"Luis might need some water."

"Of course," she said. "I will take care of him."

As she was leaving, Mitch added "I think you'll be a good nurse."

She grinned to herself as she hurried below.

***

After a couple of hours perched on the hard stool behind the wheel, Mitch started to feel groggy and stiff. He stood and forced himself to study the river. He hoped to catch some sleep after they arrived at the oil camp. If Luis felt well enough after the medic's care, maybe he could sit on the stool and steer while Mitch slept on the floor behind him. But Mitch dismissed that fantasy, borne of a desperate need for sleep. Tessa was not able to navigate on her own, so it would be up to Mitch to get them back to Iquitos.

He looked for clouds, but the hot blue sky was empty. The only breeze was from Paraiso's movement through the air, and the only change of scenery was the jungle's nuanced changes in texture or shades of green. There were no mestizo villages to see because they would only be along the Amazon's smaller tributaries this far upriver. Paths to Indian villages are always hidden, and would typically be a forty-minute or so walk uphill from the river's edge. Anyone not belonging to those tribes would be watched by lookouts, and if anything looked suspicious to them, they would release their long sharp arrows. Because all the pathways were concealed along the river, pulling up to any shore or walking into the jungle from any point carried a lethal risk.

Just around an upcoming bend, he saw what looked like swarming insects, or smoke from a small floating island. He turned Paraiso slightly toward the curious mass, and when he got closer, he saw that it was a balsa log raft. A thin column of cooking smoke wafted straight up from the iron cooking pit and dissipated behind them in the windless air. A woman squatting near the fire looked up from her steaming cook pot and blankly watched the boat. Her husband leaned on his long heavy steering pole at the stern, and nodded a somber greeting to Mitch—one captain to another.

Three barefoot children timidly came out of a tarp-covered lean-to and stared at Paraiso. A little girl—the tallest child—wore a pink tee shirt and green skirt. A boy, a little shorter, wore only dark blue shorts. The smallest boy was naked and the only one who smiled. Mitch gave them two short blasts from the boat's horn, and the children giggled with big smiles.

Mitch had seen families rafting like this on previous trips. They left from Pucallpa, a frontier town located far up the Ucayali River, which was one of two rivers that converged to form the Amazon. The rafters let the river's slow current take them to Iquitos, a trip lasting several weeks. On the way they would live on fish caught in nets on both sides of the primitive raft. After reaching Iquitos, they would either disassemble their raft and sell its huge buoyant logs, or sell it intact to make another floating shack, to be tethered to the network of other landless shacks along Iquitos's riverfront.

The raft family would also sell their most valuable cargo, coconut-sized rocks stacked on the front of the raft, used to sharpen knives and machetes. There are no stones in the Amazon basin, no pebbles, no aggregate of any kind—not even sand. There are only two forms of clay, wet muck or hard baked. Once the raft family finishes their business in Iquitos, they will return to Pucallpa aboard an overcrowded collectivo or cargo boat, and start building their next raft.

Seeing this raft family brought thoughts to Mitch about Luis's wife and children. They didn't like to see Luis leave, but they had grown used to his absences over the years, and his wife relied on the money he managed to scrounge and bring home. Before meeting Mitch, Luis had worked as a guide, mostly for gold prospectors and ancient artifact hunters. He would usually be gone for weeks in the Andean foothills, sometimes even months. The prospectors seldom found anything more than a few flakes of gold, never enough to make it worthwhile—and artifact hunters seldom found anything more than a few clay pot chards. Luis was often blamed for their poor luck. He anticipated that, and always collected half of his fee in advance, but sometimes he was cheated out of the balance.

For a while he had worked for the oil explorers, who were contracted by international oil companies. They never cheated Luis, but they did violate Luis's ethics. They drilled countless exploratory wounds into the jungle's floor. The commotion drove animals away, and the Indians had to hunt ever-farther in pursuit of their food source. Meat would start spoiling after three days, so when they faced longer round-trips, they usually relocated their villages.

Luis compared the oil company bosses to the rich rubber barons who, a century ago, ruled the economies and lives of the people in and around Iquitos. The barons lived like kings and queens, and treated the locals like peasants. Although the oil men were not ruthless, Luis was overjoyed when Mitch hired him to pilot Paraiso.

***

Mitch draped his forearms over Paraiso's steering wheel and admitted to himself that he might have made a mistake about pushing on to the camp. The only thing that should matter now is Luis's health. He wondered if he had given in too quickly to Luis's rant about completing their expedition. But that didn't matter now. Mitch knew he had to be the final judge of what's best, and that's what he was doing.

Mitch knew that Luis was no stranger to fear, suffering and survival. He was one of those hardy adventurers who could survive in the jungle like an Indian. In addition to speaking Spanish and fluent English, he spoke a bit of Portuguese for trips downriver to Brazil, and a smattering of three Indian dialects. He taught Mitch how to approach an Indian village without getting run through by deadly arrows. During one of their trips, Luis wanted to visit a friendly Indian village he knew to see if they had any jaguar fangs, worth hundreds of dollars to foreign archeologists. When Luis had spotted the familiar trail head, he had told Mitch to speak in a normal voice, and walk casually to avoid seeming to sneak up their pathway. The Indians had no jaguar teeth on that trip, but the chief offered to trade a necklace strung with piranha jaws. The chief accepted Luis's offer of a few cigarettes, then lit one at a smoldering cook fire. He took the first puff, and then let the village men take a puff and pass it around.

***

Mitch drew a breath of relief when he spotted the Yarapa River's entrance on his left. The Yarapa was one of the first tributaries to empty into the Amazon River, and a few hours farther upriver was where the oil men made their camp. Soon after Mitch entered the narrow tributary, he spotted four familiar small aluminum boats with long-shaft outboard motors fixed to the sterns. The river's gentle current made the boats tug against lines that tethered them to a long wood-plank dock. A few yards up from them, a red-and-white single-engine airplane on floats had been partially beached onto the riverbank and tied to a tree. Although Mitch had never seen the oil company's airplane here, he knew it flew in from Lima each week to deliver basic supplies, and took back test boring results to Lima. He also knew the pilot brought pocket-money advances on the workers' contract salary, and Mitch provided the important service of bringing things for them to buy. He kept his prices fair and knew what the men valued. He never charged them for the recent issues of a Peruvian English-language newspaper he always brought, which they seemed to value most.

As he drifted closer, streaks of sunlight breached through the high forest canopy and flashed off silver galvanized steel barracks and the mess hall. They all had several screened windows with no glass. Behind the barracks was a supply shed and the office. Mitch blew a short toot from his horn when he approached the dock, and three men ran to help him tie up. While that was going on, Tessa came up to the main deck and walked cautiously to the bow. She wore jeans, which was unusual for a local woman, a white blouse, and white sneakers. While leaning on the rail with both hands she scanned the grounds, and returned a wave from one of the men on the dock.

Mitch steered the boat upriver and let it gently drift sideways against the dock. One of the men hollered for Tessa to throw him a line. She ran to the coiled bowline, and cast it to him with both hands. It fell short, so one of the men got on his belly and grabbed it out of the water. As soon as Paraiso bumped against the dock, the man tied the line to a wooden dock cleat. He told Tessa to throw the stern line. She used more heft this time, and he secured that to another cleat.

After Mitch cut the engines and shut down the boat's electrical system, he dragged the wood gangplank from its place on the foredeck, opened the deck rail gate, and slid the gangplank down onto the dock. Just a few men would be in the camp at this time of day because most of the crew were working at seismic exploration sites, using sophisticated sounding equipment to measure the likelihood of deep oil deposits. This information was recorded for oil company geologists, who would use the data to calculate whether a particular area might be a candidate for drilling.

Tessa stayed aboard and chatted with the men on the dock, answering their questions about where she was from, and why she came to this place. She answered someone's question about how she learned such good English. "My father is a schoolteacher—even when he is home." That brought a laugh. Someone else asked if she was Mitch's girlfriend. She looked at the rail and quickly said, "No."

While she kept the men busy, Mitch went below to check Luis. He saw that Tessa had changed his gauze bandage. A bit of fresh blood only seeped through a few spots where the wounds were deepest. Luis was asleep on his back, breathing heavily through his open mouth. Mitch felt Luis's forehead, and thought his temperature might have decreased.

When he returned topside, he saw the three men were still on the dock. One of them invited Tessa to see their camp, but instead of answering, she looked at Mitch. He shook his head no with a stern look, and that quelled any further questions.

The camp foreman, Guy Clipe, soon strode onto the dock, and the other men left.

Clipe was an Australian who had spent most of his adult life living in harsh oil exploration camps in South America and Asia. He wore khakis pants, knee-high snake boots, a red tee shirt— faded enough to start looking pink—and a wide-brimmed drover's hat to shade his leathery face.

"I trust you haven't lost your taste for a cool beer," Mitch said.

Clipe climbed the gangplank. "When I do, they can ship my dead carcass back to Sydney."

Mitched turned to Tessa. "Will you join us?"

"I've been below most of the day. Go drink your beer. I'll wait in the wheelhouse."

"I think Luis's fever broke."

"Yes, I think so."

Clipe stepped aboard and followed Mitch down to the galley. Mitch opened a large bottle of Cristal beer and poured it into two glasses until foam oozed up, but not over the rims.

"Did you stay at Tambo Yarapa last night?" Clipe asked.

"No, we were beached in a mud bank farther down the Amazon."

Clipe took his hat off and fanned himself. "How in bloody hell did that happen?"

"By surprise. It was getting dark and we were close to the shore. When we hit, our passenger fell overboard. Luis jumped in to rescue her, and got bit up by piranhas."

"Sorry about your bad luck. I didn't know you took on passengers."

"I don't as a rule, but getting stuck wasn't her fault."

"How's Luis faring?"

"Better, but he needs a doctor. As soon as your men return for the day, I'd like to sell what I can and then start heading back. That float plane tells me they have some money to spend."

"Sorry to add bad news to your bad luck, mate. The pilot brought some provisions, but no money this time. There's been rioting and terrorist bombings in Lima. Public gathering places have been closed temporarily and banks are closed indefinitely. But that's not the worst of it. When I called our Lima office on my satellite phone, I was told to gather up all the most valuable equipment, and be ready for a boat from Iquitos in a few days. Peru's new socialist president has decided to nationalize all the oil and gas companies, which means we're through here. Nasty business, Mitch.

"No word about when the banks might open?"

"I'm afraid not." Clipe took a long draw on his beer.

Mitch picked up his glass. "Well, cheers. This has been one hell of a trip."

"Same on our end. None of us know where we'll be sent next, but maybe the company will explore for oil in some paradise like Tahiti. More likely, though, either New Guinea or Cambodia."

"I'll miss making trips here. I'll have to find new customers."

"My men will miss your visits, too. They don't really need most of the things you sell them, but spending some walking-around money breaks the monotony of camp life, and gives them something fun to look forward to. Letting them visit with your pretty passenger gave them a bonus this time."

"I guess we might as well shove off, then. Can I get your medic to look at Luis before we go?"

"Of course. I'll go get him."

While Clipe went for the medic, Mitch went to Luis's room. Tessa was helping him drink from a bottle of water, and Mitch went to the other side of the bed to prop him up so he could swallow easier.

"How are you feeling, Luis?"

"My legs are on fire."

"The camp medic is going to have a look. I'll ask if he has pain killers."

Clipe stepped into the small cabin, followed by a short rotund man with a thick black mustache.

"This is Assiz, our medic. He's originally from Port Moresby in New Guinea. He's worked with me for several years, better than most doctors when it comes to tropical diseases, snakebite, and other inconveniences we run into out here."

Assiz put his palm on Luis's forehead, then he pulled back some of the bandage. Luis grimaced with each of Assiz's careful tugs on the gauze.

"This was bandaged very well, but I must remove it to see your wounds and maybe treat them. But first I will give you something for your fever and something else for your pain."

While Tessa helped Luis wash the pills down with swallows of water, Assiz removed the gauze. He asked Tessa to put a fresh towel under Luis's legs. Then he motioned for Mitch and Tessa to follow him down the passageway to the rear of the boat. Guy Clipe went with them.

"The infection has become wild," Assiz whispered. "I will give him injections of antibiotics and morphine, then I'll apply antibiotic ointment to his wounds. But you must get him to the hospital in Iquitos very soon. He needs an antibiotic IV drip. The hospital might even have to send him to Lima if they can't help him fight the infection."

"Would it make a difference if we waited until morning. It's dangerous to travel on the river at night."

"Every minute is dangerous for him. He could lose his legs, maybe his life, if you delay."

After Assiz went back to Luis's room, Tessa said to Mitch "We have to leave now."

"I know. I'm as worried about Luis as you are. I'm also worried that the Iquitos police chief will keep us from getting him to the hospital. It sounds like Luis might not live long in jail."

Clipe said "Why don't you just pay off the bloody police chief. Scoundrels are always for sale."

"It's a bit more complicated than that."

Tessa turned to Mitch. "You can leave Luis with me in Iquitos, and I'll make sure he gets to the hospital. Then you can hide your boat, or take it to Columbia or Brazil."

"I'd need to draw money out of the bank for that. I wouldn't last long without a lot of extra fuel and basic provisions."

Mitch went into Luis's room and saw Assiz give Luis an injection into his arm. Tessa and Clipe watched from the passageway.

Mitch put his hand on Luis's shoulder. "We're heading back, my friend."

Luis looked up at Mitch. "We can sell the cargo tonight and leave in the morning. This doctor will heal me."

"The men have no money and the camp is closing down. Our business here is over, Luis. I want to get to Tambo Yarapa before dark."

Luis drew a deep breath. "I don't think we can make it there before dark."

"Then I'll find it in the dark."

"I don't need to tell you the risk in that."

"Don't worry, I'll bet a cold beer that we'll reach Tambo Yarapa safely, in the dark or not."

Luis winced when Assiz pulled away the rest of the bandage and dropped it to the floor, and then used his latex-gloved finger to daub the wounds with antibiotic ointment. Assiz finished wrapping Luis's legs. Before leaving, Assiz said to Mitch "Capitán, I left ointment, pain pills, and two extra bandage rolls in your first aid kit."

Mitch followed him to the main deck, with Clipe close

behind. Tessa stayed with Luis to help him with another drink of water.

When they got to the gangplank, Clipe said, "What's your plan, mate?"

"I'll push hard to arrive in Iquitos within a couple of days. That'll give me plenty of time to think of my next steps. Tessa suggested dropping her and Luis off at the wharf, and she can take him to the hospital in a taxi. In the meantime, I'll anchor up in a local tributary for a few days, until Luis feels up to coming for me."

"Sounds easy enough."

"We'll see."

A man in khaki cargo pants, a pale green buttoned shirt and tan baseball cap walked to the end of the dock and looked over Paraiso. He said "Beauty of a boat."

"You must be the pilot."

"Yes, sir, but not for long. I'm taking three guys back to Lima in the morning. If the weather cooperates, I'll make one or two more trips back here. Any remaining men will have to wait for a chartered boat sent from Iquitos."

"You can fly that little airplane over the Andes Mountains?

"The Cessna 210's little all right, and old. But with its turbo-charged engine, and a portable oxygen bottle, I could climb to twenty-thousand feet if I wanted to. But I don't need that much altitude to get through the mountain pass I use."

"How do you carry enough fuel?"

"I have a travel range of almost a thousand miles, but I refuel at certain airports along the way. My last fuel stop is at Tingo Maria, in the low mountains. That gives me enough fuel to reach this camp and return to Tingo Mara to refuel for the next leg."

"How long to reach Lima?"

"I leave at first light and get back around sunset."

"Well, have a safe flight. I'm Mitch Winslow, by the way."

"I'm Reggie Mandelson, but I go by Tex. It's quicker to say."

"What part of Texas you from?"

"Never been to Texas. I'm from northern Minnesota, raised on a cattle and horse ranch up there in the bogs."

"I used to live in northern Minnesota. What airport did you fly out of?"

"Bemidji Airport. I used to fly anglers into Canada for fishing trips. But during winters I squandered my earnings and wasted my time. I couldn't get ahead. But this job keeps me flying year-round. I get paid well, too. Seaplane pilots who can fly in the mountains are scarce as snowmen down here."

Mitch went to the wheelhouse to prepare for starting the engines. After Tex and Assiz left, Clipe untied the boat from the dock cleats and tossed the lines back onto the boat deck. Tessa quickly coiled them like an experienced deckhand.

Clipe hollered up to him, "This'll be our last time together, Mitch. As parting advice, you might reconsider throwing some money at that policeman in Iquitos. If you made him look like a chump when you left, he'll need to save face now. It's how the game works."

"He *is* a chump, and I don't like games"

"None of us do when we're on the paying end. Have a safe trip home."

Chapter 8

Mitch throttled Paraiso's engines for cruising speed down the Yarapa River. Dark clouds gathered overhead and their shadows concealed long stretches of the river. Luckily, the gentle Yarapa did not originate in the steep Andes Mountains, so uprooted jungle vegetation was minimal.

The sunlight dimmed faster than Mitch's vision could adjust. Without Luis's experienced eyes, he would have to guess when they reached Tambo Yarapa, the only village before entering the Amazon River. He switched on the boat's navigation lights, and turned off the dim wheelhouse overhead light to protect his night vision.

After what seemed like a couple of hours, the river still looked too narrow to be close to the Amazon. He strained to look for Tambo Yarapa, named after the river, but if it got much darker, and if the villagers had no cooking fires going, their village might not be distinguishable from the surrounding jungle. The Yarapa River emptied into the Amazon soon after passing the village, but if he got that far, he faced pressing on through the night to San Fernando, a small village located about halfway to Tamshiyaco. It was much farther down the Amazon, but residents there used kerosene lanterns, a few of which would probably remain on late. Navigating to San Fernando in the dark, however, increased the danger of hitting something.

The thickening cumulus clouds bloated and creased like aged faces, and the jungle quickly cloaked itself in shadows. Mitch scanned the shoreline with his binoculars, but they were useless now. Every few minutes, he turned on the rooftop searchlight and quickly flashed it across the water and riverbank.

He heard the steel companionway door clank shut. Tessa smiled at Mitch and walked past the wheelhouse. She had changed into a knee-high deep red dress, and she glided across the foredeck barefoot. Mitch remembered how desperate and sad she had been to leave Tamshiyaco. But instead of helping her, he had exposed her to danger and mayhem.

After studying the night-black water, she looked up at Mitch again.

"Luis is finally sleeping," she said. She went into the wheelhouse. "I was afraid he slept too deeply, but he talked to me when I felt the heat in his face. I think he is sad and feels alone. That can be the worst kind of pain."

"I'll visit with him when we tie up at Tambo Yarapa."

"Why there? If you go on to San Fernando, you will be closer to Iquitos tomorrow morning."

"You, of all people, should know the dangers of night travel on the river. We can stay in San Fernando tomorrow night. The next day I'll follow your plan. I'll leave you and Luis off in Iquitos, and you can take him to the hospital in a taxi."

"I will, and I'll stay with him until he is safe."

"I'll be heading up the Nanay River and tie up at Tambo Nanay. I'm not sure what I'll do after that, but it's the best plan I can think of for now. The original idea was for Luis to meet me up the Nanay River when his legs got better, but that might take too long."

"Maybe my friend in Iquitos can help you."

"I don't think so."

"How do you know?"

"My enemies are powerful."

"When I feel overpowered, I pray for help."

"Maybe you can pray for Luis."

"I have been. And for you."

Mitch wiped his forehead with the back of his hand and looked at her. "Then we're both doing the best we can."

Tessa leaned toward the windshield, as if trying to see through the black void ahead. The sun had already set behind the forest's canopy, but there was enough residual light in the sky to make the jungle silhouette against it. Mitch turned the search light on and scanned the riverbank, hoping to see telltale dugout canoes that had been pulled ashore. Against the awkward silence between them, the engines hummed and trembled through the boat's steel body. Mitch always thought the engines sounded rougher at night. Luis blamed ghosts for the restless noise level.

Tessa picked up the binoculars and scanned the waterline shadows.

Mitch said, "They won't help much."

"I see little lights flickering along the shore."

"Probably fireflies."

"Maybe…but they're not moving. Ahead to the right."

She handed the binoculars to Mitch, and he saw twinkles behind the vegetation. As he got closer, he turned on the spotlight, but its bright beam drowned out the lights. He turned it off and reduced the engine's power. When within a few yards, he saw a short dock come into view, and he turned the search light back on.

"It's Tambo Yarapa."

Tessa said "Their pier looks too small for a boat this big."

"We can tie the bow line to a tree and let the current hold enough of the hull against the dock. I've done that many times."

"Where are the villagers' boats."

"On the riverbank. In this area, even mestizos use dugout canoes. They buy them from the Indians with rum."

"Should I get the rope ready?"

"Yes, but please don't fall in the water again."

She waited to see if he was serious, and then held back a smile. "Don't worry. I'll stay on your boat this time."

Approaching the dock, Mitch turned off the search light to avoid disturbing the villagers or losing too much of his night vision. He kept his eye on the riverbank, and when he estimated it to be within a few feet, he turned toward the upriver shoreline. He stopped the props and let the boat drift gently against the dock.

Two men from the village came out and stood on the dock to watch Mitch gently add enough power to nudge the bow into a muddy bank that was steep enough to avoid getting hung up. He kept the engines running while Tessa cast the bow line, and the men scrambled for it. After one of them tied it to a tree on the bank, Mitch cut the engines. As Mitch predicted, the river's current rested the hull snugly against the dock.

Mitch turned off the electrical power. The red and green navigation lights faded into the blackness, and the absence of engine noise accentuated the territorial screems of nocturnal howler monkeys.

As he stepped down from the wheelhouse stairs to join

Tessa, recorded Peruvian festival music suddenly blared from the village grounds.

She looked back happily at Mitch. "They are using their valuable batteries to welcome us."

Kerosene lamplights began to glow from the open windows and doorways of thatched family huts on stilts, scattered throughout the partially cleared jungle. All of the huts were raised to a uniform height of about fifteen feet on their large log stilts. During the flood season, the hut floors would remain just above water level, and each hut became a family's island, with a dugout canoe tied to the porch railings. The largest structure in the village was the community hut, also on stilts but built over the river's edge next to the dock. It served as a gathering place for village events, but was primarily there to shelter visitors. Navigation maps always showed which river villages had one of these "government houses" by preceding the village's name with the word *Tambo*—which is an Inca word meaning *inn,* or *resting place* for travelers.

Mitch unlatched the left side deck rail gate and stepped down onto the narrow wood dock to meet four village leaders, who confirmed their status by being the first to welcome him. Tessa remained on the boat deck until Mitch had a chance to greet them and explain who his passenger was.

Mitch excused himself after greeting the leaders, but when he turned to invite Tessa onto the dock, she was gone. He went down the boat's companionway, and found her sitting next to Luis, holding a wet towel to his forehead.

"I came down for my shoes, and to check Luis. His body is still too warm."

Luis strained half-asleep to talk but only mumbled incoherently. Mitch went to the galley and returned with an opened bottle of water and gave it to Tessa. Luis seemed more alert when Mitch raised his upper body to drink, while Tessa handled the bottle.

She said, "Can you take a sip?"

Luis nodded slightly and she brought the bottle to his lips. He struggled to swallow, and it took a few minutes for him to satisfy his thirst. She took the bottle from his mouth when he stopped drinking.

Mitch gently lowered Luis to the mattress. "I think we can let him sleep safely for a while. Would you like to join me?"

"Yes, I would like to see Yarapa. I know about this village, but I've never been this far from home."

Mitch followed her to the guard rail. He stepped onto the dock and put his hand out for her. She took his hand then stepped down. Tessa introduced herself to the men in Spanish while Mitch went back to the boat. He soon emerged from below deck, straining with a heavy ice chest. Tessa went to the edge of the deck and took one of the handles, and they carried it together down to the dock. He opened a bottle of beer and handed it to the man he knew to be the governor— the local term for *mayor*—of Yarapa. The governor took a drink and handed the bottle to the village school teacher, who then passed it to the man next to him. While the beer made its rounds, someone offered Mitch a metal cup of uncured rum. Mitch took the first sip of the harsh distillate known as *aguardiente*—which translates roughly into "Schnapps," or distilled liquor. Mitch handed it to the man closest to him and the cup made its rounds.

While it wasn't Saturday night, having travelers as guests was important enough to the villagers to celebrate. Mitch knew the custom of communal sharing in mestizo jungle villages, and that one cup would eventually serve all the village men, round after round. Mitch's cooler held American-brand cola to dilute the rum, and vanilla *Inca Kola* soda for the women—that is, if and when the women decided it was a proper time to join the party.

The men furtively eyed Tessa. Mitch assumed they wondered why a pretty Peruvian woman, who didn't wear a wedding ring, would be traveling alone with a gringo boat capitán. Mitch anticipated that and explained that she was from Tamshiyaco, and how Luis risked his life to save her.

Tessa translated that in Spanish, and said Mitch was a great American boat captain who saved both her and Luis.

The village men were too polite to talk directly to Tessa, not being sure about her real relationship with Mitch, so they directed their questions in Spanish to him, and Tessa translated back and forth.

She turned to Mitch. "The village men are surprised that piranhas were swimming together in such a large river."

"Tell them the river was shallow where we beached our boat, and our struggling shook branches hanging into the water. The disturbance must have attracted them."

Tessa related this to the village men. They nodded their heads thoughtfully, and continued debating the matter between themselves.

Tessa turned to Mitch. "They think the piranha must have been feeding on something else like an animal, and Luis swam through their feast."

After the rum cup had been passed a few times, one of the village men, apparently loosened by the spirits, took the bold step of approaching Mitch and asked in English, "This woman your wife?"

"No, she is a respected passenger. Her father is the school teacher of Tamshiyaco."

The governor explained this to the other men, which

brought knowing nods. Tessa looked away as if she hadn't heard the question or the answer.

She said to Mitch in a low voice, "That was a good thing to say."

Tessa assured the governor that Captain Mitch was a Christian and would not sin with an unmarried woman. The governor gave Tessa an approving nod and the men talked among themselves about this extraordinary situation. They agreed that a Christian American boat captain and a schoolteacher's daughter needed to be respected.

One of the other men started explaining something about other guests, but he spoke too rapidly for Mitch's limited Spanish. When he finished, Tessa interpreted.

"He said an Indian chief and his wife are living in this village because they have lost their tribe. The people here are trying to help them heal their sadness. They hope the chief and his wife can start a new life here."

"How did they lose their tribe?"

"The oil explorers upriver hunt with shotguns instead of arrows, and that scares away monkeys and other game animals deep into the forest, too far away for a large hunting party. The chief had to divide his people into small groups so they could be absorbed without too much burden by villages and other Indian tribes along the river."

"Why didn't the whole tribe just move to a better hunting area?"

"They would have to cross Jivaro Indian territory. The Jivaros would kill them at first sight, and maybe eat them."

"Couldn't the chief's people live on fish?"

"They are not fishermen. They are hunters."

The village men left the empty beer bottle on the dock and started to meander away. One of the men told Mitch and

Tessa to follow him.

Mitch said to Tessa, "Should we bring the ice chest?"

"Oh, yes," she said with a grin. "The party is not over. I think they want to introduce us to the chief now. It is a great honor that he and his wife chose this village to live in."

One of the men took a handle of the ice chest and helped Mitch carry it to the village's government hut. They lifted it up a notched log ladder to the large thatch-covered platform. After they set the chest down, Mitch reached down to help Tessa with the final step. A kerosene lamp flickered dimly on a lashed bamboo table near a rough-hewn wood box. The pale amber light barely illuminated the old Indian man standing in front of the far rail. In times past, he would have worn a grass skirt, like all Indian men. But the only garment on his sinewy body was a short leather groin skirt. A leather bag hung from his waist by a braided string. The chief's straight black hair was unadorned, and he wore no necklace beads to assert his social rank.

The chief greeted Mitch and Tessa with only a thin relaxed smile. As soon as two of the village men got the cooler up to the platform, they stood silently behind Mitch and Tessa.

Mitch took a bottle of beer from the cooler, opened it, and gave it to the chief. The chief nodded his appreciation, then said something to Mitch in a strange dialect.

Mitch looked at Tessa for help, but she shrugged her shoulders. "I don't know his language."

One of the village men introduced himself as Juan, and said he understood the chief's dialect. He translated to Tessa in Spanish, then she explained to Mitch.

"He knows you are a chief," she said. "He asked about your trouble."

"How does he know I have trouble?"

"A chief has the power to know such things."

"Tell him about Luis and ask if he can help him."

This was translated to Juan, who translated it to the Indian chief. The chief looked into Mitch's eyes and replied. Juan communicated it to Tessa.

"He will look at Luis," she said.

The nimble old chief scurried down the notched log, and waited until everyone else was on the ground. Mitch led the way to the boat and the chief jumped up onto the boat's deck and waited. He followed Mitch to Luis's cabin, with Tessa and Juan close behind.

The chief strode past Mitch to Luis's bed. He gently probed Luis's facial muscles and arms with his fingertips. Luis opened his eyes deliriously, and then let them close without any reaction to the chief, as if seeing an old, almost-naked, Indian stand over him was normal. The chief opened each of Luis's hands and sniffed the palms, then held them for a moment. He said something to Mitch. The translation quickly went through Juan.

Tessa whispered, "The chief said the spirit of death waits for Luis."

"Ask him to help," Mitch said. "He must have some herbs or roots, or something we can try."

After the translation exchange, Tessa said, "Because you are Luis's chief, only your power can help him."

The old Indian left the room with Juan in tow. Mitch ran out of the cabin and said to Juan, "Do you speak English?"

"Only a little."

"Tell him I'll pay him. I have many gifts to give him if he'll try to heal Luis. I have flashlights and radios, and batteries to power them."

After this was interpreted to the chief, he smiled and gave

a lengthy reply. Juan interpreted it for Tessa, who understood English better.

She turned to Mitch. "The chief said he doesn't need those things. He already has everything he needs to hunt, and if he can hunt, he and his wife can live happily."

Mitch returned to Luis's bedside and stroked Luis's matted hair with his fingers. Luis muttered something unintelligibly while squinting up at Mitch.

Mitch said, "Stay with us, my friend." He rested a palm on Luis's warm forehead. "Your wife and your happy children need you. Fight this infection devil for their sake, and for mine. I am your friend, close as a brother, and I want you to heal."

Mitch slumped in silence for several minutes, fighting back the gloom welling in his throat. He turned to see Tessa's moist brown eyes before he sulked up to the top deck. The villagers and the chief had already disappeared into the darkness, and the cooler chest had been placed on the boat's deck. The party was over.

Mitch went to the bow rail and pondered what the chief had told him. The chief must have been talking about magic or supernatural powers, but Mitch knew that Luis needed more than that. He needed a real doctor.

Tessa stood next to the wheel house and watched him. As if sensing her presence, Mitch turned and looked at her blankly.

"His pulse is good," she said taking a step toward him. "And I think his temperature is coming down a little."

"I feel so helpless, Tessa. I'm not a chief, and I can't make miracles. He needs a doctor. You've understood that all along."

"I think we both understood it. When we get to Iquitos,

I will make sure he gets to the hospital. You will be free to escape from Peru."

"I wish I knew where to go, and how?"

"Maybe you can steal your boat back. If the police took it dishonestly, it is rightfully still yours. After that, you can go anywhere."

"I've thought of that. But the next port downriver is at Leticia, Columbia. It's too dangerous right now, and I don't have enough fuel to reach Manaus, Brazil. It's about a thousand miles, and then almost another three thousand miles to the river's delta at Belém. Even if I had the money to refill my fuel tanks, I don't know where I can buy it on those long stretches."

"Do you have enough money to fly back to the United States?"

Mitch looked down and slowly shook his head. "I can't go back there."

"Maybe my friend in Iquitos will loan you money for a ticket."

"It's not the money. I did something that was righteous— and I would do it again—but I had to break a law."

"I'm sorry if I made you remember something bad."

"It's fine. My only worry now is for Luis. It scares me to think about bringing a lifeless body back to his wife and children."

While he stood on the boat's bow, a hot breath of wind grabbed Mitches attention. A raindrop touched his cheek. He looked up and saw gathering clouds silhouetted by the moonglow behind them. Lightening flashed from cloud to cloud in the distance, but the jungle muffled its crackling thunder. Rain started to fall in tiny spatters that tapped against broad leaves, while stirring and cooling the muggy air.

The rain strengthened, and Tessa ran for the wheelhouse door. The light from a flash of lightning illuminated her running figure. By the time she reached the door, strands of wet hair began to mat against her cheeks and neck. Parts of her wet blouse clung to her body.

"Come in, Mitch." She squinted to keep the rain out of her eyes.

"I'll let the rain cool my mood."

"Sleep would be better for that. We have a very long trip tomorrow."

He stepped numbly into the wheel house with her. "I don't think I can sleep."

"I'll sleep on the floor in Luis's room," she said. "You won't have to worry about us."

"I should have turned back to Iquitos sooner. If Luis dies, it will be my fault."

"If you must find fault, then blame me. I'm the one who fell in the river. You saved Luis. You saved both of us. You did what you could, but you are not God. You *are* a chief, though, and that's not a small thing. "

"I'm like the old Indian who lost his tribe."

"Maybe, but the chief is not suffering. He did not fail his people—he saved them. He still has the power of a chief, and he is respected by everyone in Yarapa. The people of his tribe will honor him for the rest of their lives, and their children will know that he saved his people, and they will someday tell their children."

"I'm nothing like any of that. "

"Yes, you are, Mitch. You worry more for Luis and me than you do for yourself."

She stepped out of the wheelhouse, then paused to turn toward him. A few cool rain droplets rolled down her bare arms while she locked her eyes on his. She cocked her head as if listening for something. Mitch reached out and pushed back a wet strand of hair clinging across her cheek and mouth. The rain's clatter stopped as suddenly as it started, and Tessa spun around toward the riverbank.

"I just saw something move in the jungle."

Mitch turned and saw it too. A pale purple glow from a small object floated in the air and moved above the waterside grasses. It stopped briefly before the dark outline of a person emerged.

Tessa gasped. "A night hunter!"

A chill ran through his body. He remembered the shotgun in his cabin.

She smiled when the grinning Indian stepped out of the shadows and walked toward them. "It's the chief!" she whispered. "I think he's bringing something."

The chief stepped onto the dock and waited. He said something to Mitch in his strange dialect and touched his chest with two fingers. Then he held up a glowing phosphorescent mushroom the size of a man's fist. Mitch stepped off the boat and went to the chief, who handed the mushroom to him. Mitch was surprised by how dry and light it felt.

The chief backed away and touched his chest with two fingers again. Mitch thanked him, nodding slightly, hoping the chief would understand his gesture if not his words.

Mitch looked back at Tessa. "I should give the chief something in return. I'll give him my watch."

She giggled into her hand. "What would he do with a watch? He doesn't need anything you have. I think he's giving you this because he thinks you're lost in some way. Bits of these mushrooms mark the trails when they hunt at night. They can follow them back to their village. The mushrooms have spiritual powers, too, and they bring the hunters good luck."

"Maybe he wants me to give it to Luis," Mitch said.

"No, he would never give a gift to one of your people. He respects you as a chief, and only a chief can give something to his people. He knows that Luis's fate is in your hands."

Mitch touched his chest the way the Indian had. The old man twirled around three times while hopping from one foot to the other. He ran off the dock and was soon absorbed by the darkness.

Mitch kept staring into the jungle as if spellbound. He turned and said "We're clearing out."

Tessa looked at him quizzically. "Now?"

"Yes, right now. If we cruise half speed the rest of the night, I think we can reach Iquitos tomorrow by morning."

"What if we run into something?"

"My eyes will get used to the dark, and there's a little moonlight between the clearing clouds. If that's not enough, then I'll use the search light. It'll still be risky, but waiting is too dangerous for Luis."

"I will watch over him during the night, and maybe I can help you."

"You know where the flashlights are in the galley. After you get some dry clothes on, try to sleep. If you can't, you can join me in the wheelhouse to help watch the river. I'll start the engines now and hold the boat against the dock with the props while you untie us."

Mitch rushed to the wheelhouse and carefully set the phosphorescent mushroom on a flat space above his instrument panel. After firing up the engines, he switched on the navigation lights, and then the searchlight. The lights illuminated countless drips clinging to jungle leaves, and made them twinkle like tiny stars.

While Tessa untied the bow line from the tree, a small group of men and women gathered near her. She thanked them for their hospitality, and said Mitch was leaving now to get Luis to the hospital in Iquitos by morning.

This dramatic news instigated some discussion between the villagers.

Juan approached her. "A few minutes ago, the chief just told me that bad spirits near your friend's body will leave now."

"Thank you, Juan. I will tell Capitán Mitch."

"The chief said your capitán already knows."

Tessa threw the line onto the boat's deck, then climbed aboard and latched the rail gate. Mitch immediately backed away from the shore and turned down the Yarapa River. When he got to the middle of the river, he pushed the throttles to half speed.

After getting a bottle of water and flashlight from the galley, Tessa went to Luis's room with the flashlight on.

Luis blinked from the light. "Hello, Señorita."

She set the bottle on the floor and felt his forehead. "Your fever broke!"

"And the sweating stopped. Why is Mitch moving Paraiso in the dark?"

"He wants to be in Iquitos by morning. The boat is going slow to be safe."

"Where are we?"

"We just left Tambo Yarapa."

"We should stay there tonight."

"He wants to get his money from the bank before the police become busy. While he does that, I will take you to a hospital."

"He shouldn't worry so much about me."

"But he does worry about you, Luis. That's why he wants to leave now, and it's why he wants someone like me, a person with some medical experience, to take care of you. And I'll tell you about something very important. An Indian chief at the Yarapa village said you will heal."

"Did he give you magical herbs or powders?"

"No, but he gave Mitch something more powerful—a mushroom that makes purple light in the dark."

Luis struggled to prop himself up on one elbow. "The chief is a night hunter. I have heard stories about these people, but I didn't know they were real."

"They are real," Tessa said. "But you can only see them when they let you."

Tessa turned on the cabin's ceiling light, and turned off the flashlight. She carefully changed Luis's bandages, pausing whenever he winced. But his wounds were not bleeding now. Some of the smaller bites had started healing over. She felt the healthy skin on his legs, and told Luis they were no long warm from the infection.

Luis said "Did the hunter talk to you?"

"Yes, but I didn't understand his language. One of the villagers interpreted for me."

Tessa told Luis why the chief and his wife were now living with the people of Yarapa, and how the chief appeared out of the jungle with his gift for Mitch.

"Do you feel strong enough to eat something?" she said.

"Yes, how about roasted chicken with fried manioc?"

"How about a banana instead?"

"*Si, Señorita,* I will follow my nurse's orders."

On the way to the galley, she grinned to herself. Luis felt well enough now to tease her.

Chapter 9

Mitch pushed on through the night with his engines at cruising speed. Between a pale half-moon and his night vision, he could read the water well enough at that speed. When a craving for sleep gushed over him, he got up from his stool and stepped out onto the deck to let the damp breeze from the boat's movement wash over him.

Tessa came to the main deck with her flashlight on.

"You won't need that once your eyes adjust to the dark," Mitch said.

She turned the flashlight off, then went into the wheelhouse to hand him a bottle of water. "You must be thirsty. I also brought good news. Luis is feeling much better and he ate a banana. His wounds are already starting to heal, and there is no fever in his legs. None at all."

Mitch tilted his head up and closed his eyes. "Thank God"

While he drank his water, Tessa scooted the extra wood stool forward from the back. Mitch sat next to her. The instrument lights cast a faint glow, making their faces barely reflect off the windshield. When their eyes met in the reflection, she pretended to look past him.

"I've been meaning to ask," he said, "why were you angry when I first met you."

"You seemed to respect my father, but not me."

Mitch thought about that for a moment. "I guess I already had enough enemies. I didn't want the entire population of Tamshiyaco added to the list."

"Why would it matter. You don't have to live there."

"No, but I might need to do business there someday."

"Even an angry schoolteacher cannot stop business."

"What's it like to live in Tamshiyaco?"

"Mostly like anywhere else, I guess."

"Did you like living there?"

"As a child, it was the perfect place to live."

"When did it change?"

"Tamshiyaco never changes. But I did."

"Then when did *you* change?"

"When I had to face dying alone."

Mitch glanced at her and saw a faraway look. "How old were you—what happened?"

"I was twelve years old, and I wandered too far into the jungle, chasing a blue butterfly. It was very large and beautiful, and it seemed to wait for me every few meters until I could catch up, then it would fly a little farther and wait again. It kept doing that. It was before supper, and I forgot about the time. When darkness fell, I ran back toward home, afraid a bushmaster snake might chase me. I tripped and fell into a huge spider web and started to scream. I wasn't sure if I was on the right trail, so I ran faster to find out. By the time it was fully dark, I knew I had made a mistake that could end my life. I screamed for help until I could no longer control my crying."

Mitch was staring at her now, trying to picture this woman as a little girl lost in the Amazon jungle at night.

"How did you find your way out? Did someone find you?"

"No one from Tamshiyaco. I had wandered off too far and ran the wrong way. I knew that finding my way home was hopeless. I decided to stand in that very spot until morning. I couldn't see anything, not even the stars because of the jungle's thick canopy. I pleaded with the Virgin Maria to guide me home to my parents and brother. Suddenly, I saw what I thought was a spirit floating toward me. It danced in the air, as if trying to scare me. I am a Christian, but I also believe that spirits roam the earth, some of them evil. I could tell the purple light was floating directly toward me because it became brighter and bigger. It stopped and wiggled in the air for a moment, as if trying to scare me, and then it started floating toward me again. I could hardly breathe. I was so frightened that it was an evil spirit coming to kill me. I hoped it might be an angel, or maybe the Virgin Mother herself answering my prayers. But I knew miracles do not happen that way. The light floated closer, and I closed my eyes and prayed out loud so I would not think about my heart pumping wildly. When I opened my eyes, an Indian was standing before me with the mushroom near his cheek. There was only enough light to see one side of his face, as if he only had a half of a face and no body."

"A phosphorescent mushroom," Mitch said. "Like this one on the instrument panel."

"Yes, and seeing it glow a moment ago when I turned off my flashlight reminded me of that frightening night when I was only twelve. The chief we met and the Indian who saved me might be from the same tribe of night hunters. I had heard about them since I was very young. I was told that night hunters only came out during the darkest time of night, and slept with the nocturnal jaguars during the day. No one from our village would have thought a night hunter would come so close to Tamshiyaco."

"You must have been terrified to see that Indian."

"Yes, but only at first. When I opened my eyes, he was smiling at me. I said `Tamshiyaco' to him, but he didn't seem to understand me. He handed me his mushroom, then he showed me his leather bag full of them. He motioned for me to follow, but I was still too scared to move. I was afraid he might be a headhunter. He turned and smiled again, and waited for me. He was so relaxed, so at peace. I trusted that he must have been sent by the Virgin Mother, and I followed him, holding my glowing mushroom like a sacred object. He led me all the way back to the edge of Tamshiyaco. When I saw house lights, I cried like a baby and started to run toward them, but then I stopped and turned to thank the Indian. He backed away and touched his chest with two fingers, and then he twirled around while hopping happily from foot to foot. I thought he must be dancing to celebrate my safe return. Then he smiled and disappeared back into the forest as if it had all been a dream."

"Do you still have his mushroom?"

"No. It dried out and became crisp, but I kept it in my room until my mother died, three years later. They let me put it in her casket to guide her to heaven."

"You were so young to lose your mother."

"It was worse for my father and my older brother. It made them both crazy and hard. They are stubborn men, and they eventually became poisoned with hate for each other. When my brother left home five years ago, my father only had me to torment. He didn't like any of my friends. He said they dress too much like American gringas and they listened to wild disco music. He told me that no man in Tamshiyaco would want to marry me because my evil brother had shamed our family. I felt like a prisoner, and I used to pray for a way to escape. A few Sundays ago, after so many years, my prayers were finally answered. Our visiting priest delivered a letter from a rich friend who would pay my expenses to attend nursing university in Lima. That was the first of two miracles."

"What was the other one?"

"When you stopped your boat at Tamshiyaco."

Mitch had started to take another drink of water, but turned to see if she was joking. He saw her bite her lower lip—it was no joke.

"What happened to your brother?"

"He moved to the mountains. He exports produce grown there by the Quechua people. They are descendants of the Incas, and are very good farmers."

"What kind of produce—"

"I have told you so much about me. What about you, Mitch? Do you miss your family in America?"

"I don't have a family. My parents died in a car crash when I was a baby."

"Did you grow up in an orphanage?"

"No, I lived in foster homes. The government pays people to let orphans stay in their homes."

"Do you have a wife?"

Mitch stood from his stool and gazed through the windshield "I did. She died a few years ago."

Tessa got up from her stool and stood near him. They both looked ahead at the dark river in silence, glimpsing at each other's reflection in the windshield.

Suddenly feeling self-conscious, Tessa said "I should check Luis."

"Yes, maybe you should."

Their eyes lingered on each other for a moment, and he put his hands on her shoulders. Tessa took a half-step into his arms and they kissed softly and long. She rested her cheek against his for a moment, then took a bashful step back.

"It will be a long night for you. Would you like coffee?"

"That would help."

"I'll make some for you."

Tessa used the flashlight to find her way to the galley. She found a small saucepan, then stopped a moment to ponder her unexpected kiss—with a man she knew just a few days. With any other man, kissing so soon might have seemed inappropriate. But she didn't feel that way with Mitch. She remembered how the night hunter chief seemed to see right through him, into his heart. He would never have respected Mitch as another chief unless he saw purity and power.

She lit the burner with a match, and while the water heated, she peeked into Luis's room. He was on his back snoring peacefully. She stepped in and felt his forehead, making sure the fever was still gone.

She hurried back to the galley and rummaged through the crowded cabinet until she found a jar of instant coffee crystals and a tin can of sugar cubes. Both would have been treasures in her village. She let one of the sugar cubes dissolve in her mouth while the water heated, It gave her time to wonder what caused Mitch to change his mind about her. He had never flirted or teased her, like other men. Instead, he was almost rude when they first met. His kiss tonight took her completely by surprise.

But none of that would matter in a few hours. Mitch would deliver her and Luis to Iquitos and then disappear forever with his boat. Nothing would be left except a lifetime memory, as memorable as the one when she got lost in the jungle as a little girl, but for very different reasons.

After pouring the hot water into a mug, she stirred in two heaping teaspoons of coffee powder and dropped in two sugar cubes.

When she got to the wheelhouse, she handed the coffee mug to Mich. "Luis's fever has not come back."

Mitch took a deep breath and sucked in a sip of the hot coffee. "You helped him heal, Tessa, and so did Assiz. I wonder if the chief's spirit did something."

"I don't know, but I know yours did."

Chapter 10

Shortly after Tessa had gone below to sleep, Mitch reached the end of of the Yarapa River. He turned onto the wide Amazon, and cruised to the middle. After an hour or so, the emotional afterglow from embracing Tessa filled his head. Those thoughts and the muggy night air soon mellowed his energy into a trance-like stupor. Whenever he caught himself nodding off, he'd refresh with a deep breath and stand up from his stool. If any scrapes against the hull took him by surprise, he prolonged the adrenalin punch by stretching his muscles. He forced his brain to stay alert by mentally rehearsing step-by-step plans when they returned to Iquitos.

If his plan went well, Luis would continue healing and Tessa could go to her friend's house, and from there travel alone to Lima for nursing school. He hated thinking that he would never see Tessa or Luis again. He wondered if he would ever find someone, or someplace, he didn't have to leave.

The soothing mechanical dirge of Paraiso's engines soon entranced him. His eyes unfocused and his eyelids drooped, even shut for a moment. He mumbled "Help me" but didn't know who he was petitioning. But he blinked and tapped into an energy reserve that he didn't know he had, and the next few hours passed quickly.

Fresh daylight spread pink and orange highlights across puffy clouds that had grown overnight. After he stretched and loudly yawned to energize himself, Tessa startled him from behind.

"Luis is sitting up now," she said.

He turned to see her at the door in sneakers with no socks, and wearing a light green dress imprinted with tiny white flowers. She had tied her hair back with a thin white scarf and her face glowed from excitement.

"He ate a whole banana and bread with butter, and even drank coffee. He couldn't stop talking to me about his family. I think he will stay well now."

"Thank God." His voice cracked from too many silent hours at the wheel. He cleared his throat. "He beat the damned infection."

Mitch blasted the boat's horn three times to celebrate, and frightened long-legged waterbirds flapped their wide wings to soar up out of tall riverbank grasses.

Tessa stepped closer. "I changed his bandages last night. When I treated his wounds with antibiotic ointment, they were not yellow anymore."

"Things are going well for a change."

"You look so tired, Mitch. Can I steer for a while? I'll get a blanket and you can sleep on the floor next to me. I'm sure I can stay in the middle of the river. And I'll kick you if I have a problem."

Mitch had a ready laugh for her joke. He glanced at his watch. "We're almost to Iquitos. I can stay awake now, but you can scoot a stool over next to me and visit."

Tessa sat with her eyes locked on his, then she absently searched the river ahead. "Our time together will be over soon…maybe forever."

"I hope not forever."

"I will borrow money from my friend in Iquitos, to pay you for my passage."

"No need to. You're not a passenger anymore. You've become an official crewmember."

She pressed her lips to keep from smiling. "Such an honor. How much do you pay crewmembers?"

"Oh, I forgot to say, '*Unpaid* crewmember.'"

After a few minutes, she said, " I might need to stay in Iquitos for a while before I can get an airplane flight to Lima. Maybe we can meet before I leave."

Not wanting to stop the back-and-forth banter, Mitch said, "Then would I be a proper suiter?"

"Yes, but I hope not too proper." She stood still smiling. "I will make you coffee now, and bring you bread and bananas for breakfast."

"Will you have breakfast with me?"

"Yes. Of course."

Within a few minutes, Tessa entered the wheelhouse carrying a small basket of bread buns and bananas in one hand, and a mug of coffee in the other. He went to her and took the coffee, and almost dropped it when he saw Luis following her into the wheelhouse, wearing untied sneakers, a wrinkled gray tee shirt, and khaki cargo pants.

Mitch set his coffee on the floor and ran to Luis, helping him up the step.

"Sit in the chair, my friend. Do your legs hurt?"

"Not too much, but my legs have gotten lazy from too much rest. They need to work again."

"I think we'll be at Iquitos soon."

"Yes, I know that bend ahead."

Humid heat soon dominated the morning air. After a couple of hours, they could see Iquitos's colorless profile blurred by a heavy morning haze. Mitch steered toward the ramshackle riverside raft houses and wood stilt buildings that competed for space along the riverfront.

"I see the city wharf," Mitch said. "It doesn't look like anyone's there."

Luis said "Never trust what you can't see. Start heading for the Nanay River dock."

To be less conspicuous, Mitch cruised past Iquitos from a distance. Just past town he turned toward the Nanay tributary, which emptied into the Amazon River east of Iquitos. As they cruised along at low power, he scanned the area with the binoculars.

Mitch gave the binoculars to Luis. "I didn't see any boats or people at the Nanay pier."

Luis used both arms to struggle up off the wood chair, and then peered out the windshield with the binoculars. Tessa joined them on Mitch's other side.

Luis handed the binoculars back to Mitch. "An empty pier is more normal here than at Iquitos. The water is not clear in this area, so the fishermen stay away."

Mitch turned the wheel over to Luis, and walked with Tessa to the front of the boat. After Luis eased Paraiso up against the pier, Mitch opened the deck rail gate and stepped about a foot down onto the wood dock. Tessa tossed the bow line to him, and after he tied the line to a mooring pole, they went to the stern and secured that line the same way.

Luis cut the engines and stepped gingerly down from the wheelhouse step with a tight grip on the handrail.

"My legs are still a little lazy," Luis said with a grin, "but it is beautiful to be home from this exciting trip."

Mitch said, "You're not home yet." When Tessa joined them, he said, "I don't see any taxis here, so I'll walk to town to find one. Last night I thought of a slight change of plans. Luis, we'll take Tessa to her friend's home, then I'll go with you to the hospital. Then I'll stop at the bank to withdraw my money, and come back here to take Paraiso up the Nanay River. I'll anchor or tie up somewhere upriver, and you can come for me when a doctor says you are fit enough."

"I don't need a hospital or doctor, Mitch. My wife will take care of me."

"I know Gardenia will take good care of you, but please let a doctor look at your wounds first—otherwise I'll worry about you. I already have enough to worry about."

Luis nodded a surrender and pointed down the dirt road. "See that bar down the road? It's called *Pico's*. I know Pico. I'll wait here and rest my legs while you talk to him. Tell him I sent you, and I think he will drive us for a cheap price."

The unpainted, tin roofed, open-air bar was perched above the Nanay River's edge with long stilts holding it up on the river side. It looked about a city block away,

Tessa turned to Mitch. "I'm afraid we won't see each other again."

"I'll find you when I get past some of this trouble, Tessa. I promise. I don't know how or when, but I will find you."

Her eyes moistened. "I believe you will try."

Luis said, "I'll hire a speedboat, Mitch, and join you in a few days."

"Fine, but no need to hurry. I have plenty of provisions aboard, and I hope to get enough money from the bank to stay a long time."

Tessa went aboard for her pack and waited on the dock. Mitch was helping Luis to his room to pack a few belongings into his small duffle bag. Before leaving, Mitch went to his cabin and stuffed a roll of Peruvian soles into his pocket, then he helped Luis up to the wheelhouse where he could sit on the stool and watch Mitch and Tessa walk down the dusty road to the bar.

A skinny shirtless man met them as they walked into the bar. He seemed cautious at first, and more so when Mitch asked if he was Pico. Tessa told him that Luis Riva had sent them. After Mitch offered to pay him for a ride to town, he gushed about how happy he would be to drive them. Pico apologized for having such a rusty car, but he said it was reliable and the tires didn't leak air.

The conversation stopped when a police cruiser crept by, like a predator stalking prey. Mitch coaxed Tessa by the arm away from the door. The cruiser kept rolling toward Paraiso. Mitch ran to a screened window and saw another police car following at a distance. He guessed that Captain Santos would be in one of the cruisers. Only the most reliable policemen in Iquitos were allowed to drive police cars without Santos's supervision. There had been too many embarrassing accidents by drunk officers.

They stopped at the dock, and two uniformed policemen got out of each car—Santos was not one of them. Mitch and Tessa watched Luis step down from the wheelhouse and limped toward the deck rail. A policeman said something to him and Luis shrugged with his palms up. Another officer stepped up onto the deck and shoved Luis to the deck floor. A policeman from the second cruiser ran aboard and threw the companionway door open. He drew his pistol and cautiously peered inside before stepping down the stairs.

Mitch moved back from the window. "Tessa, it looks like I just lost my boat. I have to find another way out of here. I just hope they leave Luis alone."

She stared at him, speechless at first. "What should we do?"

"After the police leave, you and Pico can take Luis to the hospital to make sure he's healthy enough to go home. After that, have Pico take you to your friend's house. It might be dangerous for you to come back here."

"And dangerous for you to stay. I can't just leave you here alone."

"I know. And I'm sure my apartment will be watched. I'll stay with a friend for a while. Would you deliver a note to her to pick me up?"

"*Her?*"

"Her name is Darla Peters."

"An American."

"Yes. Just tell her to come here and get me?"

Tessa nodded, and watched Mitch write the address on a scrap of brown paper that Pico gave him. "Is Darla a girlfriend?"

"No. Just a friend." He handed her the paper. "Just tell Darla to park at the bar's entrance. I'll be watching for her."

One of police cruisers raced past the bar, stirring up a plume of reddish dust.

Tessa put a hand over her chest. "Mitch! Luis was in the back of that police car. They must have arrested him."

Mitch looked through the screened window and saw the other police cruiser still parked in front of the boat. Two officers stood guard on the deck.

"Damn. All right, a change of plans…" While thinking through ideas, he peeled off a few bills from his roll of money and handed them to Tessa. "This should be enough to pay Pico, and some extra to bribe yourself out of trouble, if need be. Have Pico take you to Darla's first, then go to your friend's house and stay put for a while."

"Is that your new plan?"

"I'm afraid it's the best I can do for now."

"What about Luis?"

"Maybe Darla can get him out of jail, or maybe a restaurant owner I know. I'll have to sort that out later."

Their eyes locked, both knowing more plans were useless now. Mitch put his hand out and she took it in hers, and they stepped into each other's arms. He kissed her forehead, and her cheek, and her lips found his. Their kiss told of love and sadness, and a parting that neither of them wanted.

Tessa said "We have to believe—"

"We will meet again, Tessa, and soon. That's what I believe."

Mitch stood just inside the entrance doorway while Tessa and Pico hurried to his car. When it rounded a corner down the road, he went back to the window to watch the police, and wait for Darla.

Mitch remembered the pain of seeing how roughly the policeman had treated Luis, and his anger grew. He felt vulnerable now, with everything hinging on Tessa finding Darla, and Darla coming to his aid. It seemed like a hasty, clumsy plan, put together with nothing but hope for a change in luck. Ideas spun through Mitch's brain. He could jump off the bar's backside into the river, but the splash could be heard. He could sneak aboard Paraiso at night and overtake the policemen, but risk getting shot. He wondered if he could just hide in the jungle until the boat was unguarded.

But all of those fantastical ideas seemed more desperate than reasoned. He decided to just stay put and rely on Tessa finding Darla. He could rely on Tessa.

He remembered her seeming jealous about Darla. He

knew that at the time, but had offered nothing more than a hasty gloss-over about his uncertain relationship with Darla. His friendship with Darla was not anything close to the way he felt about Tessa, the lovely woman from Tamshiyaco who has unexpectedly melded her way into his heart and his life. He avowed to someday, somehow, tell her that.

His mental rambling unhooked when Rafael Domingo's white pickup truck stopped abruptly in front of the bar. Darla climbed out of the passenger side, pushing her hair behind her shoulders while strutting toward the bar. She stopped just inside and removed her sunglasses, then Rafael roared off toward the boat.

Mitch got out of his chair and glared at her. "Why did you bring him? So he could see his new boat?"

"No, and keep your voice down. He's just wants to distract the cops."

"Okay, then why in hell *did* you bring him?"

Darla stiffened and her eyes narrowed. "I didn't *bring* him—he brought me, in case you didn't notice. Do you want us to leave? If we do, you'll eventually get caught and busted. The police are no doubt watching all the docks and the airport. There are no other ways to leave Iquitos, and you know it. You don't even own a boat anymore. I know you don't like Rafael, but he can push buttons for you, Mitch. He might be your only chance to get out of this mess."

Rafael drove back to the bar and parked in front of the door.

When he got into the bar, Mitch said "So, you found a way to legally steal my boat."

The look in his eyes didn't match the smile on his face. "I never wanted to steal your boat. How can you say that? I offered to buy it from you, and for a good price. Now I might have to buy it from the police at a low price."

"And why is that?"

"And why do you ask such a stupid question, Mitch? That policeman down the street just told me that the boat, and everything in it, will soon belong to the police. They have evidence that you smuggled cocaine into Iquitos, and they will have the right to seize your property."

"You know that evidence is false."

"Of course. But false evidence has put people into a stinking prison in Lima. A drug trafficking charge can mean a life sentence."

"And then you can buy Paraiso cheap."

"I still would rather buy it from you, and for a fair price."

"Well, it seems that you're too late."

"It's not too late. If I tell Captain Santos that I own the boat, he'll un-confiscate it. He doesn't want to take any boats from me, just from you. He thinks American gringos like you take too much money out of the country, and leave poor Peruvians to struggle."

"And if I bribe him, the money stays in Peru—although in his private bank account."

"Yes, and when he spends the money, it will go to other Peruvians. This system probably works the same way in the United States."

"I'm no economist, Rafael, but I know corruption when I smell it."

"I don't know what you are smelling, but I'm your best friend right now. Who else would offer to buy your boat from you when I could buy it cheaper from the police?."

Rafael smiled toward Darla. "That makes me a good guy, doesn't it?"

She kept her eyes trained on Mitch.

"No," Mitch said, "it makes you a drug runner with a lot of money. I'd rather see Santos get Paraiso."

Darla said, "Mitch, don't be foolish. Even if Santos keeps your boat, he'll still arrest you. And what about Luis?"

"She's trying to help you," Rafael said. "But that guard won't. I gave him a few hundred soles to leave us alone for a while, but if you don't leave with me and Darla, you better be a fast runner."

"Okay, what's your offer?"

"I'm offering to help you and Luis be free from arrest."

"How?"

"In exchange for your signing your boat over to me, I'll get Luis released to his family. Then I'll put you safely aboard an airplane I've charted to deliver some cargo. It will make a couple of stops, then take you to the United States."

"How about Costa Rica instead?"

"You're planning a vacation now?"

"I can't return to the U.S. I left behind some legal problems. But I know someone in Costa Rica."

"I can tell the pilots to let you off in Costa Rica. It's on the way."

"And I need a thousand dollars."

"Why should I pay you anything more?"

"Because I'll sign the Paraiso over to you. That way you'll have legal ownership proof when you register the boat with the Peruvian government."

"I can register anything I want to—and for a lot less than a thousand dollars."

Darla dropped her gaze from Mitch and looked at Rafael. "He needs the money to buy some kind of flower farm in Costa Rica. I wish you'd pay him if you can so we can get out of here."

"The airplane is ready to leave in a few minutes," Rafael said to Mitch. "We have to take you to the airport now, or it leaves without you."

"What about the thousand dollars."

"I don't have that much with me. I'll arrange for the pilots to pay it to you when they land."

"Why should I believe that?"

"Why should I care?" Rafael left the bar and strode to his pickup truck.

Darla scowled at Mitch. "You're so damn stubborn. Can't you understand that you're screwed if you stay here. If you don't like Rafael, fine, but I think he'll make good on his offer."

They both heard Rafael's truck door slam shut.

"I have to leave, Mitch."

"Why's Rafael bothering to help me?"

"I really don't know. He sure doesn't need to."

"Then why did you bring him?"

She gave Mitch a puzzled look. "I didn't bring him. He brought me. Rafael came to my apartment and said you were here, and in big trouble with the police."

"That was in my note."

"He didn't show me a note."

"I sent it with Tessa."

"Tessa? Who's she?"

Rafael tapped a short horn beep.

Darla said, "Maybe your new friend can help you, but I'm getting out of here."

She rushed outside and climbed into the truck. As if on cue, a police car drove past the bar toward the boat. Mitch ran out of the bar and got into the truck's back seat.

Chapter 11

Rafael sped through Iquitos to the airport, and past armed security guards leaning against the open airport gate. They stared with blank eyes while Rafael drove onto the tarmac and down a row of assorted airplanes. He pulled up to a small twin-engine business jet at the end. Two crewmen sat in the shade of its wing, and strained to get up on their feet when they saw it was Rafael. He got out of the truck and went to them. Mitch tried to hear what he was saying, but their Spanish was too fast and too far away. Darla cranked her window down a few inches, and Mitch leaned forward to listen.

"What are they saying?"

"Rafael said you're his American *corredor*—a runner."

"A drug runner?"

Darla gave him a sarcastic look in the rearview mirror. "Gosh, do you think?"

"Why would he say that about me?"

"Probably so you'll get some respect instead of a bullet. Runners have more status than desperate gringos."

"I thought Rafael only traded in raw coca."

"The Columbians have been ripping him off, so he's started processing his own coke in the mountains. Now he's trying to work out trafficking routes to other countries. That's what this flight is about."

"You know a lot about his business."

"Rafael talks carelessly when he's been drinking." She glanced at him in the mirror again. "Just like all men."

Rafael climbed up the airplane's fold-out stairs. After a few minutes, he came back to the truck and opened the rear door for Mitch.

"Time to go, my friend. The plane's full of cargo, but there's a seat for you. It's not a luxury flight but you'll be safe."

"Did you tell them about the thousand dollars?"

"Yes, and the captain will give it to you enroute."

"Why not now?"

"They're too busy with preflight checks and flight plans."

"And they're letting me off In Costa Rica, right?"

"Yes, of course."

One of the ground crewmen motioned for Mitch to get aboard the airplane. The cargo bay was crowded with stacked black plastic bundles, each wound with clear shipping tape. They were about a foot square, all of them strapped together. Mitch had to shuffle sideways to get through the narrow space between stacks. The cockpit door was closed, but he heard switches clicking and the pilots calling off checklist items in English. There was no ventilation, and the windows had been neatly taped over with duct tape.

Mitch stood still until his eyes adjusted to the darkness. A thread of light from the bottom of the cockpit door allowed him to find two webbed seats attached to the rear bulkhead. He sat down and clasped the seatbelt, hardly able to breathe in the steamy air. His tee shirt started soaking up sweat, and salty droplets from his forehead stung his eyes. He became woozy after several minutes of waiting, and unfastened his seatbelt to lay on the metal floor with his eyes closed.

The engines' whine startled Mitch from a delirious drift into sleep. He had no idea of how long he had been on the floor, but the sunlight was still bright around the cockpit door. The engines began to scream louder and he felt the airplane haltingly creep forward.

Squeaking brakes checked the airplane's momentum, and eventually stopped it. The engines revved to a shrill while the airplane shook, then the airplane lurched, and Mitch slid back. He knelt and felt for the seat, but when the airplane pitched up into a steep climb, his body slammed against the bulkhead. He got up and sat in one of the webbed seats, then tried to find the seatbelt. The landing gears growled while pulling the wheels up into the airplane's aluminum belly.

The engines soon reduced power, and Mitch could feel the airplane leveling. He wondered how they reached cruising altitude so quickly—they'll soon have mountains to climb over before reaching Central America.

He buckled himself into the seat. The cabin began to cool and he soon had to cross his arms against a chill he wasn't used to. When the cold and monotony grew intolerable, Mitch unbuckled and worked his way toward the front of the airplane. He felt for the cockpit door latch and twisted it. As soon as the door opened, both pilots jerked their heads around.

"You're not allowed in here," barked the pilot in the left seat. "Close the door and take your seat." His perfect American English carried a slight southern accent. Neither of the pilots looked like Peruvians.

"I just wanted to know how soon before we're in Costa Rica."

"Our next stop is for fuel."

"Where at?"

"Belém."

"That's in Brazil, on the east coast. I thought you were heading north to Central America."

"There's bad weather in the mountains, so we're making a detour. Now get back in there and sit down. Don't open this door again, and stay in your seat when we stop to refuel."

Mitch took a step back and started to close the pilot's door. "Okay, no problem."

"Yes, there is a problem. We don't get paid to take on passengers who could later talk to the wrong people. You're lucky we didn't shoot you and throw you overboard as soon as we left Iquitos. So, sit down, stay small, and shut up."

Mitch quickly closed the door and felt his way back through the stacks of plastic-wrapped packages. His mouth and throat were dry, but he didn't ask for water.

Chapter 12

The two policemen who had arrested Luis brought him to the hospital, and followed a nurse to his room with three beds, all of them empty. After she helped Luis into one of the beds, one of the policemen handcuffed him to the bed's iron-rail headboard. When the attending doctor arrived, he protested about having a patient handcuffed, but his complaint was ignored. When the policemen started to leave, the doctor said he would call his friend the mayor if they didn't remove the handcuffs immediately. The policeman unlocked the cuffs with a sarcastic grin.

After the policemen left, Luis said "Thank you, Doctor."

"You are a patient here, not a prisoner. That looks like fresh blood through your pants."

"The wounds had started healing, but the police treated me roughly."

When a nurse came in to dress his wounds, the doctor helped her cut away Luis's tattered pants. Luis tried to distract the pain with thoughts about his wife and his children.

After his legs were bare, the doctor looked the wounds over. "What happened to you?"

"Hungry Piranhas happened."

"Were you swimming?"

"I was helping to save a woman from drowning."

"And the police arrested you for that?"

"No, the police arrested me for no reason."

"I see…" The doctor let it go and went back to his examination.

The doctor instructed the nurse to treat the wounds with antibiotic ointment, and he prescribed antibiotic tablets before he left. While carrying out his orders, she offered to call Luis's wife for him, but Luis decided against alarming her yet. He didn't want Gardenia to see him this way. She had already suffered too much, too many times before. He would sometimes come home from expeditions cut and scraped, with broken bones or snake bites. Once he was electrocuted almost to death when he stepped on an electric eel in the shallow water of a jungle puddle. It took him two weeks before he could walk without help. He wanted to spare Gardenia from more tears this time, at least until his legs were bandaged.

After treating his wounds, the nurse covered him with a sheet and gave him an antibiotic tablet with a plastic cup of water. When she left, Luis slipped into a deep sleep.

***

After a few hours, Luis woke from someone gently wiggling his shoulder. He looked up at the doctor. "Am I well now?"

"Not quite. The bleeding stopped, but the wounds could still open easily."

The doctor pulled the sheet off Luis and carefully felt his legs and forehead. "I didn't see any infection. Someone took good care of you."

"Yes, a young woman who wants to be a nurse. She should work here."

"Maybe she can."

"She will be happy when I tell her that. Can I go home now?"

"Do you have someone at home to take care of you?"

"Yes, my wife, Gardenia."

"Then you should go home before the police return. I'll tell the nurse to give you a bag with ointment, antibiotic tablets, and gauze. Do you have a way to get home?"

"I can walk home. I live only a kilometer or so from here."

"You can't walk that far yet. I'll pay for a taxi, but wait here until the nurse brings your medications."

"My wife can soak some crushed roots in beer for a healing tonic."

The doctor nodded thoughtfully. Many of his patients, while valuing modern medicines, still relied on ancient home remedies.

"Please try my medicine first. If it works, you won't have to waste your beer."

"That is very wise. No wonder you are a doctor. I'll get dressed now."

"The nurse had to throw away your pants. There were too many tears to mend and too much dried blood and puss to wash out. You can keep your hospital gown."

Luis creased his forehead. "People will think it's a dress. They'll say I'm under a spell, or even crazy. And what if a priest sees me?"

"It looks like a hospital gown, not a dress. Anyone can see that."

"But it's on backwards, as if I'm too stupid to wear a dress properly."

"It's just for your ride home. I'll have a nurse sneak you out the back door, and pay the driver extra to keep your secret."

After he left, Luis carefully lowered his legs off the bed without too much pain. His feet felt cool against the tile floor, and that worried him.

When the nurse returned, he said, "Can my feet die before I do?"

"I've never heard of that problem. Do you have any feeling in them?"

"Yes, but it's a cold feeling."

"Oh, then your feet aren't cold—it's the floor that's cold."

Her smile made Luis wonder if she was telling a clever lie. She said "I'll get you some hospital stockings."

Luis surrendered with a nod—first a dress, now stockings. He wondered, What next? Will they want to tie a pink ribbon in my hair?

He tried standing, but a flood of pain grabbed him by surprise. He clenched his teeth and reminded himself that this was not the worst pain he had ever suffered, and everything would be fine, now that he was going home to his family.

After the nurse left, he wondered if the police took Paraiso and put Mitch in jail. Before his imagination could run with those questions, the nurse appeared at the door with ankle-high socks and a wheelchair.

"I have a taxi waiting for you at the back door."

"Wheelchairs are for feeble people. I can walk to the taxi."

"Wheelchairs are also for important people, like professors and cinema stars."

Luis was now convinced that she was lying, just to make him happy.

"Maybe I'll try riding in it, then."

The nurse slipped on his socks and wheeled Luis out of the hospital's backdoor. She helped him get situated in the taxi's back seat. After handing Luis a paper bag with his medications, she paid the driver.

They drove through Iquitos's central market district, and within a few minutes they arrived at the front door of Luis's home. The driver helped Luis hobble to the front door, and then left when Luis opened the unlocked door.

Gardenia gasped when she saw him. "Luis, what happened to you? Are you sick? Are you hurt? "

"Both. I fell into the river and piranhas attacked me. I won the fight."

"Piranhas? Oh, my God, Luis. I always pray that you won't kill yourself someday but you keep trying."

"The doctor said I was healing well."

"It was bad enough to find a doctor?"

He didn't want to open worries about being arrested. "Mitch wanted me to see a doctor. He worries for us, you know."

"Yes. Mitch is a good man."

"Where are the children?"

"The boys are with my mother this afternoon. They are helping her make dried fruit sweets."

Luis shuffled over to his favorite wood rocking chair, and sat down heavily.

"We made no money this trip, Gardenia. I'm sorry." Luis braced himself for her complaints. How could she love him if he didn't bring home money?

"Don't worry. We still have some money."

Without saying anything further, she went to their cramped little kitchen and poured him a cup of papaya juice from an unglazed pitcher that had been covered against insects with a white cloth, and kept cool from the pitcher sweating. She brought the cup to him and sat facing him in her favorite cushioned rattan armchair.

"What else happened on this trip, Luis?"

He told her about Tessa and how she almost drowned, and that the oil explorers are leaving their jungle camp, maybe forever.

She said, "Can you and Mitch find other business for his boat?"

"That's another problem. He lost his boat."

"He can't find it?"

"Not that kind of lost. Policemen came for us after we returned to Iquitos. They said cocaine was found aboard the boat, and they were confiscating it. When I disrespected his lie, he handcuffed me and said he would take me to jail for resisting him. Since he lied, I lied back. I said I was dying from contagious jungle rot. After he saw my bloody pants, he and another policeman took me to the hospital—to get rid of me, I think."

"You were a better liar than that policeman, Luis."

"Thank you, dear."

A pounding at the door startled both of them. Gardenia bounded out of her chair and opened it just enough to peeked out. She said "Please come in," and then stepped aside.

Luis stopped rocking and glared at her.

Darla said, "How are you getting along, Luis? I heard you were attacked by piranhas."

"How did you know about that?"

"I went to the police station to look for you, and they said you were in the hospital with a terrible disease. The nurse who helped you told me what really happened to you, and told me where you live."

"Does Rafael own Paraiso now?"

"I don't know."

"I guessed that Rafael's girlfriend would know."

"You are guessing too much, Luis. Rafael already has a girlfriend, but it's not me. He has said very little about her, except that he wants her identity kept a secret. He's afraid his enemies might kidnap her for a ransom."

"How does he hide her?"

"She only stays with him when she's in Iquitos, which is not very often."

"She must live in the mountains."

"Maybe, but I didn't come to discuss Rafael's girlfriend. I just wanted to tell you that Rafael helped Mitch escaped from the police. In exchange for giving him title to Paraiso, Rafael gave him passage out of Peru on one of his chartered jets."

"Where is the airplane going?"

"I don't know the final destination, but the pilots will drop Mitch off in Costa Rica. Rafael also agreed to give Mitch a thousand dollars so he could buy a flower farm there."

The room went silent for a few moments. Gardenia finally said, "I think Mitch's dream is finally coming true."

Chapter 13

Mitch stayed in his seat after the airplane landed. The pilot who had threatened him strode out of the cockpit, glanced at Mitch, and opened the side door. Amber late-afternoon sunlight flooded the cabin. While Mitch adjusted his eyes, the pilot lowered the electric folding stairs down onto the tarmac. He carried a zippered canvas pouch, presumably to pay for the fuel.

Mitch unbuckled his seatbelt and stood back from the doorway, looking for something to identify their location. Within a few minutes, a fuel truck with *Gasolina Brasil* on its tank pulled up next to the airplane.

Mitch guessed that they would have reached Costa Rica by now if they had flown a direct route, and this airplane was surely able to fly in any weather. Why did they make such a long detour? Maybe their plan was to deliver some or all of the cargo to some Caribbean Island north of Belém, Brazil, and then head west to Costa Rica. It's the only thing that made sense. But he dared not ask the pilots.

***

After the airplane left Belém, Mitch drifted in and out of a shallow sleep on the floor. His dreams became remarkably vivid. He caught himself half-awake mumbling something aloud to Tessa. Once, he thought he could see her, but the hallucination disappeared when the familiar grinding of the landing gears announced the approach to their next landing. The touch-down was hard this time, and Mitch could feel the tail wagging from side to side for directional control down the runway. The jet's reverse engine thrust howled wide open, and with hard off-and-on braking the airplane jerked to a quick stop. While the airplane taxied, Mitch got up off the floor and sat in the web seat, but without his seatbelt on. He was intuitively on guard, ready to escape. Nothing about this bizarre flight made sense to him. First, the pilot's lethal threat meant he was probably armed. Then, the inexplicable route they had taken, crossing the South American continent in the wrong direction for fuel— because of bad weather in the mountains? He readied himself and resolved to make a run for it if this stop wasn't in Costa Rica.

As soon as the engines went silent, the cockpit door swung open. The pilot who threatened him at the beginning of the flight stayed in his seat, while the co-pilot unlatched the cargo door, using his weight to pull it inward. He flipped a switch that slowly unfolded the mechanical airstairs to the ground. The pilot started down the stairs, then paused and turned to Mitch. "You'll be staying at this airfield until the next airplane arrives. You'll continue on with them."

"How will I know which airplane?"

"It'll be the next one that lands here."

"Where are we?"

"Nigeria."

"Africa?"

"Yeah—that's still where Nigeria is."

Mitch ignored the snipe. "What about Costa Rica? Is the

next plane going there?"

"You'll have to ask the next crew."

"Where are you going?"

"We'll fuel up at the international airport, then head back to Iquitos."

"What about the thousand dollars Rafael said you'd pay me? Or was that bullshit, too."

"Listen, our only job was to fly here from Iquitos with cargo, and then fly back empty—and that means without you. That's all we know, and that's all we want to know."

The other pilot startled Mitch when he rushed out of the cockpit. He glanced at Mitch, and then said to the co-pilot "There's a rough-looking bunch of soldiers out there. Let's unload and get the hell out of here."

Mitch went to the open door and saw an asphalt runway, cracked and blistered, with a multitude of tar-patched potholes. He took one careful step at a time down the lowered stairway, and looked at a surrounding area composed mostly of bare dirt and weeds. He counted twelve solders silently eyeing the pilots, as if waiting for something. The only people working were six men wearing desert camo military trousers, floppy hats, black boots, but shirtless. They used machetes to hack down knee-high grass bordering the runway, swinging their blades in unison, advancing one step per swing. A long swath of hand-mowed browned grass lay behind them. Now and then one of them would try to glance sideways at the airplane while maintaining the cadence of his companions. Beyond the airport, a vast plain reached a cloudless blue-sky horizon. Tall umbrella-like trees sparsely littered the landscape, and Mitch saw a lone giraffe in the distance, grazing on one of the tree's leafy high branches.

Two soldiers in a military jeep roared in from somewhere

behind the airplane, and pulled up in front of the pilots. The pilots climbed into the back of the jeep, and Mitch watched the driver take them to the airport's only building, a one-story rectangular concrete structure with a corrugated tin roof. It had a wood door near the middle, and two small windows, one on each side, with screens and shutters. Two big army-green trucks with canvas-covered backends sat in the front of the building, casting shade for a few men in civilian shorts and shirts. About half of the men climbed into the back of a truck, while the others squatted or stood in the building's scant shadow.

Mitch looked around to the other side of the airplane and saw only more of the endless barren plain. He stood in the shade of the airplane's high tail and idly watched the machete men mowing. He considered asking them where the nearest town was, but a glint of sunlight off one of the machetes reminded him to be careful, at least until he had a better measure of this place.

After a few minutes both of the large military trucks lumbered down the decrepit runway, stopping just short of the airplane's low wing. Heavy steal tailgates banged down, and six men from each truck scrambled out of the open backend. Two of them in uniform wore sergeant's stripes on their arms, and barked orders. The other men climbed up the airplane's stairs and began handing the square bundles down to the other men on the ground, who strained to get the packages on their shoulder, and then carried them to the back of the trucks. Two men inside each truck's bed stacked them.

One of the drivers got out of his truck and blankly watched the loaders. The entire process looked as if it were a routine procedure. Mitch could see the driver seated in the other truck, slowly, nonchalantly, peeling an orange.

Mitch didn't recognize the strange language that the men spoke between themselves. He asked aloud if anyone spoke English, but other than getting a few glances, he was ignored.

After all the packages had been transferred and stacked inside the trucks, the men helped each other up into the back to squeeze into available spaces. The last men in slammed the tailgates shut. The drivers throttled the engines to smoky life, and both trucks sped back toward the cement building.

It wasn't long before the military jeep returned to the airplane, with the pilots aboard, , swirling a confusion of dust before reaching the runway. The driver stayed seated while the pilots got out and headed toward the airplane.

Mitch hurried alongside the pilots. "Let me go back with you guys, okay? I'd rather take my chances in Iquitos."

The pilot in command didn't slow down, and said "You're staying here, chances or not. And if you get any closer to the airplane, I told the officer in that jeep to shoot you in the back."

"I don't believe that."

"Go ahead, bet your life that I'm wrong. Or, you can just wait for the next plane."

While the pilot-in-command started a preflight walk-around inspection of airplane, the co-pilot got out of the jeep and walked over to Mitch. "Don't worry, bud, we made a deal with these guys that will keep you safe."

"What kind of deal?"

"They collect a landing fee of a few thousand dollars from every crew that flies in here to pick up the cargo we deliver. But last time, the pilots took off as soon as they loaded up. That officer sitting in the jeep is still pissed, and he wanted to confiscate our airplane until someone pays him. I convinced him that delivery flights don't carry any money. I promised they'd get paid when the pickup aircraft arrives. In the meantime, they'll have the cargo, the arriving crew—and you—as collateral."

"So, I'm a hostage. How is that deal good for me?"

"It'll keep you alive. I told the commanding officer in the jeep that you're a big boss, and there would be no more landings, and no more landing fees if you're harmed. I think he bought it."

"What if the other crew won't cover what's already owed to him?"

"They'll pay. This cargo is worth a hell of a lot more than the landing fees."

"And my life hinges on that theory working out."

"It's the best we can do."

"When's the other airplane coming?"

"Probably tomorrow, unless there's trouble on their end."

"Where's their end?"

"I can't say."

"I'll find out eventually. I'm supposedly going there, right?"

"Okay, it's an outfit out of Belgium. Owned by an American. I don't know where this cargo is going, but they'll probably take you to their home base in Belgium after delivering it. You better get in that jeep now before the driver gets nervous."

"Just one more question. What if the other crew won't take me out of here?"

"Then stay as close to the military as you can. This part of Nigeria is infested with kidnappers and you don't want to end up as ransom bait. A white American would be a jackpot for them."

While both pilots stepped up into the airplane, Mitch hollered "Aren't you afraid I'll tell somebody about all this?"

The pilot in command narrowed his eyes. "Be careful. That *somebody* might not be your friend."

After the airplane hatch closed, Mitch looked back at the jeep driver, who head-motioned for him to get in. As Mitch got into the passenger seat, the driver said, "My name is Musa. I am an army captain and I am in charge of this airport."

"I'm Mitch."

"Welcome to Nigeria, Mitch."

"What happens now?"

"I will drive back to the terminal."

"I mean after that. What will happen to me?"

"You will eat supper and sleep here tonight. The airplane from Europe might be here tomorrow"

"What if the next pilots don't pay you?"

"I don't know yet. But I heard what those pilots were saying to you. I think you were tricked."

"How so?"

"You cannot trust the pilots from Europe."

Musa drove back to the terminal building, and told Mitch to wait inside. Mitch walked past two men squatting in shade from the overhang. Their dispassionate eyes were the only things that moved, following him to the wood door until he went inside.

The almost-bare room appeared large enough to take up about a fourth of the building. A ceiling fan slowly churned the stale air. Under it stood a simple unpainted wood table, with two wood chairs tucked under it. Two more matching chairs were against the back wall, next to a large cork bulletin board where fly-specked official-looking papers had been neatly tacked into place. They were either typed or hand-written in English, and appeared to be standard procedures, duty rosters, and event schedules. A few feet to the other side, an open doorway revealed a rudimentary kitchen.

Mitch looked out the window to see if anything had changed. The machete grass cutters appeared to be the only activity on the field, and had almost worked their way to the end of the runway.

After what seemed to Mitch like an hour or so of sitting and pacing, Musa came in.

"This will be your quarters for tonight. You must stay inside this building. You will be safe here, but nowhere else."

Mitch looked around. "Where will I sleep?"

"You will be given a blanket."

Musa looked into the kitchen, "I see water and bread have been left in the back room. I will bring better food later."

After Musa left, Mitch went into the back room. It had a tile sink and a single faucet. He gulped copious amounts of water directly from the faucet, realizing how dehydrated and foggy-brained he had become. He shooed flies away before lifting a yellow cloth off a ceramic bowl next to the sink. It contained round bread buns. A careful first bite tasted like stale doughnuts. He stuffed down three of them while looking through the only glassed window he had seen since arriving. He saw two men working on an old Land Rover outside, with a few others idly watching. The front wheels had been raised up on plank ramps, and the back wheels were chocked in place with cement bricks. While one of the men lay on his back underneath, another man handed him tools when he asked for them.

Mitch took a chair and sat in front of the window, becoming another spectator for what seemed to be the most interesting thing going on for miles, even though he couldn't see anything the mechanic was doing. It soon became boring, but still better than staring at plaster walls. After an hour or so, when the late-day shadows grew longer, the workmen gathered up the tools and left. Mitch felt disappointed to see the only signs of life leave.

He stood near the front door, and thought a few minutes about pushing it open, just enough to peek around. But Musa startled him by pulling it open, He carried a basket in one hand, and two rolled blankets tucked under his arm. He set the basket on the table and pulled a chair out, then head-motioned for Mitch to come and sit down. Musa took a newspaper-wrapped package out of the basket and opened it to reveal two half-moon-shaped pastries, each about the size of a man's hand.

"Meat pies," Musa said with the first smile Mitch had seen from him. "Very lovely. My wife makes them."

Mitch sat and wondered what kind of meat—giraffe? Dog? Then Musa took out a pint-sized jar of dark brown liquid and unscrewed the lid. "Warm cocoa," he said, setting the bottle on the table. He picked up the blankets and draped them across the chairs against the wall. "Good for sleeping. Nights can be cool here."

Mitch thanked him but Musa stood expressionless, as if waiting for something.

"I don't have any money to pay you," Mitch said.

"You do not pay for my hospitality. You are a guest."

"Are you going to join me?"

"I have already eaten."

Mitch nodded and bit into the flaky pie crust, which enclosed warm meat, potatoes and carrots, buttery and sweet. Mitch smelled the contents of the brown bottle before tasting it. The rich cocoa was still warm. While he ate, energy slowly oozed through his body and brain.

"One of my soldiers will stand guard outside your door.

He is there to protect you, but do not be foolish enough to try leaving. You will be safe here, but nowhere else."

That put Mitch's appetite on hold. Was that a threat, or just good advice?

Mitch said, "Are all these soldiers here just to collect landing fees?"

"No, we are protecting this airfield from Boko Haram and other revolutionaries. They are very dangerous in this area."

"So, the airport is owned by the government?"

"Yes.

"Many of the men are not in uniforms."

"They are not soldiers, but they are good fighters. They are paid to help us defend the airfield."

"Your government hires mercenaries?"

"No, I hire them. I pay them with the landing fees. The army doesn't give me enough money or men to protect this airfield, so I have to find a way."

"Why would revolutionaries attack this airfield?"

"To kill my soldiers, and stop the army from sending more soldiers. They do not want to be stopped from kidnapping children for ransom."

Mitch took another bite of the meat pie while trying to piece that together.

"So, in a sense, drug traffickers are helping you protect your airfield."

"They do not protect anything except their drugs and money, and they protect no one but themselves. Do you like the meat pie?"

Mitch swallowed his bite. "Yes, very much. Please give my thanks to your wife."

"I will."

As if dismissed, Musa went to the door and left. Mitch

finished eating the pies and drinking the rich cocoa.

The ample meal and setting sun made him drowsy, so he placed all four of the room's chairs next to each other against the wall, and draped the two blankets across them. But before trying to sleep, he opened the front door to peek outside. A soldier stood guard a few feet away under the roof's overhang. A rifle with a wood stock and detachable ammo magazine was slung over his shoulder. He regarded Mitch with a brief lifeless stare, and then gazed off toward the almost featureless flatland beyond the airport.

The plastic-wrapped bundles from Iquitos had been stacked on the other side of the guard, up against the whitewashed building's wall. Mitch wondered what the soldier was really guarding—him, the stacked contraband, or both?

He ducked back into the building and closed the door, then went to the back room. He couldn't see anyone in back now, and wondered about his chances of escaping when it got dark. But where to? He didn't know where he was, except somewhere in Nigeria, which was somewhere in Africa. And if Musa was telling the truth, the area around the airfield was crawling with kidnappers.

Mitch tried to distract himself from these unanswerable questions by trying to get into a comfortable position on the row of chairs. After deciding that was impossible, he spread the blankets on the cement floor. Even though the windows were screened, he wondered if rats, snakes, or insects could find a way in after nightfall. If this was in the jungle, he would never sleep on the floor without insect netting.

His scattered thoughts finally narrowed on Tessa, and he found comfort there. He remembered her sparkling brown eyes, a smile that windowed her soul, and the feel and scent of her soft hair. When he promised to return to her, he had meant it, but now danger challenged that promise. As drowsiness overtook him, he dismissed the problem for now. Like Musa, he would decide what to do tomorrow.

Chapter 14

Mitch woke to the thunder of jet engines. He struggled to his feet and ran to the screened window in time to see a twin-engine business jet complete its landing roll. It was larger than the one from Iquitos, and used almost all of the runway to stop and turn around.

He went outside and saw the man who had guarded his building run to join other armed soldiers heading toward the runway. Both of the canvas-covered army trucks raced past them, loaded with other armed men in the back, some uniformed, some not. Mitch walked toward the airplane, worried that he might be challenged for leaving the airport building.

He saw Musa charge his jeep past the trucks. He had three armed soldiers with him, and he parked in front of the approaching airplane to prevent it from moving. Musa and the other soldiers jumped out of the jeep, and the two soldiers aimed their rifles at the cockpit windshield. Musa used a cut-throat gesture for the pilots to stop the engines. The trucks pulled up behind the jeep and the armed combatants piled out of the opened tailgate, all with rifles at the ready.

While the engines wound down, the airplane's cabin door slowly opened from the inside. No one could be seen until an electric motor unfolded and lowered the stairs. When the stairway came to a rest on the runway, a man in jeans and a wrinkled white shirt with rolled up long-sleeves came to the doorway. After nervously scanning the crowed of armed men, he said "Take it easy. We're just here for the cargo. We need help loading it. A storm is coming, and we need to leave right away.

Musa walked up to the man and said, "Your cargo will be loaded after landing taxes are paid—once for this landing, and once for the time you cheated us."

"We'll pay for this shipment, but we didn't handle that last one."

"That's too bad for you."

The pilot looked back into the cabin and whispered for a moment with someone. He turned back to Musa. "If you try to keep our cargo, you'll never see another flight come here. Understand?"

"Musa said. "I understand. And you need to understand that if you don't pay us, we'll keep your cargo, *and* your airplane—and you."

The pilot stared at Musa and bit his lip. "All right, you win.."

The pilot disappeared back into the unlit cabin. No one on the ground spoke, and the soldiers began to shoulder their rifles.

The standoff silence frightened Mitch, like standing in the placid eye of a vicious hurricane. His instincts told him to move carefully toward the front of the airplane, away from this quiet, but volatile showdown. When he got just past Musa's jeep, two men in tee shirts and jeans came to the airplane's doorway with short Uzi-style machine guns. One fired a burst into Musa and his three riders, then they sprayed the soldiers with fiery streams of bullets. Expended brass casings streamed onto the runway like metallic hail. Mitch ran back to Musa's jeep, his only protective cover, and squatted out of sight. When he heard rounds snapping by and popping off the asphalt, he dropped flat against the runway with his face hugging the hot surface, listening to non-stop gunfire filling the air like thunder that wouldn't stop. While peering from underneath the jeep, he could see soldiers topple to the ground like lifeless ragdolls. All the mercenaries had already run away, and most of the soldiers followed them. Several stumbled from gunshots in their backs. As soon as one of the pilots ran out of ammo, he would eject the empty magazine onto the floor and slammed in a full one from a cardboard box. Mitch assumed they had been well-prepared for trouble, and were experts at delivering it. The few soldiers that had dropped to a knee to return fire were immediately ripped apart with bullets.

One of the wounded soldiers who had ridden with Musa crawled slowly on his belly back to the jeep with Mitch. He glanced painfully at Mitch before reaching up and taking a hand grenade from under the jeep's driver's seat. He then crawled slowly, moving only as needed to get under the airplane without being noticed. Once underneath, he struggled up on his hands and knees and got under the airplane's ground stairway. Mitch watched him pull the pin, let the handle fly free, and after a couple of seconds, he stood and tossed it into the cabin. The blast's concussion hammered through Mitch's bones. His ears rang. He got up on his knees and saw the space where the cargo door used to be, the metal around it peeled back like a shot-through tin can.

Some of the soldiers who had fled now crept back to the smoking battle scene. Those who still had weapons held them more or less ready, with fear in their eyes. Every last mercenary had disappeared. A few soldiers looked into the giant jagged opening that was once a cabin door, but there was apparently no sign of life inside. Still, Mitch was afraid to get up. A surviving soldier, still dazed, might mistake him for a crew member, or might be in a mood to shoot any foreigner.

The scent of something burning signaled a new danger. Mitch knew that if flames reached the wing's fuel tanks, he'd never survive this close to the airplane. He got to his feet and stood still for a moment to check his balance, then he ran for his life. He looked over his shoulder and yelled "Run!" but the few soldiers who could function were busy checking the fallen bodies of their brothers in arms. After pausing to yell a second time, a soldier picked up a rifle aimed it at him. Mitch reflexively started to duck, but an explosion slammed him to the ground. He choked and gasped from crude black smoke, then drew on what little strength he had left to crawl away from the blazing wreckage. The ringing in his ears became louder, his vision narrowed as if looking through a tube that kept getting longer, and he soon blacked out.

Chapter 15

Tessa distracted herself by tidying up the second-floor living quarters of Rafael's spacious river-side house. His household and business staff lived on the first floor, and out of respect, they tried to stay out of her way whenever she was in Iquitos.

She took a glass of iced lemon water to the rooftop terrace and sat in a cushioned lounge chair. Local boaters cruised back and forth, enjoying Sunday on the Amazon River, but Tessa couldn't enjoy anything about this day. Rafael had bragged about how he helped Mitch escape from Iquitos. She was grateful that Mitch got away safely, but her gratitude was overshadowed by a painful doubt that she would ever see him again.

Tessa reflexively flinched when the stairway door slammed behind her. She turned to see Rafael wearing a troubled expression, something unusual for him. She set her glass on the side table and sat sideways on the lounge chair. "What's wrong?"

"We both have to leave Iquitos, Tess—today."

"I can't go back to Tamshiyaco...not yet, anyway."

"I know. We're going to my house in Huaraz."

"You know how I hate the mountains. Besides, I have to

start school in Lima."

"That'll have to wait, Tess. Trouble's coming—trouble for you, too."

She stood slowly while staring at him. "What kind of trouble are you talking about?"

"A deadly kind."

"You have bodyguards for that."

"I just got a satellite phone call from Lima, from a government official on my payroll. He said a professional assassin has a contract on me. He's working for the Cubans, and he might be in Iquitos already."

"Why do I have to go?"

"You could be taken hostage, or forced to tell where my Huaraz house is. You'd be easy to find, Tess, whether you're in Iquitos, Tamshiyaco, or at university in Lima. My team in Huaraz are all locals and they've been with me longer than the people here. We can trust them."

"You're scaring me. What have you done to make someone want to kill you?"

"I've been successful, that's what. The Columbian cartels are not happy about my new ability to compete with them. I now have processing camps in the Peruvian mountains, so the coca growers there won't need to do business with the Columbians. I've started to ship processed *coca* from Huaraz to Iquitos with small planes, and then by jet all the way to Africa. From there I contract an underground transport operator in Belgium to fly shipments anywhere in Europe, even into the United States."

"I wish you would quit this dirty business. Don't you have enough money?"

"Even if I quit, it won't stop an assassin from earning his fee. But there's another problem, Tess. I told you Mitch was on one of my flights to Nigeria. I just found out that the pickup crew was from Havana, not Belgium. They tried to cheat the soldiers at the airport. An argument led to a gun fight, and it ended with their airplane exploding."

Tessa stood and held her breath. "Maybe Mitch returned on the Iquitos airplane."

"I thought about that. But no, he didn't."

"Maybe he wasn't in the destroyed airplane."

"It would have been his only way out of Nigeria. The Nigerian government sent soldiers to the airport a couple of days later, and found most of the dead had been decimated by wild animals. An unidentified party had already flown in to remove the bodies of the flight crew."

Tessa's lips parted slightly while she stared at Rafael. "Did anyone survive?"

"A few soldiers. All the surviving mercenaries had long-since fled from the area."

Tessa sat back down and gazed unfocused at the floor with her elbows on her knees.

"We need to leave now, Tess. I charted an airplane from Lima, and they're waiting for us at the airport. I'll see you downstairs, all right? Please hurry."

She couldn't look at him, or answer him. When she heard him walking down the steel stairway to the second floor, she put her face in her hands and cried. With her eyes still closed, she clutched her necklace's medallion once again, and held it to her heart. When her sobs started to subside, she sniffed and wiped her eyes with the back of her other hand, and slowly, absently, walked to the stairway.

Chapter 16

Mitch winced against the sunlight when he started to open his eyes. He caught a glimpse of someone standing beside him.

He said, "Who are you?"

"My name is Miss Ibrahim. I am a nurse. If your next question is about where you are, the answer is that you are in a safe house in Abuja, which is Nigeria's capital city."

"A safe house?"

"The United States Embassy maintains this apartment for special visitors."

"What makes me special?"

"I'm not told what I don't need to know. I'm only here to help you recover from a plane crash. You slurred a few words in your sleep last night, so I thought you might be opening your eyes soon."

"I remember the airplane burning, but I don't think it…"

"More pieces will fall into place. Give it a little time."

Miss Ibrahim pressed a button to raise the back of a hospital bed that had been set up in the middle of a small studio apartment. Furniture had been moved against the walls to make room.

She said, "Would you like something to eat?"

"I'm starving."

"I'll get some warm beef broth and bread from the kitchen. It's light to start with, but better than being fed through that tube in your arm."

"Can I speak to someone at the U.S. Embassy?"

"Of course. I'm supposed to call them as soon as you're awake. I'll do that while your broth heats."

After Miss Ibrahim left the room, Mitch tried to sit up. All his muscles felt like they had been pounded raw. After a painful attempt to sit up, he surrendered and lay back against the bed. Bright daylight squeezed through the window's translucent woven shades, which had been pulled all the way down. A wall clock showed the time to be a bit past two o'clock.

Fragments about the savage chaos at the airport began to surface. He remembered seeing the captain named Musa lie bleeding on the blistered runway, his lifeless eyes wide open, most of his skull torn away. For a horrible moment, the carnage scattered around Musa's body came into focus and broadened. He remembered machine gun fire, terrible screams, soldiers running. The nurse said the airplane crashed, but he didn't remember it that way.

Miss Ibrahim brought a tray and set it on his lap. It held a brown ceramic bowl of broth and a spoon, and a saucer with a bread roll on it.

"You're not supposed to have solid food yet, but you can dunk that bun into the broth to soften it." She brought a glass of water from the bathroom. "I'll leave you ddto eat in peace. Just push this little red button on the bedrail if you want me."

"Did you call the embassy?"

"Yes, and I was told an official was on the way."

The food restored Mitch's energy and thinking ability.

After he finished, he pushed the red button.

Miss Ibrahim stopped at the doorway. "I'll take your tray. Is there something else I can help you with?"

"I'd like to get up and walk. Can you remove these tubes from my arm?"

"Someone's here to see you first. After she leaves, I'll come back to remove them."

A few minutes after Miss Ibrahim left, a woman in a dark gray business skirt and tan blouse appeared at the door. She knocked twice on the door frame while passing through it.

"Hello, my name is Martha Mindel. I work at the American Embassy in Abuja. To whom do I have the pleasure of speaking?"

Mitch thought he detected a Spanish accent. "I'm Mitch. I lost my passport. Can the Embassy get me a new one?"

"Of course." She pulled a chair up to his bed, and took a pen and small notepad from her purse. "What's your full name, Mitch?"

"Mitchel Johnson."

While writing she said, "Mitchel...Johnson. And your middle name?"

"I don't have one."

"All right." She tucked her pad and pen back in her purse, and took out a mobile phone. "I need a photo for your passport."

She got up and stood at the foot of the bed and clicked off three photos while he posed with a half-smile.

"Is there anything else I can do for you, Mitch? I understand you survived a terrible airplane crash. That must have been a horrible experience."

The memory came back in an instant—the airplane exploded at the end of the runway, but it wasn't a crash.

He wondered why she wouldn't know that. "It was pretty bad, but it happened so fast. Luckily, I was thrown from the airplane."

"Yes, lucky you. Either I or one of my associates will be back tomorrow. We should have your temporary passport ready by then. If you need anything in the meantime, just tell your nurse, all right?"

"Sure…oh, there is one other thing. My wallet must have been lost in the crash. Could I get some cash for travel expenses? I would sign a promise to repay it."

"We'll do whatever it takes to get you home, Mitch. Just get some rest and don't worry."

But after she left, Mitch did worry. That seemed too easy. Why didn't Mindel ask how an airplane could crash without colliding into something, like trees? If it crashed on landing, it would have left a trail of debris on the runway. And what about shot-up soldiers scattered all over the area? How could she not know about that?

He decided that if things still seemed weird tomorrow, he'd have to get out of the country some other way. If Nigeria had a seaport, he might be able to sign on as a deckhand with a no-questions-asked rogue cargo ship.

After pushing the red button, Miss Ibrahim soon appeared at the door.

"Yes?"

"You said you would take this needle out of my arm."

She walked in and looked at the drip bag. "Yes, it's almost empty. I can remove it now."

"I'm not familiar with Nigeria…do you have a seaport?"

"Nigeria has six ports. The closest is Lagos."

"How long does it take to get there?"

"About one hour" she said while pressing an adhesive

bandage over his needle wound.

"On foot or by car?"

Miss Ibrahim laughed. "By passenger jet. A car would take three days to reach Lagos. You are in the middle of Nigeria."

After Miss Ibrahim left, Mitch hobbled to the window blind, but the window behind it was made with translucent glass blocks, impossible to see through—and were likely bulletproof. He looked in the closet for his clothes, but didn't find them. He paced nervously around the room until he couldn't take the pain anymore. He spent the rest of the day in bed, reading a Nigerian English-language news magazine, and napping when that became too boring. As the sunlight began to fade, Miss Ibrahim brought him two meat pies and tea.

***

The next morning Miss Ibrahim brought in a breakfast of what she described as "spicy pureed beans over custard," along with the familiar bread rolls, and tea.

"I looked for my clothes," Mitch said, "but the closet was empty."

"The clothes you arrived in were tattered and soiled beyond repair. Someone is bringing you new clothes."

"Then can I leave?"

"I don't decide that. You can ask the Embassy official who comes today."

Later that morning, a knock on the door startle Mitch from a stuporous nap.

"Come in," Mitch said groggily.

A man about Mitch's age, wearing dark green pants and a black tee shirt, pushed the door open and walked in with a cardboard file box.

"I'm Zakk Renshaw." He set the box on the floor. "I was sent by the American Embassy.

"I'm Mitch…Johnson."

"No, you're not. You're Mitchel Winslow. We'll get along a lot better if you stop trying to con me."

Mitch sat up. "How did you find my name?"

"The FBI ran a recognition scan for us, using the photos Martha took yesterday. They also matched the fingerprints we lifted from your drinking glass. You have an interesting background."

Renshaw opened his box and removed a pair of jeans, a tan shirt, belt, socks, underclothes, and gray sneakers, and set them on the foot of the bed. He sat in a side chair and said, "Go ahead, get dressed."

"Are we going somewhere?"

"It's my job to ask the questions."

"Fine, but if you want answers, don't be such an ass."

"This is my friendly side. You don't want to see my hard-ass side. Get dressed."

Mitch got out of bed and started putting on his new clothes.

"Let's start with your current problem, Mitch. You were involved with the transport of illegal substances, namely cocaine."

"I was just hitching a ride, that's all. I had no idea what the cargo was."

"You didn't just hitch a ride. You were pressured by someone to board that flight. Do you know why?

"The guy was supposedly doing me a favor."

"You're not that stupid. You know that Rafael Domingo doesn't give favors without a hitch. He certainly didn't give a damn about you, and I think you know that."

"Okay, let's say I'm stupid. Then why did he help me leave Iquitos?"

"I can't tell you."

"Can't, or won't?"

"I ask the questions—remember? Let's get back to your current situation. The Nigerian government wants to arrest you and lock you in one of their filthy prisons for the rest of your life, which is the normal sentence for drug trafficking in their country."

"Can you get me a lawyer?"

"Sure, but that's just the beginning of your trouble. As soon as you leave the protection of this cozy little bullet-proof apartment, the Nigerian police will also arrest you for multiple counts of murder. They don't like it when people kill their soldiers, especially when drug runners do it. The sentence for each count, by the way, will be hanging."

"I wasn't even armed."

"A minor detail. You were an accessory, and Nigeria's prosecutors are under pressure to pin someone for that airport catastrophe. I'm afraid you're their bad guy."

"I'm also an American citizen. Can't you get me out of the country?"

"I doubt it. But even if we could, you wouldn't get a warm reception in the U.S. There's a warrant against you for first degree murder and interstate flight to avoid prosecution. The FBI will arrest you as soon as you step one foot off the airplane."

Mitch sat on the side of the bed looking at the floor. "Okay. I'm screwed. Is there any way out of this?"

"Not an easy one."

"Nothing's ever been easy for me."

Zakk said, "Then you might like our offer."

"What offer?"

"Before going into that, I need to put things into prospective—to get us on the same page, if you will."

"I'm still listening."

"Let me start with what will happen if you accept our deal. First, federal charges against you will be dropped. The Drug Enforcement Agency will drop trafficking charges against you. As for the first-degree murder charge against you in Minnesota, we'll work with the district attorney to drop charges because you acted in self-defense. If the DA won't cooperate, then the United States Marshals Service can make you a protected witness, and you can live under an alias in a state they choose for you."

"How about in another country."

"Depends on which country."

"Costa Rica."

"We might be able to give you an alias passport, but if you're living outside of the U.S., we can't give you protection."

"Fair enough. What do you want for all of those Christmas gifts?"

"Tell me everything you know about the recent spike of cocaine trafficking out of Peru. The alarming amount of coke arriving in the U.S. has pressured Congress to investigate. That's the reason you and I are talking to each other. Your inside information could give the that investigation a head start.

"I only know what I experienced on a plane from Iquitos, Peru. I was promised a ride to Costa Rica, but I ended up here. The cargo was a bunch of square packages, which I assume was cocaine, and they were unloaded at a remote airport somewhere in this country. I was left at the airport, and the next day a plane from Belgium landed, presumably to transfer the cargo and me to somewhere in Europe. That plan went bad when the pilots tried to stiff the Nigerian soldiers out of some money they owed—they called it a *landing fee*—and then a gunfight started. The last thing I remember is an explosion."

Zakk said, "We already know all that."

"Do you know who shipped the cargo from Iquitos?"

"Rafael Domingo."

"How do you know that?"

"We have an undercover officer in Iquitos."

Mitch said, "Then you probably know more than I do."

"Maybe, and we also know that an assassination has been organized against him. One of our Peruvian contacts leaked that information to him.

"Where do I fit in?"

"You are in a position to deliver an offer to Rafael, and we think he's in a position to consider it. We know he is no friend of yours, but he does know you and we hope he'll trust you enough to at least agree to a meeting. If you can arrange that, you'll be able to offer him amnesty and asylum if he agrees to walk away from his trafficking network. The Peruvian government is in on this deal, and they'll leave him alone if he agrees."

"Okay, and when he tells me to go to hell—which he will—then what?"

"Then Plan B kicks in. Tell him if he doesn't take our offer, we'll hunt him, his family, and his girlfriend, and we'll make them all disappear."

"Who is his girlfriend?"

"We don't know. Her identity is a well-protected secret."

"Seriously, Zakk, if I deliver your message, it won't interest Rafael, and he doesn't scare that easy

"I know."

"Then you must know this assignment is a waste of time."

"Yes, I know that, too. But that won't be your real purpose. Your real task will be to gather information for us. We need to know where his mountain hideout is, who works for him, and the location of his processing camps. You discovered one trafficking route, but he's likely trying others. Find out who his collaborators are, and who his enemies are."

"If he thinks I'm just panning for information, he'll make sure I can't report it to anyone."

"We'll provide you with protection."

"Oh, right. Did you know that Iquitos is like a secluded island, hidden in the jungle with no access except by boat or airplane?"

"We weren't planning to land soldiers on the beachhead. You know how to use a firearm, right?"

"Oh, please. I'm not going to shoot anyone."

"You've done it before."

"In self-defense, and I think you know that."

"The victim was unarmed and was shot in the back with a load of buckshot. That's what I know, and it doesn't sound like self-defense."

"The guy was going for his hunting rifle. Some people in that area keep their guns loaded."

"And you just happened to be armed."

"Yes, and I knew I'd never explain my way out of killing him. That's why I ran."

"Can you tell me what happened?"

"There's not much more to tell. I drove from northern Minnesota that night, straight through to Louisiana. I slept in my car for a few hours at a seaport, and the next day I signed on as a deckhand with a Chilian cargo ship leaving for Belém,

Brazil. From there, I worked on a Brazilian ship heading up the Amazon, and got off at the final port at Iquitos, Peru. I got terribly sick in Iquitos and the ship left without me. I didn't think anyone would ever find me in such a remote place, so I stayed."

"What about family members?"

"After my wife, Maggie, was gone, I had no family."

"What about when you were a juvenile?"

"I grew up being tossed from one foster family to another. I was officially a 'maladjusted' child, but I thought the foster parents were more maladjusted. Anyway, I lived up to my title just to piss them off. When I hit eighteen, I was on my own—until I met Maggie. Her parents were alcoholics, and when we got married, we promised to help each other enjoy our lives, forever. We moved from stressful city life in Minneapolis to Minnesota's peaceful north woods. We bought an older house on the edge of a small town and spent time together fixing it up. Maggie was a nurse, and found a job right away at a nearby clinic. I worked for the county as a heavy equipment operator, mostly grading gravel roads in the summer and plowing snow in the winter. Those two years together were the best years of our lives."

Zakk leaned toward him. "And then your wife's life was taken."

"And my child's. We had recently found out that Maggie was pregnant."

"I'm sorry, Mitch. I have no business asking anything more about that."

Mitch stared at the floor. "That's okay. It's a load off to finally tell someone what happened. On a January night about three years ago, I got home around two in the morning after plowing snow. Our living room light was on when I drove up, and that worried me. It meant Maggie might still be awake. When I got in, I said her name while removing my boots—not loudly, though, in case she was asleep. Oddly, the bedroom door was closed. Maggie always left it open when I worked late. I opened the door and said her name quietly. The bed looked empty in the dark. I flipped the light switch and saw the bed sheets covered with blood. She was lying on the floor next to the bed on her stomach. Her bloodied pajamas were partially off. I ran to her and rolled her on her side, yelling 'Maggie, Maggie' over and over, as if I could wake her from this nightmare. She wasn't breathing. I checked for a pulse, but found none, so I called 911 and started CPR. Sheriff's deputies soon began to fill our little house, and one of them took over the CPR. The ambulance seemed to take forever, but time had stopped for me. The deputies muscled me out of the bedroom while the ambulance crew taped electrodes to her chest. I barely remember sitting in the living room, stuck in a mental haze while watching the first-responders wheel Maggie out into the below-zero cold to the waiting ambulance."

"How did go from that to shooting some guy with a shotgun?"

Mitch got up and paced the floor to steady his composure. His breath became strained, and he barely felt the deep bruises and cuts still ripe from the airplane's explosion.

"I didn't go anywhere that night. I lied awake all night on our sofa, broken up. I couldn't keep a straight thought."

"How did you know who murdered your wife?"

"I couldn't imagine who'd want to kill Maggie. A few days later, a sheriff's deputy I knew told me unofficially that they knew who likely assaulted and murdered her. The suspect was a repeat sex offender who had recently moved into the area. I thought I knew who the deputy was talking about, and when I mentioned the guy's name, the deputy nodded, but added that he couldn't say anything more while the investigation was underway. He said finger prints had been wiped by the perpetrator, and the only circumstantial evidence they had so far was a matching tire track on our driveway, but it wasn't enough to assure a conviction. Without more evidence, they'd need a confession. I became wild with anger. If the rules of law really let this guy go free, then I should break the rules. I went to the guy's remote trailer home, which sat on blocks in the middle of nowhere, and confronted him at the door with the shotgun aimed at his stomach. I said I'd pull the trigger if he didn't sign a confession on the spot. I'll admit that I thought about just killing him anyway, and being done with it. I didn't care about myself anymore and I had no one else to care about. He swore at me, and when he turned and ran for his rifle…well, you know the rest."

"You were either smart or lucky—buckshot isn't easily traceable to a specific shotgun. The expended shells can be, but you obviously picked up the empty casing."

"It was my only gun, and I used it for grouse hunting. Out of mindless habit, I picked up the empty casing from the floor and threw it into a ditch on the way home."

"I don't blame you for what you did. But I have to leave soon, so let's get back to your current problem, and ours. Maybe we can work together to help prevent cocaine from ruining American lives."

"Okay, but Rafael and I are not exactly friends, and if I show up in Iquitos, the police will arrest me on a trumped-up drug smuggling charge."

"Our high-level contact in the Peruvian government will make sure all charges against you are dropped."

"My boat was confiscated by the Iquitos police. Can you help me get it back?"

"Consider it done."

"Okay, then. I'll be your delivery boy. What's the message for Rafael?"

"Tell him that if he agrees to our terms, he can retire now as a rich man. He'll get a pardon from past crimes, and guaranteed safety for him and his family."

"I wonder if he has a family."

"He does."

"And when he turns the offer down, then what? And forget about me shooting him or anyone else."

"Don't worry. Your job will be done at that point, and the United States does not assassinate people. But you can tell him that his life, and the lives of his family, will be in constant danger, not just from the Peruvian government, but from powerful foreign cartels."

"So, let me sum this up. You want me to march into Iquitos and threaten one of the most powerful drug lords in South America, and when he laughs at me, tell him that someone might snuff him and his family unless he retires. Really, Zakk? After having a good laugh, he'll make sure I don't leave alive. And I think you know that. Something's missing here."

Zakk stared at Mitch with cold unblinking eyes. "That's where the gun comes in."

"So, that's what this is really about, isn't it? You're looking for someone to assassinate him. Well, I'm not your guy."

"You're adding your imagination to this, Mitch. It's just that if Rafael realizes you're working for us, you might need to protect yourself. I didn't say this would be without some risk. No matter whether you're with us, or not, you'll be facing some danger."

Mitch eyed Zakk for a moment. "What if I just tell Rafael I was blackmailed into scaring him. We could both walk away free."

"Yes, but you'd lose your boat for good, and you'd be on the run from us for the rest of your life, no matter where you go. It might not be a life worth living, and it could end badly."

"I know you're not supposed to do this, but why not just pay a professional killer."

"Even if we could legally—which we can't—we don't have access to Rafael like you do. He knows you, Mitch, and probably trusts you. All we want is a chance to make him stop producing coke."

"And I deliver the rewards."

"That's right. Look at this as an opportunity, Mitch. You're in the unique position to escape to a better life after your mission is complete. You won't face murder charges in Nigeria, which would put you in prison for life, or more likely get you hanged, and you won't be extradited to the U.S. and face first-degree murder charges. Take this chance, Mitch. You won't get a second one."

"I'd need enough money to take my boat down the Amazon River and out of South America, and more money to find a place to hide."

"We'll pay you a hundred-thousand dollars. Anything else?"

"How do I get paid?"

"The money will be deposited in a special account at the bank in Iquitos. You'll get instructions for drawing it out when we verify that your mission is complete."

Mitch got up and paced back and forth across the small bedroom while mentally processing the most bizarre and dangerous arrangement he had ever heard of. He stopped and turned to Zakk.

"Where do I get the gun?"

"From one of our operatives, who will meet you after you arrive in Lima and get you through Peruvian customs. There won't be any other security checkpoints when you fly to Iquitos."

"Okay, I'll take your offer."

"Fine. When you feel up to it, we'll give you a new passport and a ticket to Miami. You transfer to an American airliner to Lima, Peru."

"Why don't I just fly to Peru from Nigeria?"

"Because we'd lose operational control. The flight to and from Miami will have an undercover U.S. marshal on board."

Zakk stood and said, "Do you think you'll be ready in a couple of days?"

"I'm ready now."

Chapter 17

Two days later, Mitch sat through an uneventful flight that landed in Miami, Florida, late in the afternoon. After clearing U.S. customs, he saw a 30-ish woman with dark brown hair holding a paper sign that said "Mitch W."

When he approached her, she said "Mr. Winslow?"

Mitch assumed she knew what he looked like, so he just smiled.

She didn't smile back. "Are you Mitch Winslow?"

"Yes."

"May I see your passport, please?"

"I already cleared customs."

"I have to confirm your identity."

He gave her his passport, and after a cursory look, she handed it back. "Come with me, please. My name is Alicia."

Mitch's muscles and joints still ached, and he had to push himself to keep up with her. They rode a shuttle to the main terminal, then Alicia briskly maneuvered through the crowd with Mitch following.

When there was enough room for him to walk alongside her, she said, "You'll spend a few hours at a secure motel near here. You'll be given a travel bag, already packed with clothes that should fit you. You can shower and change after a briefing, and you'll have some time to rest."

"I've been resting for hours. I'd rather have some excitement."

Alicia didn't respond for a few seconds, and then said "Be careful what you wish for."

A black Lincoln Town Car waited outside the terminal. Alicia opened the back door for Mitch, and then got in next to him. The driver glanced at him in the rearview mirror before pulling out and into the steady chao of airport traffic. They rode in silence to a small old one-story motel named *The Sky Blue Motel,* not far from the airport. The driver parked in front of one of the rooms.

Alicia knocked on the door and a gaunt middle-aged man with receding hair opened it. He nervously scratched his hawkish nose and looked Mitch over. Two disposable ink pens peeked out from his crisp white shirt pocket. "Everything's ready," he said to Alicia after she walked in past him.

"This is Mr. Winslow," she said and fell into a worn stuffed chair next to the droning air conditioner.

"This might seem hasty," he said to Mitch, but we have to keep to a strict schedule. "

"Alicia said "Maybe you can show Mr. Winslow what you've got for him."

"Yes, of course. My name is Claremont, by the way. It's my first name."

"Glad to meet you."

"All right, let's start with your travel bag. It will fit in an overhead compartment, so do not check it in under any circumstances. If the flight crew insists that there's no room for it in the cabin, get off the airplane and we'll book you on a later flight. While you are in the airport terminal, keep hold of this bag at all times."

Claremont unzipped the black bag. "There's enough underclothes, trousers, and shirts to last a few days. There are basic toiletries, a small water-filtering straw—we don't trust tap water in Peru—and an empty water bottle. There are a few granola bars in case you miss meals." He unzipped a compartment behind the clothes. "Here's a thousand dollars' worth of Peruvian soles, and an itinerary for a connecting flight from Lima to Iquitos. You'll be given a boarding pass when you arrive in Lima."

Claremont took a paper from the side table and pulled a pen from his shirt pocket. "I need your signature on this receipt."

After Mitch signed it, Claremont left. Alicia went to the door, and looked back. "I'll be back in a couple of hours."

After they left, Mitch sat for a few minutes, then decided to take a walk. It had been a long time since he walked on American soil. But the door knob would not turn, and there was no phone to call the front desk. He was sure the windows could not be opened, and tapping them produced a muffled thud instead of the clink of normal window glass. I assumed they were smash and bullet proof. He looked up and around for a surveillance camera. He couldn't see one, but was convinced he was being watched.

Mitch showered and watched American TV for the first time in years. After a few minutes, he turned the TV off, realizing that he hadn't missed much. He lay on the bed and let his fragmented thoughts come and go.

A knock at the door stirred him from a deep sleep. The door barely opened and Alicia asked, "Can I come in?"

Mitch turned on the bedside lamp. "What if I said no?"

She rolled her eyes and pushed the door wider. "Very funny. Are you ready?"

"All packed and ready."

The evening traffic was thin on the way back to Miami's International Airport. Mitch didn't bother trying to converse with Alicia. He didn't like her, and he had nothing to say. Instead, he shifted his thoughts to Tessa. He hoped she hadn't left for school in Lima yet. He wanted to see Luis, too. But first, he wanted to get his business with Rafael over with. He planned to tell Rafael upfront that he was only a messenger forced to deliver a ridiculous message. Maybe they could have a laugh together and be done with it.

They pulled over to the airport terminal's curb. Alicia got out and waited on the sidewalk while Mitch slid out the other door with his government-issue luggage in hand.

"This is where we part," she said. "You'll soon be on an overnight non-stop flight to Lima. Customs officers in Peru have been notified that you are on official business for the United States government, but with a regular passport for cover reasons. An undercover U.S. Marshals Service officer will be on your flight. Another officer will escort you through Peruvian customs, and will make sure you get on a flight to Iquitos. After that, you're on your own."

"That'll be good."

"One more thing. I haven't been told what your mission is, but the amount of official oversight tells me it's something big, and probably dangerous. Anyway, good luck."

Shortly after Mitch arrived at the gate, the loudspeaker announced boarding for Lima. All the Peruvian passengers got up at once and rushed toward the gate, nudging each other into a tight wedge while trying to protect their bulging shopping bags, mostly from Disneyland if they had children with them, and from brand-name specialty stores. Mitch let the crowd stuff themselves into the airplane before boarding.

He found his assigned seat next to a window, with no one occupying the two seats next to him. After he stowed his travel bag in the overhead compartment, he closed his eyes. The nightmare of the last few days was coming to a head now.

Chapter 18

The flight to Lima turned into an airborne bingo party after supper was over and the resulting trash had been collected by flight attendants. Because this was an international flight, alcohol was free, served from quart bottles by attendants with aisle carts. After a couple of passes, an open bar was set up in the aft galley. Mitch knew that Peruvians have a passion for bingo, and game after game was played late into the night for cash prizes and free airline tickets to Peruvian cities. The cabin lights dimmed soon after someone won the grand prize of fifty dollars. A few men continued visiting in the galley for free drinks. When the bottles were empty, the men staggered back to their seats to sleep the party off. The cabin lights went out.

***

A voice through the intercom startled Mitch from a thin dream that immediately faded from memory. Lights had been turned back on, and the captain announced in both Spanish and English that they were starting their descent to the Lima airport. The captain asked everyone to fill out declaration papers, which would soon be distributed by the flight attendants. Mitch opened his shade and squinted out at the brilliant sunlit sky.

The airplane dipped a wing into a steep bank as it descended through a dense cloud layer. As the cloud darkened, turbulence jostled the airplane. Mitch soon saw patches of ocean breaking into rhythmic whitecapped waves along the coast. The water looked gray at that altitude, but soon turned bright blue-green as they descended. Lifeless rounded-domed sand mountains dominated the view, until the pilot made another steep bank into a short final approach to the airport. After settling onto the runway with a smooth touchdown, the pilots received a grateful applause from the passengers.

Mitch followed the other passengers down a steel stairway that had been pushed against the cabin door with a ground tug. He got into the line for foreign visitors, indicated by a sign over the terminal entrance. There were only five people ahead him. He straightened his sleep-snarled hair with his fingers while shuffling along with his luggage in the slow-moving line.

When it was Mitch's turn, he handed a stocky customs agent his passport. The officer looked at the photo, and quickly thumbed through the empty pages. He told Mitch to sit on a nearby bench and wait. After stamping the last foreign passenger's passport, the officer told Mitch to stay seated, then he left with Mitch's passport.

Mitch sat alone for several minutes, crossing one leg then the other. All the passengers on his flight had already been processed through customs and had gone to find their luggage at the baggage claim conveyor. He stood to look around, when the customs agent returned and handed Mitch his passport, then said to follow him.

Mitch was taken to a small room containing only a small

metal table and two armless chairs. There were no file cabinets, and the walls were bare. The agent said to wait there, and then left and closed the door behind him. Mitch set his bag on the table, and as soon as he sat down, the door opened.

A man wearing blue jeans and an untucked gray polo shirt walked in, carrying a large brown shoulder bag. "Mitchel Winslow?"

"That's right." Mitch remembered seeing him on the airplane, seated near the front.

The man took a small black leather wallet from his shirt pocket and flipped it open for Mitch to see his photo ID. "I'm Jed Donahue, with the US Marshals Service."

"I saw you on the plane."

Jed sat in the empty chair. He unzipped his bag and removed an envelope, then handed it to Mitch.

"That's your boarding pass to Iquitos. Your flight leaves from here in about three hours, but you'll have to stay inside the terminal."

"Can I just step outside for some air?"

"No. You'll be carrying a firearm illegally, and as soon as you step outside that door, you'd be vulnerable to possible search and arrest. Inside, our Peruvian counterparts can keep an eye on you.

"Don't worry—I don't have a firearm."

Jed pulled a gray plastic case from his backpack and slid it across the desk toward Mitch. "You do now. I've been told that you're familiar with firearms and you're not afraid to use them."

Mitch stared at the case. "Well, I used to have a shotgun…"

Jed flipped up two catches on the plastic case, and opened it.

"This is a Glock 26. The hammer is internal, and the safety

is built into the trigger so you don't have to fumble with finding it. Just point and shoot—but keep your finger off the trigger until you're ready to fire. The magazine is already loaded with nine rounds of 9 mm cartridges. When you get some private time in Iquitos, pull the slide back all the way and release it to chamber a round and cock it. Keep it on your person at all times. The pants that were packed inside your travel bag in Miami have large double-stitched front pockets, and the gun is small enough to not show its shape."

"It looks like you thought of everything. Have you thought about what happens when I refuse to carry a gun?"

"It's just a precaution, in case self-defense is required. By the way, we'll want it back when your assignment is completed. Is there anything else? I have to catch a flight back to Miami in a few minutes."

"There is something. After I meet with Rafael, and he turns down your wonderful retirement package—which he will—am I to believe that I can just go my merry way?"

"That's right. Withdraw the money we've deposited in your name at your bank, and start a new life—anywhere but in Peru."

"What if I change my mind and disappear before meeting with Rafael?"

"Then you will have breached our agreement. We don't reward failure, Mitch, and we don't let betrayers hide."

Chapter 19

Mitch got a window seat on the midday flight from Lima to Iquitos. He watched the Andean terrain change from drift-sand mountains on the west side, to higher barren mouintains that transformed into verdant valleys underneath craggy snow-capped peaks. On the east side, thick clouds blanketed lush rainforests until the Amazon basin came into view, with its dense canopy hiding everything except the sparkling rivers that cut through it, reflecting the brilliant blue sky.

The hour-and-a-half flight ended too quickly for him. Stress gripped his stomach as the airplane started its final approach to the airport. He would soon face a confrontation that seemed foolish, hastily planned by people he didn't know or trust. He wondered if the U.S. government was really naive enough to think his brief visit with a powerful drug lord could end cocaine trafficking from Peru.

He decided to find Luis as soon as the airplane landed. He hoped Luis and his wife, Gardenia, would be privy to the latest rumors about Paraiso, and they might know how he could find Tessa. After visiting Luis and Gardenia, finding her was his next order of business. Then he would look for Rafael and get that over with.

While the airplane taxied to Iquitos's terminal, Mitch thought about the best way to approach Rafael. He decided to tell Rafael how he was forced to return to Iquitos. Start with candor, turn all the cards over. He would make it clear that he was only a messenger, with no vested interest in Rafael's decision. After that meeting, he would look for his boat, hoping Zakk's promise back in Nigeria to "consider it done" really meant the return of Paraiso.

He took a taxi from the airport to Luis and Gardenia's small house on the north side of town. After knocking on the door, he could hear their two boys calling for their mother. When Gardenia opened the door, her mouth drooped open.

"Mitch, you are alive! Luis and I have worried so much about you. Come in, come in. Luis is resting, but I will wake him."

"Let him rest, Gardenia. I can wait."

"He would be angry if I let him sleep while you are here. He can sleep another time."

Before getting Luis, Gardenia told their two boys to go outside and play. When Luis emerged from the bedroom with her, he gave Mitch a groggy look. "Mitch, how can that be you? Did you die and return to life?"

"It almost seems like that. Are you healing well?"

"Yes, my legs are very beautiful now. They are ready for our next trip.

Gardenia said, "Your legs might be ready, but you're not." She turned to Mitch. "Sit down, Mitch. Tell us what happened to you."

Mitch told them about leaving Iquitos in a jet with Rafael's cargo, the chaos and horror in Nigeria, and then being rescued by the US Embassy.

After a moment of stunned silence, Luis said, "I don't know

why you came back to Iquitos, with all your trouble here."

"I have a secret to tell you. It will help you understand."

Gardenia started to stand. "I can wait in the bedroom."

"Please stay, Gardenia, but neither of you can tell anyone what I am about to say. I'm am being forced by the U.S. Government to deliver a message to Rafael. It's an offer to give him safety and money if he gets out of the drug business."

"How is your government forcing you to bring this message? I don't think Rafael will like hearing it."

"I'm wanted for a serious crime in the United States, and that's what brought me to Iquitos in the first place. The U.S. government is offering me immunity, and they said the Iquitos police will drop their false charges against me."

Luis said, "Did you really commit a crime in the United States?"

"Yes. I killed a man because he murdered my wife."

Gardenia said, "You avenged your wife's murder. It was justified."

"Not according to the law, but I would do it again."

"I will go with you to see Rafael," Luis said. "I can bring my shotgun to keep you safe."

Gardenia's eyes froze on her husband. "You cannot leave your family for such a ridiculous idea."

Mitch said, "You are right, Gardenia. Luis has no business with Rafael, but I do. I will deliver my message, and then leave. After that, I'll try to find Tessa. My plan is to work aboard an ocean freighter for a few months and make enough money to settle in Costa Rica. I hope Tessa will wait for me, but I can't expect her to. I don't have a very good reputation for plans working out."

Luis said, "She will believe in you. I think she understands you better than you think."

"She was going to stay with a friend somewhere in Iquitos. I hope she hasn't left."

Luis said "I don't know about Tessa's friend, but Darla might. Iquitos's secrets usually find their way to her."

***

Mitch took a taxi to Darla's home just off the riverfront street. He knocked on her door, waited, and knocked again. When he finally turned to leave, he saw Darla walking toward him along the side of the road.

"My God, Mitch, how did you get back so soon?"

"It's a crazy story."

"Come in." She unlocked the door and led the way in. "Have a seat and I'll be right back."

While Darla was in the bathroom, he set his pack on the floor and sat in a ratan chair in the living room. She soon returned with freshly brushed hair, and he sat on the sofa.

She said, "When I watched you leave on that flight out of Iquitos, I was worried sick about you. How in the world did you get back here—and why did you return?"

Mitch drew a long breath and searched for where to begin. He summarized how Rafael's cargo was confiscated by the Nigerian soldiers, how the arrival of another jet turned into a battle scene that ended in an explosion.

"After that, I woke up in an American Embassy safe house in Nigeria's capital city. A representative from the embassy informed me that I faced murder and trafficking charges, and would probably be hanged by the Nigerians. He said they could get me out of the country, but for a price."

"He wanted a bribe?"

"No, a mission. I have to deliver an important message

to Rafael."

Darla barely nodded, as if it was something she had expected. "And what would that offer be—or is that a secret?"

"I can tell you. It's sort of a retirement plan. If he agrees to stop processing coke and trafficking it out of Peru, he'll get amnesty and a lot of money. If he refuses the offer, they'll hunt him, his family and girlfriend down, and kill them."

"You must know he'll flat-out turn you down, Mitch. And if you threaten him and his family like that, he'll shoot you on the spot. Don't think for a minute that you can scare him with some cockamamie assassination plot. He has more protection than the president of Peru—unless you're the assassinator."

"No, I'm just here to warn Rafael, and then get out of the way. I don't really care whether he goes for the deal or not. But first I have to find him. By the way, do you know where I can find the woman that we brought from Tamshiyaco?"

Darla's eyes stayed on his. "Tessa Cortina."

"You didn't know who she was when you and Rafael came for me."

"I asked Rafael about her after we left you at the airport. He said you sent her to find me, but she went to him instead."

"Why him?"

"I don't know. Maybe because she knows him. She doesn't know me."

"Is she Rafael's girlfriend?"

"I don't know that, either. What if she is?"

"Just curious. I better get going."

"If you're going to Rafael's house, save your taxi fare. He left Iquitos two days ago. He brought his entire staff with him, so I don't think he's planning to return anytime soon."

"Do you know where Rafael went?"

"I assume to his mountain compound. But if you go anywhere near that place, be careful. It's seriously guarded."

"How can I meet with him?"

"Go to the city of Huaraz, in the Andes Mountains. Don't nose around too much, but ask hotel workers or taxi drivers where you can find him."

"Does Huaraz have an airport?"

"Yes, but commercial flights have been cancelled recently. The winds are too dangerous to land in.

"Then how do I get there?"

"You'll have to fly back to Lima and take a bus up into the mountains. The bus is a reliable way to travel, and it only takes a day. Tickets are cheap, so book the seat next to you for more privacy."

Mitch stood and picked up his travel bag. "Thanks for your help."

"I didn't help you, Mitch. I just told you how to find more trouble."

Chapter 20

Mitch stayed in a hotel that night, and by the time his early flight arrived in Lima, sunlight had burned off most of the ocean's morning fog. He took a taxi to the bus station, and worked his way through the busy terminal. Following Darla's advice, he bought two tickets, then stood in the waiting area with the rest of the passengers, most of whom sat silently with full baskets, gunnysacks, or fabric travel bags. The children sat with numbed boredom, and pretended not to notice the tall gringo who just joined the crowd.

A bus pulled up to the open gate and its brakes hissed to a stop. Heads turned toward the gate attendant, who stared back at them as if in a standoff. When the bus's pneumatic door whooshed open, everyone jumped up and rushed toward it. Mitch held his travel bag against his stomach and squeezed into the mob. He started to worry that all the seats would be taken, even though his tickets promised specific seats, but this crowd didn't seem to care about orderly procedures. The driver got out and let the chaos sort itself out while he shoved assorted bags and boxes into the bus's cargo underbelly. Mitch kept his backpack with him, and shuffled in line down the bus's aisle. His two reserved seats were vacant, so he sat next to the window, placing his backpack on the seat next to him. After the passengers settled into their seats, a wave of sleepiness swept over him. He slid his arm through the bag's shoulder strap in case he nodded off.

The driver got in and the bus's engine growled to life. Air brakes released their hold and the bus shuddered in low gear through the gate, then surged into the street traffic. Andean flute and guitar music started over the intercom speaker and Mitch closed his eyes.

He woke each time the bus stopped to pick up passengers who waited along the road out of Lima. The bus driver collected cash from them and stuck it into his pocket while they looked for an empty seat. Mitch kept his bag on the seat next to him, and put his arm around it.

After about an hour, they stopped at a tiny village. The driver let a crush of vendors aboard, who sold candy, bread, and cheese. Mitch clutched his bag tighter to protect it and stared out the window, afraid eye contact might suggest an interested customer. Food and body odors turned his empty stomach, but the vendors soon left, and the music resumed.

The bus sped up a highway that was seemingly scooped through a mountain of smooth sand. Far below on the left, frothy ocean waves lapped at the bare coastline. On the right, a featureless sand dune ascended high above them toward a naked blue sky. The mountain held no vegetation, no rocks, just immense wind-blown dunes that made the distant highway ahead look like a dainty black slit to nowhere.

Mitch saw a distant speck on the road. He squinted and guessed it was a truck of some kind. After several minutes it was bearing toward them down the middle of the highway, with no room to pass on either side. The bus driver pulled over the center of the highway in a faceoff. Every passenger silently watched to see who would move over first, while the recorded Andean flute and guitar music fluted and strummed in the background. Mitch could now see the faces of two men in the truck. The vehicles closed at high speed, and then dodged each other to their respective sides at the last moment. No one gasped or moved or cheered—just a brief amusement to break up a very long, monotonous ride.

The bus slowed when it entered the next small town, but this time there were no waiting vendors. It stopped in front of a row of shops, and a few passengers got out, including Mitch with his bag's strap over his shoulder. He went into three shops before finding one that sold bottled water with sealed plastic caps. He bought two liter-sized bottles and a small pack of crackers, and took a long drink of the lukewarm water before he returned to his bus seat. After everyone seemed to be accounted for, the driver slid into his seat and drove off.

The highway gradually narrowed as the grade steepened. A few scraggly trees dotted the grassy foothills and they occasional passed by sheep farmers' hovels while pushing up the steady ascent into the Andes Mountains.

After a few more hours—with each one seeming longer than the last—the bus stopped in front of a small house perched between the road and a steep canyon behind it. A leathery-skinned man and woman sold bread and sheep cheese to the passengers who stepped off the bus. The farm couple's round faces and colorful clothing told Mitch that they were Quechua Indians, descendants of ancient mountain civilizations like the once-mighty Inca. A baby hung on the woman's back in a cloth bundle, and a little girl came outside and held onto her mother's ground-length skirt. The man was bare-headed, but his wife wore a black brimmed bowler hat.

Mitch left the bus to join some of the other men who

were urinating in the ditch on the other side of the road. He went back to his seat to take a drink of water and saw that the plastic water bottles had bulged from the decrease in atmospheric pressure. He loosened each cap carefully to let compressed air whoosh out.

The driver called for everyone to board, then crawled in low gear up the steep road, turning back and forth from switchback to switchback to hairpin turns up the next few miles of mountains. The curves started to widen, and after a few hours, rolling grassy hills were replaced by steep mountains that rose above them, many with terraced fields at their base, occupying every patch of ground not hampered by stone outcrops. The road began to descend and follow a stream that meandered toward a valley.

The driver spoke through the bus's speaker system for the first time during this seemingly-endless trip, identifying the area ahead as *Cordillera Blanca*—a group of parallel snow-capped mountain ranges.

The bus rounded a curve, and Mitch saw red-tiled roofs sprawled across a basin of velvety green. The driver announced that they were entering the city of Huaraz. He explained that the city had been shaken into rubble by an earthquake in 1970, and had been rebuilt since then. Bushy green trees ushered the bus into town. Above them, three snow-white mountain peaks glistened in the brilliant sunlight.

Huaraz's bus depot stood near the center of town. Young men crowded toward the arriving bus holding newspapers and food to sell.

A man with disheveled hair and thread-worn clothes pushed his way through the Peruvian passengers to reach the bus's only gringo. He stood in front of Mitch beaming a big friendly smile with a few teeth missing.

"You want a good hotel my friend? I take you."

Mitch nodded but wouldn't let the man take his travel bag. They agreed on a price for the ride and Mitch got into the back seat of the driver's faded and dented '60s-something Pontiac Bonneville. A couple of coarsely-woven wool blankets had been tucked in over the seats, to either hide or preserve what was left of the original upholstery.

The driver introduced himself as Torres. On the way through town, he pointed out the central square, city hall, and a museum. He pointed to a small building with a painted sign above the door that said, Restaurante Del Mundo—*Restaurant of the World*. The driver had to pump the brakes furiously before each stop sign before the car would finally slow to a hesitant stop. Mitch tried to tell him he needed brake fluid. The driver smiled politely and responded in Spanish, which Mitch could barely understand— something about American cars being the best taxis.

Torres stopped in front of the Blanca Hotel and jumped out. "*Muy bueno hotel.* No much money." He wanted to carry Mitch's luggage, but Mitch shook his head no.

Mitch registered at the front desk, and paid Torres. Before Torres left, Mitch asked in Spanish if he knew about some people from Iquitos who were supposed to be nearby. Torres cocked his head as if to consider the question, then pursed his lips and shook his head sadly. He promised to ask his friends. Mitch gave him a tip worth about one U.S. dollar and Torres grinned widely. He said he would ask many friends and his cousins about Iquitos people, and promised to tell Mitch immediately when he discovered something. Torres lingered for a moment, then he wished God's blessing for Mitch and left.

Mitch felt the effect of thin mountain air when he climbed

the single flight of stairs to his hotel room. He stopped at the top of the stairs and let his breath catch up before walking down the hallway.

His room was small but clean and had a private bath. Dark hardwood floor planks were oiled to a satin sheen. Mitch dropped his bag onto the bed and opened French doors to a small tiled balcony, where a pot of red flowers overflowed down the cement railing. A late afternoon breeze felt cool, a sensation never felt in the jungle. The balcony overlooked small single-family homes, two-story apartment buildings, and neighborhood shops, all roofed with the same half-round red clay tiles. Behind the sprawling town, Mitch could see Mount Huascarán—which he knew was Peru's highest and most famous mountain. Its white peak gleamed regally against the deep blue sky.

He went back inside and ate one of the granola bars that had been packed into his travel bag in Miami. He opened the gray plastic box and removed the small pistol, remembering that he was supposed to keep it on him at all times while in Huaraz. He removed the black ammo-filled magazine from its compartment and pushed it up into the pistol's hand grip, then he pulled the slide all the way back and let it go to load a round into the chamber. He slid the gun into his right front pocket, where it fit perfectly, and walked around the room to feel its surprisingly heavy weight. He stashed most of his money and his passport into an undergarment money belt that he found in his pack.

He left the room and locked the door behind him, and walked down to the front desk. He approached a young man sitting behind the counter.

"Do you know the man named Rafael Domingo?"

The man stood up. "Your name?"

"No, I'm looking for someone by that name."

"My name Tomas."

Mitch tried to explain in his best possible Spanish. "*Señor Rafael Domingo esta in Huaraz?*"

The man gave him a hopeless shrug and sat back on his stool.

"*Personas de la selva?*" Mitch asked.

The man's eyes lit up. "Jungle men?"

"Yes, where are they?" Mitch asked.

The man shook his head and said he knew nothing about jungle people, but Mitch saw the lie in his face. The man suddenly absorbed himself with some papers from behind the counter, as if Mitch was no longer there.

Mitch waited a moment then said, "The jungle people are here in Huaraz."

"Ask at *aeropuerto.*" He turned and strode into the back room.

There were no taxis in front of the hotel, so Mitch walked a few blocks and found the town's central square. Typical of Peruvian towns, the block-long square park was originally a place where Spanish soldiers would make a last stand during ancient wars with the Incas or other mountain peoples. It was decorated with large terracotta pots containing shrubs and yellow and red flowers, and offered several cement benches. Sidewalks crisscrossed the dark green lawn.

Old American cars showing rust, dents, and sun-faded hoods, represented the town's taxi fleet, and were parked in an orderly line along the street on the other side of the square. The drivers sat idly or talked among themselves. All of them stood except two who sat on the hoods of their cars. The talking stopped when they spotted Mitch walking toward them. When one of the drivers—the one who presumably was next in line—stepped onto the street, Torres's beat-up Pontiac cut him off. Mitch could see Torres desperately pumping his brake pedal to a stop, and while doing so, the passenger door swung open on its own. Torres beamed his goofy-tooth smile. "Where you go, my friend? I take you very quickly."

Mitch climbed into the front seat and slammed the door shut three times before it finally latched. "Can you take me to the airport?"

"Si, aeroporto. I know it very good!" Torres gunned the engine and the Pontiac lurched ahead down the street.

They hadn't agreed on the fare, but Mitch decided that since Torres had claimed him as his regular customer now, he might not inflate his fare too much.

On the way through town, Quechua Indians sauntered along the narrow road, some with bundles over their shoulders, and mothers with their babies in cloth slings in front or wrapped pouches that hung on the mother's back. The men wore colorful wool ponchos and straw hats, and the women wore long skirts, shawls, and black bowlers. Torres told Mitch that the Indians walk many kilometers every day. He did his best to explain that farmers grew potatoes, maize, and coca in the high mountains, and farmers from the lower hills grew quinoa, vegetables, and fruits. When Mitch asked about coca, Torres explained by mimicking how the Indians stuffed coca in their cheek then licked lime ash to unlock its spirit. He flexed his bicep and said the coca helps them work hard all day.

"Do you chew coca, Torres?"

"No, no, Señor," he said waving his hand dismissively. "Only Indians and tourists."

The airport's single asphalt runway extended along

the floor of a wide, shallow canyon. A control tower and rudimentary terminal sat at one end of the runway, where a single-engine turboprop airplane and a twin-engine business jet were parked. Torres pumped his brakes and turned down a road to the airport. He shifted the Bonneville into low gear to help slow the descent down a series of switchbacks toward the bottom of the canyon.

Halfway down, the car's engine quit. Torres stopped and jumped out of the car and put a rock in front of the driver's side front tire before throwing open the hood. He stepped onto the front bumper and climbed into the engine compartment. Mitch got out of the car and worried that it might start rolling down the steep road. By the time he got to the front of the car, Torres had a shoe off and was banging the carburetor with its heel. The big V-8 engine looked small inside the copious engine compartment, with enough spare room to see the road underneath. Torres smiled and wired the air filter back in place. He got out and slammed the hood shut, then kicked away the rock chock under the tire. Torres got in the car, and after a few mechanical groans on the starter, the engine sputtered to life. Mitch jumped in and they continued down the twisty road in low gear.

Torres parked next to the airport's control tower. They tried to open the white metal door, but found it locked. An armed uniformed guard near the twin-engine jet watched with apparent apathy from behind his gold framed aviator-style sunglasses. After Torres knocked on the door, the guard stepped away from the comfort of the airplane's tail shadow and transferred the sling of his automatic rifle to the other shoulder.

Mitch walked toward the guard but stopped several feet away. "Where can we find Rafael Domingo?"

The guard pointed to the road without answering.

Mitch put his hands on his hips and asked again, louder this time.

The guard just stared at him with a perturbed expression.

Torres whispered hoarsely from behind, "Mister friend. We go now. It's not good to make him angry."

Mitch turned and followed Torres back to the control tower, as if it was a safe zone.

Torres said "That man a *trafficante*. No good for us. It is better to visit a mountain lake today. Very much peace and beautiful."

Mitch went back to the tower door and banged on it several times. Torres glanced back at the guard, then at Mitch.

"No good, mister friend. Maybe the police come."

Mitch banged on the door again and stopped while Torres and the guard watched. Mitch raised his fist again, but the door opened.

A severe looking man with years of hard weather in his face peeked out. He wore black slacks and a wrinkled white shirt.

"Do you speak English?" Mitch asked.

"Yes. You have to leave here."

Torres was already in his car, trying to start it.

Mitch said. "I'm looking for, Rafael Domingo, who flew here from Iquitos."

The man stared at Mitch for a moment, then head-motioned toward the road they came on. "You can find him in Huaraz."

"Where in Huaraz?"

The man shrugged, and then pointed to the jet. "That airplane is from Iquitos. Maybe the guard knows."

"He might know, but he won't talk to me."

"That is a problem between you and him. I must return to my duties now."

After the door closed, Mitch returned to Torres's car. It idled roughly, and quit running when Mitch got in. Torres jumped out, threw open the hood, and repeated his shoe-banging repair.

On the way out of the canyon, Torres said, "This *aeroporto* not good for tourists. I can take you to a museum today, and tonight best bars for dancing."

"Take me to the best hotel in Huaraz. I think my friends would be staying in a place like that."

"I understand. We will find your American friends."

Mitch said, "They are Peruvians."

"Peruvians?" Torres said with uncertainty. He kept his eyes on the road, apparently trying to sort out Mitch's confusing request while navigating up the steep grade in low gear. "I understand," Torres said. "I will find Peruvian friends for you!"

Mitch wasn't sure if Torres really understood, but hoped some trial-and-error searching might pull things together.

On their way into town, they stopped at three hotels on the north end of Huaraz. None said they had guests from Iquitos. They continued through town toward Mitch's hotel. Mitch wondered if Torres had given up the search, but he started braking again. He pulled over at a small two-story building enclosed with a whitewashed concrete wall. Unfriendly-looking broken glass was embedded into the wall's top surface. A closed driveway gate, made of ornate iron grillwork and painted black, discouraged visitors.

Torres parked outside the gate and stayed in the car. "Very good guesthouse for tourists."

Mitch went in by himself through an unlocked service

door next to the driveway gate. The lobby was decorated with glossy ceramic pots of various colors, and were filled with plants and blooming flowers. Several stained-glass windows filled the room with tinted sunlight. A cheerful young man wearing a pressed blue open-collar shirt greeted him.

"Do you speak English?" Mitch asked.

"Yes. A little."

"I'm looking for my friend who came from Iquitos a few days ago. I was supposed to meet him, but I don't know which hotel he's in."

The young man smiled and bobbed his head. "You are looking for Rafael?"

"That's right."

"Rafael always stays at our hotel his first night in Huaraz. More people came with him this time. They took six rooms."

"Are they still here?"

"No, sir, they checked out."

"Was one a woman?"

"There were two women, one old and one young."

"What was the young one's name?"

"I don't know. Rafael signed for all the rooms."

"Oh, of course. Where did they go?"

"To his villa, I think."

"Where's that?"

The man's smile faded. "If you are Rafael's friend, then you would know better than me."

"Yes, but I know him in Iquitos. This is my first time here and I don't know the roads."

"You have to take the road to Mancos, but that is all I know."

"Is his house in Mancos, or nearby?"

"I do not know, sir. I have never been there."

Mitch left wondering if the young woman with Rafael was Tessa. But how could that be? The woman he loved staying with a drug lord? He remembered her sweet kiss, and couldn't believe it had been a lie.

Torres was sitting on his car hood when Mitch came back, and he jumped off to open the passenger door.

Mitch said "The man in the hotel told me about a villa near Mancos. Do you know where that is?"

Torres nodded. "Yes, Mancos is one hour north."

"Can you take me there?"

Torres looked away and shifted from foot to foot. "My is car very old for those bad roads."

Mitch waited for Torres to complete his thought.

"I think that place is bad for you, mister. And for me. I know the villa. It is owned by a jungle king."

"I know him. He's not a king, and he won't hurt us."

"Maybe not you, but maybe. I am not his friend like you. Please, mister, let me take you somewhere safer."

"Just take me close to Mancos, and I'll walk the rest of the way."

"I cannot get close, and you cannot walk there. There are many dangerous men."

Mitch took several soles from his money belt. Torres's eyes locked on the money, then he looked at Mitch's face.

Torres shook his head sadly. "I want to be your friend, mister, but what you want has much danger for me. My wife and daughter need me too much."

Mitch handed the dollars to Torres. "That's for today. I'll walk back to the hotel."

"Be careful. *Banditos* wait everywhere for rich tourists. You will be watched."

When Mitch got to the city center on his way back to

the hotel, he stopped to look at beautiful Quechua tapestries hanging from makeshift wood racks along a sidewalk. Each one depicted some daily aspect of Quechuan life. No two were alike, and were apparently hand-woven from dyed wool yarn. He saw native women sitting on the sidewalk together, hand-spinning wool relentlessly while they tended babies and visited with each other. A young woman who was packing folded tapestries into large woven bags looked up when she noticed Mitch watching her. Her shy furtive smile made him think about Tessa again, and a deep sadness tightened his throat. He wondered if she had ever really loved him.

He walked dejectedly through what looked like the remains of a marketplace earlier in the day. He stopped at a booth that offered leaves from woven baskets. He picked out a leaf and asked what it was.

"Coca," replied the stocky round-faced woman. She picked up a bag of commercially packaged coca tea bags and gestured for Mitch to buy it. He knew unprocessed coca was nothing more than a mild stimulant, like caffeine. He said, "No, *gracias,*" and walked on.

Mitch couldn't shake off the painful realization that he might never see Tessa again—but if she was with Rafael, he didn't want to see her. He felt naïve for thinking she could love him just because they shared a few days aboard Paraiso. While he wandered down the street, the sun slipped behind the mountains. He saw house lights flicker to life, and the drifty evening breeze carried faint cooking scents. Children ignored him while they chased each other through the neighborhood, using up their last measure of energy for the day.

As he walked along, Mitch touched his pants leg to feel the pistol in his right front pocket. It felt out of place in this homey setting, and the thought of shooting anyone anywhere chilled him. Confronting Rafael with a lethal threat seemed ludicrous, a dangerous fantasy cooked up by out-of-touch government phantoms.

But ridiculous or not, meeting with Rafael was his ticket to freedom. Mitch hoped that the people forcing him into this will leave him alone once they somehow confirmed that the meeting took place.

When he reached his hotel, he got his key from the front desk, then walked into the hotel's tiny restaurant. He ordered fried local trout and steamed quinoa, and then sipped a pisco sour while he waited. After supper, he went to his room, short of breath again from the thin mountain air. After locking the room door behind him, he slid his shoes off and collapsed onto the bed without getting undressed.

***

Mitch awoke shivering in the dark. He groped his way across the room to shut the balcony's French doors, then returned to the bed. On the edge of sleep, he heard something tapping on his door. After waiting a few seconds his eyelids drooped shut, and he heard it again. Someone was knocking.

"Hang on…"

He felt for the side table lamp switch, and winced when its tiny bulb flashed to life. On the way to the door, he checked his watch—almost midnight.

"What?"

"The hotel sent me up to tuck you in."

Mitch recognized Darla's voice and opened the door.

"What are you doing here, and at this hour?"

"You didn't meet with Rafael yet, did you?"

"No. Why? How did you get to Huaraz so soon?"

"After you left Iquitos, I flew to Lima on the next flight.

The strong winds had eased up in Huaraz, and I was lucky to find a connecting night flight from Lima. After getting here, I booked a hotel room a couple of blocks from here, then checked other hotels to find you."

"Okay, nice to see you. Now back to question number one. What in hell are you doing here?"

"I'm part of your team, Mitch."

"I have a team?"

"I was in on planning this operation."

"You could have mentioned that in Iquitos."

"I couldn't say anything until you arrived here. We needed to see a show of commitment to the mission."

Mitch sat on the edge of the bed. "So, you're here as my babysitter. How long have you been in the spy business?"

"I've been working undercover in Iquitos to gather intel about Rafael's operation. You must have at least suspected that. I was surprised anyone believed the fish farm cover. You at least guessed that it was bogus. And why else would I befriend a scum like Rafael?"

"Or someone like me?"

"I *am* your friend, Mitch. When you first arrived in Iquitos, I received a background report on you, but you were never a person of official interest to me, or to U.S. Intelligence. So, when Rafael unexpectedly went out of his way to help you escape from Iquitos, it raised questions. We had to find out if you had a relationship with him that we didn't know about. That catastrophe in Nigeria gave us the opportunity to do a deep background investigation, to find out what you and Rafael have in common."

"And you found nothing, right?"

"Wrong...sort of. We discovered a wildcard by the name of Tessa Cortina. Can you tell me how she fits in?"

"No, I can't. I mean that."

"Well, it doesn't matter at this point. We have enough information to corner Rafael, and you are a perfect—if not enthused—messenger. You're not a government official, you're impartial, and he seems to like you."

"I might have thought your fish farm was a dumb idea, Darla, but this cockamamie plan is laughable, and I think you know it."

"Maybe, but it's worth a try. There's been a spike in illicit drugs on American streets. That gives drug gangs more power, money, and the ability to buy politicians and cripple law enforcement. You have to convince Rafael to shut his operation down, Mitch—for the good of America, and I hate to say this, but for his own good. He's gotten greedy and he's juggling too many balls."

"I keep wondering what happens if my meeting with him goes down in flames."

"It would mean my cover has been blown, so I would be reassigned, probably to a place even less tolerable and more dangerous. I don't know exactly what my superiors have promised you, Mitch, but I think you will get some cash and your boat back."

"That's a happy forecast for me. What about the fact that Rafael might shoot me?"

"That's why I'm here, Mitch. I've been assigned to protect you. I'll take you to Rafael's compound tomorrow, and tell him I'm just acting as a go-between. He knows both of us, so there shouldn't be any trouble at that point. Once you've presented the offer to him, you've done your job. We'll encourage him to think it over, and then we'll leave. He can get a message to you in Iquitos if he's interested, and you can let me know. That will set things in motion, and the rest will be out of your hands."

"And then I can go my merry way."

"That's right. By the way, that gun in your pocket was never intended for your use. Rafael's guards will pat you down and take it away, and Rafael would need to know why you brought it."

"Then why was it given to me?"

"To deliver to me. I've very proficient with the Glock 26, and I'll use it only if the meeting gets out of control. But don't worry. I doubt that Rafael will feel threatened in any way—he usually keeps a cool head."

"Why didn't the U.S. Marshal in Lima tell me I was just delivering the gun?"

"Because then he would have had to tell you about my role. You didn't need to know that until now."

Mitch pulled the gun out of his pocket.

"I'm glad to get rid of the damn thing."

Darla pulled her loose trouser leg up over her knee, revealing a black plastic holster held in place with a stretchy band over her calf. She took the gun from Mitch, pulled the slide back just enough to confirm that a round was chambered. She slid the gun into her snug holster, and dropped her pant leg.

Mitch said, "Does Rafael know we're coming?"

"Yes, I told him. I said you are being forced to deliver a message to him. He thinks I'm coming along to help you find his house."

"You're making this sound like a friendly get-together. Why should I trust you? No offense, Darla, but I'm wondering if I can trust anyone, including you."

"I don't blame you. But why shouldn't you trust me?"

"Because you just admitted to not being honest with me."

"Don't you understand, I couldn't until now."

"You called Tessa a wildcard. What did you mean by that?"

"It's just that we don't know anything about her."

"Do you know where she is now?"

"I honestly don't"

Mitch drew a deep breath and walked out onto the balcony. Stars glimmered brilliantly in the clear high-altitude air. Darla came out with him and crossed her arms against the night's chill.

"Mitch, I know you feel something for Tessa. But I think she knew Rafael long before she knew you."

"I can't stop wondering why she went to Rafael instead of you for help."

"It's because I wasn't home, so she went to Rafael for help. He told me this on the way to get you. He saw me walking home, and asked me to come along."

"So, helping me leave Iquitos was a favor to Tessa, or you. Such a nice guy. But he also got my boat, and almost got me killed."

"He didn't set you up for that Nigeria massacre. He lost an entire shipment of coke because of it."

"Well, it doesn't matter now. I'll just be glad when tomorrow's over."

"Don't worry, Mitch. It'll be fine. I'll stop by at dawn to pick you up, if that's good for you. Rafael's place is only about an hour from here."

"I wonder if I'll see Tessa there."

"Do you want to?"

"I didn't think so, but now I don't know."

Chapter 21

After Darla left, Mitch lay awake for a while, then drifted restlessly in and out of sleep. After what seemed like only a few minutes of sleep, he heard a rooster's crow announce the new day.

Mitch went to the balcony door with the bed blanket caped around his shoulders. A little yellow bird hopped around nervously on the balcony rail, as if begging for some breakfast crumbs, and then finally gave up and flew away. Rising sunlight ignited Mount Huascarán's snowy peak, spreading pink light across the wispy morning clouds. Mitch scanned the disappearing stars overhead and barely saw the Southern Cross on the horizon, opposite from Huascarán.

A lone car sputtered slowly past the hotel and made him wonder when Darla would arrive.

He soon heard a car's engine pop and rumble, agitating the morning's peaceful silence. Mitch saw Torres's old Bonneville pull up directly across the street. Torres got out and stood in the street, looking around. He spotted Mitch on the balcony, squinted to make sure, then waved exuberantly. He jabbed his finger toward his car and grinned. Mitch signaled that he would come down. He got on his shoes went downstairs.

Torres was waiting for him just outside the hotel door. "I

thought about your trip to Mancos, and I was wrong. The road will be fine for my car. I can take you there."

"I already have someone to take me."

Torres's smile faded. "Another taxi?"

Before he could answer, a silver pickup truck pulled up in front of the hotel. Darla got out and left her door open. With nothing more than a quick glance at Torres, she said, "Are you ready?"

"I'll be right there."

Mitch saw a worried look cross Torres's face. When he walked over to him, Torres whispered, "Is that woman your friend?"

"She's taking me to my business meeting."

"I think she can be trouble for you, mister Mitch."

"It's all right. I know her."

"She is Cuban."

"How do you know?"

Torres concentrated for the right words. "Her Spanish speaks like Cubans do."

"How do you know how Cubans speak?"

"We are high in the mountains, and get Radio Havana. That is how I know Cubans hate Americans."

"She speaks perfect English to me, with no accent.

"Yes, but she speaks Spanish to me. She's been to Huaraz before. I once gave her a ride to Mancos, to a big house. I think that's where your jungle friends went. If you are going there be careful."

"I will."

Mitch hurried to his room and locked the door, then left the key behind the front desk. When he got back to Darla's truck, she started the engine without looking at him.

"What did that taxi driver want?"

"He keeps wanting to show me a mountain lake."

"What lake?"

"I don't know. Does it matter?"

"Rafael lives near a mountain lake."

"And…?

"He might be a spy. I'll watch to see if he follows us."

"Is this really something you're worried about?"

"Not worried, just being careful. Rafael has enemies, and they have spies in Huaraz."

Darla drove through town and headed north along a valley. Thin cirrus clouds tore free from the snowy mountain peaks above, and glided across the intense blue sky, sending faint ghostly shadows down the high hillsides.

After leaving Huaraz, Darla stayed on a narrow blacktop road through the valley. She seemed preoccupied with monitoring the rearview mirror. Her nervous silence started to feel awkward to Mitch.

He said, "Thanks for helping me."

"Sure."

"Have you been here before?"

"Just once, a long time ago, while you were on one of your river trips. I told Rafael I needed some time away from the hot jungle, and he invited me up here for a few days. It gave me a chance to see his house and meet some of his staffers"

"When did you become a U.S. Marshal?"

"I didn't. I'm a contractor. I was a Peace Corps worker in Peru for a few years, then I got a job with a company that wrote intelligence briefs for the Embassy. That led to better paying undercover assignments. I was assigned to Iquitos a few years ago to report on the increased amount of cocaine moving directly out of Peru."

"Thanks to that disaster in Nigeria, I now know that

Columbia is being bypassed."

"We already knew that. Everything's being shipped by air now instead of by sea. We just weren't sure of the routes and who the players were."

"Does your job take you to other countries?"

"No. My only expertise is in Peru."

After a few minutes of silence, Mitch said, "I wonder how Rafael will react to our visit."

"He already knows you're coming, and that you were forced to bring some kind of message—a threat, he guessed. I said all your bad luck was his fault because he put you on that chartered jet to an untried pickup point. He doesn't blame you for cooperating with the U.S. government. But he does worry about a bigger problem."

"Is it because I know about his trafficking route?"

"No, it's because you've been compromised by U.S. officials. Keep in mind that he doesn't know I'm working for them. But he knows you do."

"Now, I'm worried."

"Don't be. I've got a plan. After you deliver whatever the offer is to Rafael, tell him he should take time to think about it, and he can deliver his answer through me. I'll take Rafael aside and assure him that you won't leave Huaraz alive."

"What!" Mitch twisted in his seat to face her. "So that's why you took my gun."

"No, it's because Rafael's security goons will probably pat you down, but they won't search me. After the meeting, I'll make sure you get safely to the bus station in Huaraz, and when you get to Lima, fly back to Iquitos. Get your money at the bank, and get your boat if you can, then get the hell out of Peru however you can."

"What'll happen to you?"

"I won't have a cover anymore, so I'm done in Peru—for good."

"This is getting weirder than I thought, Darla."

"Welcome to my world, or should I say *underworld*."

"I wonder if I'll see Tessa before I leave."

"Don't even bring that up. You need to understand that she's not your friend, no matter how nice she was to you. When she needed a ride to Iquitos, you were her only option. And that's the end of it."

"I can't believe that's all she cared about."

"It doesn't matter now. I don't think Rafael will let you get anywhere near her."

When they arrived in the town of Mancos, Darla turned to the right onto another road that headed directly toward the foothills of Mount Huascarán. She slowed to pass through the middle of a small tired village, where squat buildings were huddled in clusters along the road. Hand-printed signs hung near the doors of shops, and terraced fields blanketed the surrounding foothills and slopes. After a few hundred feet, the village ended and Darla sped up. They soon saw a black truck parked sideways in the middle of the road. Two men armed with military-style automatic rifles stepped forward to meet them. Darla slowed to a stop.

"Damn. I wasn't counting on this," she said, and bit her lip.

"Who are these thugs?"

"Local militia."

One of the soldiers walked toward her door and she rolled down the window.

Mitch wished he still had the Glock. Would Darla have the guts to use it if necessary? Two American gringos would likely bring a fat ransom. If the men tried to kidnap them, he hoped Darla would at least have the nerve to turn the pickup truck around and make a run for it.

The man told Darla in Spanish that she would have to pay a road tax for the nearby medical clinic and school. He looked at Mitch and said the amount would be 50 U.S dollars.

Darla said, "I'm taking this man to meet with Rafael Domingo. Do you want Rafael to know his guest had to pay your tax to see him?"

"No, but—"

The other man came to the window and took over.

"I am sorry, señorita. The government does not help our families, so we have to collect our own taxes."

"That is very noble," Darla said. "But Rafael has helped all the people in this area by giving money to schools and clinics. If you need something more, you should talk to him. That would be better than disrespecting his friends."

The man stepped back hollered for the truck driver to back up. The driver ground the truck's gears and rolled back enough for them to get through. Both of the men with rifles backed away enough to make room. She increased her speed gradually. After a few meters Mitch looked back at the truck re-closing the road.

He said "Quick thinking."

"Pissing Rafael off would be very unpopular in this area."

"Who do these bandits work for?"

"Themselves. They're freelance extortionists. They work an area for a day or two, then move to another spot. Some of their loot will find its way into the local magistrate's pocket.

"Rafael is tax-exempt, I take it."

"Not at all. I meant it when I said he gives money to medical clinics, and schools—even to churches. And those militiamen know it."

"It makes Rafael seem so wholesome. It would make

American cocaine addicts feel proud of their source."

Darla broke a smile. "It's just part of the business. Even American corporations and unions pay off politicians and political parties. Americans are more corrupt because they openly allow that kind of bribery."

A few minutes later, Darla slowed to shift the pickup truck into four-wheel drive, then she turned up a steep gravel road. The short road ended at a driveway that was blocked with a gated chain-link fence. Darla stopped at the gate and shut the engine off. She removed the ignition keychain and found the key she was looking for, then unlocked a padlock on the gate door. She swung it open and drove the truck through, then she got out and relocked the gate.

A two-story red brick house soon came into view. It had a bright blue steel roof, and the window frames were painted white and green. Nearby, two smaller one-story buildings were constructed from the same materials. A tiled gazebo sat empty outside the big house. A picnic-style table sat in the middle, with four white plastic chairs arranged on one side. The red and blue color theme was complimented throughout the grounds with clustered flowers of the same colors.

"Well, here we are," she said.

"I expected the place to be swarming with Rafael's people."

"Most of his employees live in their own houses nearby. A husband and wife are permanent caretakers, and a few trusted bodyguards live here. In addition to those people, some of his Iquitos staffers sometimes travel with him."

After Darla parked next to the open-air shelter, Mitch went with her to the main building. She used the brass knocker, cast in the shape of a curled fish, to tap on the door. The door swung open, as if someone had been waiting behind it.

An elderly woman stood aside for Darla and Mitch,

averting eye contact and not saying a word.

"This is the cook," Darla said as she led the way in.

The woman closed the door and left. Mitch said "She seemed ready for us."

"I'm sure she knew we were coming. We've been watched by armed lookouts since we got within a mile of this place."

A short big-chested man with gray-steaked black hair came in from a back room. "Hello Darla. And you must be Mister Mitch. I am Raul."

Mitch said, "You speak very good English."

"Thank you. I worked at a busy New York hotel counter for two years. Rafael will see you in the outdoor gazebo, but before he arrives, I would like permission to search you. This is just a formality."

After Raul patted him down, Mitch and Darla walked to the gazebo.

Mitch said "What does Raul do here?"

"He prevents problems and makes trouble disappear."

"Am I considered trouble?"

"If you were, you'd already be gone."

Darla scooted the four plastic chairs away from the table. "Can you help me turn this table sideways?"

"Sure, but why?"

"So that no one has their back to the villa. Rafael likes to see what's going on around him. So do I."

"Who's the fourth chair for?"

"I don't know. It's just an extra, I guess."

A heavy wood door slammed and Mitch turned to see Rafael walking toward them.

Rafael stepped into the gazebo. "Please sit down."

"Thanks for meeting with us," Darla said.

"Of course. I always like to visit with friends. We will be

joined by someone else in a moment, but tell me, Mitch, what brings you back to Peru after all that happened to you? Do you want money, revenge—maybe a job?"

"Right now, the only thing I want is to leave Peru—for good this time. But I was blackmailed by dangerous people to deliver a message in person to you, so that must come first."

"I like your honesty. Now I'll be honest with you. What happened in Nigeria was a surprise to me, and it wasn't because you were on the airplane. It was planned by people who want to put me out of business."

"I can believe that."

"Good. Then we are both being honest. Now, what is your message?"

"The United States and the Peruvian government both want to put you out of business."

"You came all this way to tell me something every-one knows?"

"No, I came to tell you that they are jointly offering you a pardon from your crimes, and safety for you and your family. In return, you must retire from your business."

"Do you trust either government?"

"Not really."

"More honesty. I'm getting to like you even better, Mitch. Now, what are they giving you?"

"The same thing they're offering you. Freedom. And maybe I can get my boat back."

"We have much in common, Mitch. We both already have freedom, and neither of us has your boat."

"My reward is just for coming here. Yours depends on retiring."

Rafael said, "Wait here, Darla. I want to show something to Mitch."

Mitch and Rafael walked across the lawn for several meters to the edge of an overlook.

"You are wise, Mitch, but there are things you do not understand. If I *retire,* as you call it, nothing will be accomplished. The Cuban communists have been helping me expand my operation, but they will immediately take over the *cocaína* business in Peru if I am gone."

"I thought the Columbians were your worst enemy."

"Not anymore. They have the same enemies I do. The Cubans are opening cocaína processing camps in Columbia and Venezuela as fast as they can set them up. They have been helping me set up processing camps and distribution connections. But they will become dangerous if I'm not needed—or not careful. The Columbian lords became rich, but then they got lazy, and they are being run out of international markets everywhere—even in their own country. A few weeks ago, Cuban terrorists bombed a government building in Bogotá as a warning, and Columbian traffickers are being hunted down and assassinated by Cuban spies. The Cubans are very organized, Mitch. They still make rum and cigars for tourists, but a radical group of communists is getting rich on the streets of America and Europe. They are taking over Venezuela's government, and they are the ones who made all that trouble in Nigeria. They thought they could steal my cargo and scare off the Nigerians, but they paid for that mistake with their lives."

"Then maybe it really is a good time to clear out."

"It's a terrible time, Mitch. Look at the land below us. There are coca fields throughout that valley. The Columbians used to control coca prices because they controlled the processing of raw coca. But now, I'm taking over processing and finding trade routes. I'm paying our farmers a fair price and I'm protecting them from the Cubans."

"Can't the Peruvian government control the Cubans?"

"Even the Cuban government cannot control this radical communist cartel. They are sly, like jungle snakes. They stay in Havana and collect and deposit cryptocurrency through the internet instead of banks. They have no relationship with the U.S., so they don't have to launder their profits. They work through a network of foreign partners and spies, so they don't even have to step foot into South America. This is why I can't just walk away from my business, Mitch. If I lose my power up here, the communists will make sure I can never return."

Rafael glanced back at Darla, who still sat in the gazebo looking bored. He took a half-step closer to Mitch and spoke a little louder than a whisper. "I have a good friend who is a powerful government official in Lima. He warned me that an assassin has been sent to Iquitos to kill me. That's why I left Iquitos so quickly and made Tessa come with me. We are better protected in the mountains, at least for now. I tell you this because you have been good to Tessa, and I think I can trust you. You and I both face the same dangers, from the same people."

Mitch said, "What do you mean?"

"First, tell me why you brought Darla?"

"I thought you sent her to bring me." Mitch wanted to warn Rafael that she had a gun, but he no longer knew whose side either of them were on.

Something caught Rafael's eye, and he said, "It looks like someone's coming to say hello."

Mitch saw Tessa striding toward them while beaming a smile. When she got close enough to hear, he said to Rafael, "I didn't come here to visit your girlfriend."

Tessa's smile sagged and she said, "I'm not his girlfriend."

"Are you married?"

"You didn't know he is my brother?"

"No...I thought..."

Not wanting to embarrass Mitch any further, she scrunched her mouth to hold back a smile.

Rafael said, "Let's go back to the gazebo before Darla falls asleep."

While the three of them walked across the lawn, Rafael said to Mitch, "My type of business shamed our father, so to spare him further humiliation, I moved to Iquitos and changed my name from Estevan Cortina to Rafael Domingo. I haven't been back to Tamshiyaco since. I am always happy when Tess comes to visit me."

"This is my first time to the mountains," Tessa said. "Estevan insisted that I come here to be safe. That's why I couldn't wait for you in Iquitos."

Mitch turned to Rafael. "Why would someone want to harm her?"

"To get to me. She could be taken hostage."

As soon as they sat down, Darla sprang up from her chair, knocking it over behind her. Her hand was wrapped around the small pistol and she pointed it at Rafael's chest. Tessa screamed as two shots exploded, both tearing Rafael's chest open before he dropped face first onto the table. Darla immediately aimed at Tessa and a single shot cracked the air—but not from her gun. Darla's arms fell and she instinctively released one last shot that ricocheted off the gazebo's tile floor. She dropped backward onto the plastic chair before rolling lifelessly onto the floor.

Tessa yelled "Estevan!" and ran to him. She cried and hugged his lifeless body, and tried to lift him back in his chair but his body fell onto the floor while blood pooled and dripped off the table.

When Mitch saw Raul shove a gun under his belt, he stooped down and grabbed the Glock pistol.

"Leave it on the floor," Raul said. "There is no one left to fight."

Mitch dropped the gun and Raul kicked it aside. He went to Rafael and solemnly bowed his head while Tessa knelt over his body and pleaded '*Estevan—Estevan*' as if she could wake him from death, or wake herself from a nightmare.

Mitch tried to take her arm, but she wouldn't let go of her brother. When Mitch tried again, she whipped around with tears streaming and yelled "Why did you bring her?"

"I didn't—"

"Get away from me!" She ran from the gazebo.

Raul said to Mitch, "Let her grieve for her brother in her own way. But as soon as she is ready, you must take her away from this place. Our only job was to take out Rafael, but I wasn't told Darla would also kill his sister. Tessa is innocent and I couldn't let that happen. But someone else might come to finish Darla's assignment. That means Tessa is still in grave danger. And so are you."

"Danger from who?"

I can't tell you that exactly, but both of you know too much about Rafael's operation, and now you also know too much about his enemies. Go as far and fast you can. I don't want my next assignment to have her name or your name on it."

"Aren't you concerned about the fact that I am representing the United States government?"

Raul shook his head with an amused grin. "You were recently in Nigeria and Miami, but everyone you talked to was a Cuban operative. It was a game of deception, Mitch—

a game you have lost."

Mitch stared at Raul. What Raul just told him didn't seem likely—but didn't sound like a lie. "What about the rest of the household staff?"

"They will all answer to me now. A storm of power is shifting in Peru, Mitch, and we must either bend or be broken. My new superiors had helped Rafael build a strong empire, but now he is no longer needed. That's why we are here together today. But you and Tessa are left caught in the eye of the storm, and that makes you both vulnerable, no matter which way you turn. You cannot protect yourselves. You can only get out of the mountains as quickly as you can. Return to Iquitos if you can because it will always be relatively safe there."

"What about Rafael's body?"

"Arrangements have already been made to have his remains flown back to Iquitos for a proper burial. You must go quickly now, but stay away from the airport and the bus station. There will be people watching for you. You can't trust anyone from now on."

"Could the police help us?"

"I hope the police do not find you. I will have to explain what happened here today, and our story is that you assassinated Rafael. You left your fingerprints on the gun when you picked it up."

"How will you explain Darla?"

"There will be no evidence that she ever existed."

Mitch said, "So, we can't even trust you."

"That's right, I am in an awkward position. But you can believe me when I tell you to get Tessa out of here, quickly. Take Rafael's pickup truck. Leave it anywhere in Huaraz. It will find its way back to us."

"Could we drive it to Lima?"

"You wouldn't get far. The police will be watching that road."

"Then how do we get out of Huaraz?"

"I don't know. That problem belongs to you. I will open the gate for you now. After you drive through it, you will be on your own. That's the best I can do, Mitch. And for your sake and Tessa's, I hope I never see either of you again."

After Raul left the gazebo, Mitch saw Tessa standing nearby, staring at the valley below.

"Did you hear any of that?"

She drew a deep breath to collect herself. "Most of it. I can hardly believe Raul would betray Estevan this way. I'm sorry for blaming you, Mitch. I didn't know Darla had tricked you, too."

"You and I were both caught in a deadly plan."

She turned to him in tears. He nudged her against his chest while she cried into his shoulder.

She said, "You got caught in so much danger, only because you took me aboard your boat in Tamshiyaco. I have been bad luck for you."

"Taking you aboard my boat was the luckiest thing that ever happened to me."

She stepped back and wiped her eyes with her sleeve. A smile peeked through her pressed lips.

"I can't leave my brother, Mitch. Not like this."

"You heard Raul say he will send his remains to Iquitos. We have to believe that, Tessa. There might be more people as crazy and dangerous as him."

"Where can we be safe?"

"I don't know, but I know it's not here."

They walked together to the silver pickup truck, still

parked near the driveway gate where Darla had left it. The keys were still in the ignition and the gate had been left open.

Mitch climbed into the driver's seat and Tessa got in the passenger side. She started to cry, and between sobs said. "Let's go Mitch...please hurry...I can't stand being here now."

Mitch started the engine, then roared out of the compound, turning onto the road back to Mancos. When a sedan came toward them in the distance, Mitch and Tessa exchanged worried looks. He slowed and hugged the edge of the gravel road to let the sedan pass, ready to speed ahead if it didn't. The driver passed with a friendly wave and a rooster tail of dust.

Mitch said, "I want to get rid of this truck as soon as we can. People might know who it belongs to."

Mitch slowed just before they reached the outskirts of Mancos, and he crept down a narrow street toward the city center. The street opened to a small tidy plaza with flowers and shrubs and a sparkling central water fountain. The plaza was surrounded by two-story apartments and townhouses, with a large church at one end. He braked a little too hard, and when the tires grabbed at the pavement, he eased over and parked next to the plaza.

"What's wrong?" Tessa asked.

"That car in front of us belongs to a taxis driver I know from Huaraz. His name is Torres. I wonder what he's doing here?"

Mitch got out and went to the car. Torres was curled up asleep on the back seat. Mitch tapped the window, and Torres slowly looked up and blinked, and then quickly sat up.

Mitch opened the door. "What are you doing here?"

"I found someone who wanted to see a mountain lake. He is from Utah, America. I don't think they have any lakes there."

"Where is he now?"

"I think seeing the lake made him thirsty. He went across the plaza for a beer in the Video Bar."

"We need a ride to Huaraz and we're in a hurry."

"What happened to the woman who brought you this morning?"

"She had to stay and I had to go. I'm with another woman now."

"You catch women like a cinema star."

"Her name is Tessa, and I met her on the Amazon River. But now we have to get back to Iquitos. It's a town in the jungle. I borrowed the truck behind you, but we have to leave it here. Can you help us?

Torres got out of his car. "This sounds like a big problem. After I bring the Utah man back to Huaraz, I will come back for you."

"We have to leave now. You warned me about the woman who brought me here, and you were right. She shot Rafael, who is Tessa's brother, and she tried to shoot Tessa, too. One of Rafael's men killed that woman, but Tessa and I are still in danger. That's why we have to leave now."

"I want to help you, my friend, but I can't leave my American rider."

"I'll give him the truck key to drive back."

"He might not agree to that."

"If he doesn't disagree, will you take us then?"

"Yes, of course. I think."

"All right. Wait near the front door with Tessa in your car. Be ready to leave very quickly."

Mitch dashed across the plaza and went into the bar. A blond-haired man sat at the bar with a bottle of beer, watching a soccer match on a TV behind the bar. He and the bartender were the only ones in the bar.

Mitch stopped a few feet from him, "You're the Utah guy, right?"

"Yeah…who are you?"

"I like to help American tourists like you. You can drive my nice silver pickup truck back to Huaraz, and you don't have to pay me anything. It's parked on the other side of the plaza. You can leave it anywhere in Huaraz, and I'll find it later."

"Is this a Joke?"

"I offer to help you, and you call me a joker?"

"Okay, I'm sorry—but I already have a taxi waiting for me."

"I think you know that old taxi isn't safe." Mitch slid the key down the bar to him. "At least think it over. If you decide against my offer, just leave the key on the driver's seat."

Before the confused man could think of a question, Mitch spun around and walked out of the bar. When he got outside, he ran to Torres's car. Torres had the engine running and Tessa was already in the back seat. Mitch scooted in next to her and said, "Let's go! I gave him the truck key and he didn't give it back, so let's get out of here before he has time to think about it."

Torres gunned the engine and sped down a street toward the road to Huaraz.

Mitch put his arm around Tessa. She slid closer to him and rested her head on his shoulder.

"I am very sorry to hear about your brother," Torres said in Spanish.

Tessa looked up at Mitch.

"I told Torres about your poor brother."

She nodded and caught a tear with her fingers.

Mitch said, "Torres, how can we leave the mountains without going to the airport or the bus station?"

"There are two roads out of Huaraz, a good one to Lima and a bad one down the east side of the mountains."

"Where does the bad road go?"

"There are a few towns along that road, but it ends in Pucallpa, in the jungle."

Tessa said, "Pucallpa is a frontier town on the Ucayali River."

"And the Ucayali flows into the Amazon," Mitch said brightly. "Torres, can you drive us there?"

"I wish I could, my friend, but my brakes are not good enough for that road, and my old tires will slip if it rains. Sometimes the road to Pucallpa is so crazy and steep that you have to drive back and forth like a drunk man, and then sneak around corners like a thief. Even with a good car, it would take at least fifteen hours of *miseria,* much of it through the rain forest before reaching Pucallpa."

"You know a lot about that road," Mitch said.

"My brother drives a truck from Huaraz to Pucallpa each week to deliver potatoes that grow in these mountains. He and his companion driver have many stories about their dangerous trips."

"He goes through all that just to deliver potatoes?"

"Potatoes very valuable in Pucallpa. From there they are taken by boat down the Amazon River to Iquitos, and other places along the way where gringo tourists want mountain potatoes instead of manioc."

Tessa said, "Torres, will your brother give us a ride to Pucallpa?"

"I don't know when he is making another trip, but I don't think his boss, the potato farmer, will let him take passengers.

All the room in the back is used for potatoes. And there is only room in the front for the two drivers."

"Maybe we could sit on top of the potatoes," Mitch said.

"I think it would be terrible for you *and* the potatoes."

"What other choice do we have?"

"There are no other choices, my friend."

After a moment of silence, Torres said, "I will take you to my brother's house. I can talk to him."

Torres drove through Huaraz's business district to a residential area on the south side of town. Narrow concrete streets were lined with small one-story and two-story houses, each constructed from either course brown bricks or smooth red bricks. The better houses were roofed with red clay half-round tiles, and the lessor dwellings were covered with sheets of corrugated metal. A tangle of power and telephone wires drooped from square cement poles on both sides of the street, along which skinny feral dogs wandered or lounged on their sides in patches of direct sunlight, their ribs showing through mangy hair. There were few pedestrians, most of them children.

Torres pulled up in front of a single-story brown-brick house. The varnished wood door was protected by ornately welded iron grillwork, in contrast to the two front windows' austere iron security bars. Red flowers grew along the front, surrounding a plaster statue of the Blessed Virgin Mary.

"Wait here," Torres said. "I will see if my brother is home."

While Torres pounded on the door frame with the side of his fist, Mitch put his arm around Tessa and she slid closer. He said, "Will you mind riding like a potato?"

She smiled without looking at him. "I won't mind as long as you're in the same potato sack." Then her smile faded and her lips tightened.

He said, "What's the matter?"

"I'm sorry, Mitch. I can't stop thinking about how lonely and horrible Estevan looked. I should not have left him like that. I know he would have arranged my funeral if I died that way."

"We can't always choose when to leave a loved one behind. I was married once, Tessa, and I came home one night to find my wife brutally murdered. I avenged her death by killing the murderer, but that's not why I went to his house. I wanted him to confess to his crime, but when he turned to get his gun, I had to shoot him. Because it looked like murder, I had to escape from my home and my country. I still feel bad that I could not arrange her funeral."

"I'm sad for you, Mitch. Losing your wife that way must have been terrible."

"Worse than I can put into words."

"I don't need words to understand."

Torres opened the car door. "We are lucky. My brother is making his weekly trip to Pucallpa tomorrow. He wants to know how much you can pay him if he takes you."

"I will give him half of all the money I have with me."

"How much is that?"

"I have twenty U.S. dollars."

"Not very much for such a long ride. Gasoline is expensive."

"He has to buy gasoline anyway, and if he doesn't take us, he will lose ten dollars."

"I'll remind him about that."

Mitch could see Torres holding the house door open and talking. When he returned to the car, he said, "All right, he will do it, but his driving partner will want money, too."

"Tell your brother that I know a Catholic archbishop, and

the next time I see him I will tell him about your brother's good deed, and I will ask the archbishop to pray directly to God for a special blessing for your brother and for his driving partner. Ask your brother if money is more valuable than his soul."

"Yes, I understand," Torres said with serious expression. "I will ask him."

Torres went back into the house and shut the door behind him.

"Do you really know an archbishop?" Tess asked.

"A little. I met him once when he was in Iquitos."

"His priests use speedboats to say Sunday Mass in mestizo villages like Tamshiyaco."

"The next time I see him, I will ask him to pray for Torres's brother and the other driver. That intention makes my offer honest."

Tessa giggled and said, "Americans always have to be honest."

He teased her with narrowed eyes. "Not always, my dear."

Torres opened the door again and got in behind the wheel. "My brother agreed. His name is Carlos. He will pick you up at my house at three o'clock in the morning. It will take about an hour to load the potatoes at the nearby farm, and then they will start their journey. You should arrive in Pucallpa about seven o'clock tomorrow night."

Tessa squeezed Mitch's hand but said nothing.

"Can we stay at your house until then?"

"Yes, of course," Torres said.

"I need to keep the rest of my money to get back to Iquitos. I must be the worst customer you ever picked up."

"No, not the worst." He glanced at Mitch in the rearview mirror. "But the next time you see your friend, the archbishop…"

"I will ask him to pray for you and your family."

"That will be enough payment."

***

Torres parked in front of his house, located a few blocks from the center city's Plaza De Armas. His house was set back from the sidewalk, squeezed in between a three-story brick apartment building and a whitewashed cement house with a slanted corrugated metal roof. The small front yard of mostly dirt had a few weeds, but healthy red flower bushes were spaced evenly along the front of the house.

Torres introduced Mitch and Tessa to his wife and pre-teen daughter. His wife went to work making temporary beds of blankets on the floor. Torres encourage Tessa and Mitch to walk around the area, but return at dusk to get some sleep before they left. Mitch said it would be safer for him and Tessa if they stayed inside the house.

Torres's wife served a supper of *puka picante*— a pork and potato stew seasoned with red pepper and beets—along with course-ground corn cakes. Their daughter was dispatched to a neighborhood snack shack to buy a liter bottle of iced beer for Mitch and Torres to share, and three bottles of vanilla-flavored *Inca Kola* for the ladies. After supper, Mitch and Tessa entertained them with stories about life in the jungle and on the Amazon River—both places considered exotic and wild to mountain people. Tessa interpreted Mitch's accounts of running a boat business out of Iquitos. She told how they first met, just a few weeks ago, and how piranhas had attacked Luis. Their daughter said she would tell that exciting piranha story at school. After they got up from the table, Torres's wife whispered to Tessa, asking if she wanted her bedding in their daughter's room. Tessa said Mitch was honorable and she could trust sleeping in the living room near him.

***

Torres flipped the living room light switch on, waking Mitch and Tessa.

He said, "Carlos will be here soon. We wrapped a few of the left-over corn cake *humitas* to take on your trip. My wife filled a bottle of water for you, and you can refill it when you make stops."

While helping Tessa roll up the blankets, Mitch said, "How many stops are there?"

"You will pass through at least four towns that I know about, but I have never made that trip. You can ask Carlos."

They soon heard the deep rumble of a large engine. Torres went outside to tell Carlos his passengers were ready. Tessa came back from the bathroom with freshly-combed hair, and her green shirt tucked neatly into her jeans, looking ready for a weekend vacation.

"You look pretty," Mitch said. "I think we'll soon be safe."

"We might never be safe, but I'm happy to be pretty for you."

When they got outside, Mitch was surprised by the size of the truck. The red cab was large with oversized fenders, but the cargo area was just a little bigger than that of a pickup truck. The sides and tailgate were raised about a meter high with wood slats, almost doubling the storage capacity.

Carlos got out of the driver's side to meet Mitch and Tessa for the first time. He was shorter and stockier than Torres, and wore a green baseball cap. He pointed to the cab's rolled-down passenger-side window and introduced the other driver as Tuco, a round-faced man who gave them a friendly grin.

Carlos said, "Tuco is from the Quechua people. Their ancestors were the Incas, and they understand everything about the mountains."

Mitch wondered how Inca DNA might help him drive trucks down dangerous mountain roads. "Will there be much room in back when it's loaded?"

"Enough room," Carlos said. "When we load the potatoes, we will make an empty space for you. We have blankets in the back if it gets cold, and a tarp cover if it rains. I think we will get both of those weathers today. The trip will take about fifteen hours, unless we have trouble. If it rains too much, it could be closer to twenty hours."

"That's a long time to drive,"

"Yes, the roads would wear out even the best driver. That's why Tuco comes. We each drive until we need the other man to take over."

While Mitch gave Carlos a ten-dollar fee, Tessa asked Torres to thank his still-asleep wife for her hospitality. Mitch shook Torres's hand and wished him happiness and health. "And I will remember to ask the archbishop to bless you and your family."

Torres gave Mitch and Tessa a plastic bag full of the corn cakes from last night, and the bottle of water. Carlos lowered the tailgate for Tessa and Mitch to climb aboard, then he slammed it shut.

Huaraz's silent pre-dawn streets were vacant, and the cool air smelled fresh. Carlos sped through Huaraz and stopped outside of town at a brick and cement farm house surrounded by fragrant eucalyptus trees. They parked in back where dozens of gunnysacks had been filled with potatoes. Carlos said they were dug this week and brought down every day from a terraced mountain field behind the house. Mitch could see a small dwelling far up at the end of the trail and asked Carlos who lived there.

"That is their potato field *cabina*. The farmer and his sons live there with a neighbor during the week, and on Saturday they make the journey back down to go to church the next day."

"Who brings the potatoes down?"

"Their two oldest daughters. They bring two donkeys pulling carts to the cabina, and take them back full each day. When we come each week, they have a full load ready for us."

Carlos and Tuco helped the farmer and his young son load the potatoes into the truck, stacking the twine-tied gunnysacks on their sides like big sandbags. They left space in a rear corner of the truck bed, just big enough for two people.

"We usually leave a little extra space," Carlos said, "in case we find passengers along the way. This time you are the only ones."

Mitch and Tessa stepped up onto the truck's bumper, then sat in the space left for them. He gave her the bag of corn cakes and water bottle. Carlos handed them a folded green plastic tarp and an armful of blankets. Tessa spread the tarp on the floor then carefully layered the blankets on top.

After Carlos closed the tailgate, a woman dressed in a multi-colored shirt, bright red skirt, and a black brimmed hat strode out of the house yelling. Tuco and the farmer stopped what they were doing while she seemed to be berating them about something.

Mitch turned to Tessa. "I don't understand anything she's saying."

"Neither do I," Tessa said. "She must be speaking in Quechuan."

Carlos heard Tessa and said, "The farmer's wife says it is shameful to make a lady ride in the back of a truck with potatoes."

Mitch wrinkled his brow to fake disappointment. "What about men?"

"You can ride with potatoes, but your lady must ride in the cab with me and Tuco. We will be respectful and there will be enough room. She can sit next to the window, and we will stop anytime she wants to."

"I'll ride with Mitch," Tessa said.

A sign of anxiety ran across Carlos's face. "I'm sorry, but the farmer's wife will not allow it, Señorita. She said we will have to unload everything and leave if we treat you like a potato."

"Don't worry about me," Mitch said to Tessa. "This will give me more room to stretch out."

Carlos opened the tailgate, and she jumped down. Mitch took a drink from the water bottle and removed one of the corn cakes before returning the bag to Tessa. "I'll let you take care of this. I have plenty of potatoes back here if I get hungry."

***

Predawn roosters tried to out-crow each other while Carlos sped south through the suburbs of Huaraz. Mitch saw no pedestrians this early, but he had to brace himself whenever Carlos swerved around occasional stray dogs that wandered nonchalantly into the street. After leaving the residential area, they followed a road south through the valley. Mitch watched the giant snow-capped mountains gradually look smaller as they got farther away.

After about an hour they turned up a steep curvy road

heading east. Mitch pulled a blanket over his shoulders as they ascended into ever-colder air. The road switched back and forth through the rocky terrain then eventually started to descend. After another hour or so, short grass patches and bushes began to appear. They reached a fork in the road, and turned left onto the road with a sign that said *Highway 3N*. It was more of a trail than a highway, twisting through serpentine curves and switchbacks, up and down steep grades. Carlos downshifted on steep downhills to save on the brakes. The road began to straighten and eventually entered a small town. By the position of the sun, Mitch knew it was midmorning.

Carlos pulled into a gas station and stopped at one of the pumps. Mitch tossed the blanket off and jumped off the back of the truck. He hurried on stiff legs to see Tessa through her window. She pushed the door open and climbed out.

"My jungle stomach doesn't like mountains," she said to Mitch. "Did you feel sick, too?"

"I got used to being tossed around while working on ocean ships. Did you have enough room?"

"Enough to breath, barely. I want to ride in back with you now."

"The air is cold back there and the floor is hard. I'm afraid it might make you sicker."

"What if I still want to ride with you?"

"Then Tuco will get in trouble with his angry wife."

Tessa tried not to reward his teasing, so she smiled at the ground. "How would she know?"

"A good husband would admit it to his wife, wouldn't he?"

"I don't know. I've never had a husband."

"*Vamos!*" Carlos said to them after paying the station attendant. "Our next stop is five hours away, at Huanuco.

If you need to stop, Mister Mitch, pound on the side of the truck." He said to Tessa "And if you need to stop, Señorita, you can pound on Tuco."

They all released a needed laugh, except Tuco, who apparently heard his name but didn't understand what Carlos had said. On the way to the truck cab, Carlos interpreted his joke. Tuco gave him a perplexed look as if it made no sense.

This section of the highway had fewer turns, fewer settlements, and no landscape interesting enough to break the monotony. Mitch caught himself nodding on the edge of sleep while he leaned against the potato sack next to him. He bobbed awake briefly whenever Carlos hit a deep pothole, or downshifted the growling transmission gears, but sleep eventually prevailed.

Soon, the gentle scent of fresh foliage did open his eyes. Unlike the craggy snow-capped mountains, these lower rounded mountains were covered with dense growth from the top on down. The air felt warmer, even without a blanket, and Mitch knelt and stretched his arms up into the truck's invigorating slipstream.

When he sat back down on the crunchy plastic tarp, he started to worry about what would happen to him and Tessa once they reached Pucallpa. It was a frustrating worry because he had no knowledge of that area, located far beyond the Amazon River's headwaters. He had no way to formulate a plan—even though his plans never seemed to work out. He began to think about Rafael's horrible death, and how the same fate almost took Tessa. He wondered how many times she mentally replayed that horrific scene while sitting quietly next to Carlos and Tuco.

More on-and-off sleep blurred his thoughts. He was jostled awake when the truck slowed and turned off the road.

A sign said they arrived at Huanuco.

While Mitch and Tessa freshened up in the gas station's building, Carlos bought a large bottle of water for each of them at its small café, and cheese and bread for all of them to take along.

Carlos started to open the plastic tarp and Tuco got into the truck bed and shifted some of the potato sacks to even out and lower the cargo's profile. Then they fastened the tarp over the truck bed.

Carlos said to Mitch, "It rains more on this side of the mountain range. I think the tarp will keep you and the potatoes dry. If not, pound on the truck to signal us."

They left a tighter space for Mitch, which cancelled any thoughts Tessa might have about riding with him when it got warmer.

She stood close to him with a sad face. "I want to take turns in the back, Mitch. I worry too much about you back there. I know you must be suffering, even though you make jokes about it."

"I think Tuco will like it better if you ride next to him instead of me."

She gently pushed his arm with a grin. "Oh, you are a terrible joker. You would send me away just to please Tuco? I thought boat captains were supposed to be men of honor."

"Would there be honor if I let my lady ride in the back of a potato truck."

She looked down at the gravel. "I like it when you say I am your lady."

After the truck was refueled, Carlos joined them. "Our next stop is Tingo Maria. It's only three hours from here, unless the rain is too heavy. Tuco will drive that route. He's a good mountain driver in the rain."

Mitch said "Does it rain all year on that stretch."

"It can rain anytime in the foothills, but much more during the summer, which is November through March. We will keep getting rain off and on now—mostly on—for the rest of the way to Pucallpa. You'll see how the rivers along the way gather and grow into giants all the way to the Ucayali River, and from there into the mightiest of all rivers, the Amazon."

Mitch said, "Have you ever been to the Amazon River?"

"No, it is too awful for mountain people. We are not used to the heat, the insects, dangerous Indians. You can't get lost in the mountains, but you can easily get swallowed by the jungle.

"We left in such a hurry, I forgot to ask how we can travel downriver to Iquitos."

"You might be able to pay a cargo boat captain for passage, if he has room for two passengers."

"We don't have hammocks, and we don't have any money with us."

"Of those two problems, no money is the bigger one. We will be loading our potatoes tonight onto a boat that leaves for Iquitos the next morning. I'll ask the captain if he has room to take you."

"Maybe I can help him. I have experience with cargo boats."

"I will tell him."

Carlos and Tuco finished tying the tarp down over the back of the truck, except for a short section near the back corner. There, he let Mitch tie or untie the corner from the inside. Before taking her place in the cab, Tessa lifted the loose corner to peek in at Mitch. She whispered, "Carlos and Tuco have been nice to me." A tear started down her cheek. "But when I'm sitting in the front with them, I'm afraid to think about Estevan. I might cry too much. I keep thinking that no one deserves to die such a terrible way."

Mitch reached out and put his hand on her cheek. "When we get to Pucallpa, you can cry while I hold you in my arms."

Chapter 22

As Carlos had predicted, after about an hour of driving, low clouds scattered a gentle drizzle. The sky became dark as night as they drove in and out of denser showers. Mitch could feel Tuco make corrections when sudden gusts blew against the side of the truck and shuddered the tarp.

When they arrived in Tingo Maria, Tuco pulled up to the fuel pump under an overhang that shielded them from the light rain. Carlos untied enough of the tarp for Mitch to stand and climb down to stretch his legs. But Mitch felt nauseated from all the back-and-forth turns, and his head felt tortured from carbon monoxide that slipstreamed into his compartment from the truck's exhaust. While getting out of the truck bed on weak legs, he gripped the tailgate with all his available strength to avoid falling.

Tessa had already gone into the station store to use the restroom, and she strode to the back of the truck with a look of renewed energy. "Carlos said this will be our last fuel stop," she said. "Only five more hours to Pucallpa!"

Mitch turned away from her and vomited onto the gravel. Since he had eaten so little in the last few hours, his repeated gagging produced mostly mucus.

Tessa put her hand on his back. "Come inside the truck

and sit down. The rain and wind have made you sick."

"I'm already feeling better. Too much engine smoke comes into the back of the truck with the tarp on. I'll tell Carlos to tie it better over my corner, then I should be fine."

"But you won't be able to see out."

"See what? More fog and rainforest? The potatoes are more interesting. I'll save my sightseeing for Pucallpa."

"I feel fresh, Mitch, so please let me ride in the back for at least a little part of the way. Sitting in the front will make you feel better, and it will give me a break from sitting in the truck with two sweaty men."

He gave her a brave smile. "You are a very strict nurse."

"I am not your nurse. I am your friend."

"And I am your friend, so let's let Carlos fix the tarp, and I'll finish the trip in the back."

"And get sick again from poison exhaust? It might even be worse this time."

"Letting you get sick instead isn't a solution. I am sorry, dear nurse."

"Stop calling me a nurse. You mock me."

Mitch felt dizzy and leaned against the back of the truck. "I'm sorry. But please let me decide. If I get sick again, I promise to pound on the side of the truck so Tuco will stop for a while. All right?

"No, that's not all right. You might be too weak to pound loud enough."

"I don't want to argue with you, Tessa, but I won't let you take my place."

Tessa stormed off to the truck cab and got in with Tuco. Mitch told Carlos about the exhaust problem, and Carlos ran the tiedown rope down through a bumper bracket and back up to the tarp.

"If you pull this rope, the tarp will close tighter. If you loosen it, the opening will get larger. If this doesn't work in the wind, pound on the truck side and I will try something else. I have to pay for the gasoline now, and then we will leave."

Mitch hurried to the station restroom while Carlos paid the attendant for the gas. When Mitch returned, the truck was gone.

***

Tessa slept more from boredom than sleepiness, bracing her head against the side window. She woke with her head back and her mouth open.

"Carlos, how long ago did we leave Tingo Maria?"

"Maybe two hours. We should be in Pucallpa in about three hours."

"I think I hear pounding signals from Mitch."

"I didn't hear anything. I am sure he is fine."

"There, I just heard it again."

"The tarp might be a little loose. I fixed it so Mitch can pull it tighter if he wants to."

The rain had subsided, and shards of sunlight pierced through new openings in the low clouds, and glazing the wet highway with pools of light. They passed through an area rich with orchids, mosses, and other rootless plants that get water from their leaves instead of from roots. Patches of fog added mystery and gloom to their beauty. Carlos told Tessa that this wild place hides tribes of indigenous people who have never made contact with outsiders.

She had never been to the rainforests of the Andes foothills. Not only were they wetter than the canopied forest she was familiar with, but the flora was strikingly different. The underbrush was thicker here, and trees were bushier and shorter.

She wondered if Mitch was seeing any of this, then she started to worry again about whether the exhaust was still poisoning him. Maybe he was too sick to bang the truck. He could be dead. Her worries spiraled into unstoppable panic.

"I want to check Mitch, she said. "Stop the truck, please."

"We are running a little late, Señorita."

"It will only take two minutes, and it will keep me from becoming afraid and angry."

Carlos told Tuco in Quechuan to stop the truck. Tuco found a place where the shoulder was a little wider, and there was no steep ditch or cliff next to it.

Tessa worried that they might take off without her. "Carlos, come with me please, in case I need your help."

"Of course."

They walked in drizzle along the gravel shoulder. When they got to the back, they saw the dangling rope unraveled into muddy strands. Carlos threw the tarp aside."

"Oh, my God,' Tessa screamed. "He fell out!"

"I don't think he would do that. We must have left him at the gasoline station."

"We have to go back."

"We cannot, Señorita. That would make us reach Pucallpa too late at night. We cannot load the boat if the crew has left, and they will have no time to load the next morning."

"You can't just leave Mitch behind."

"We will stop for him on the way back."

"He has no money to stay overnight, and he might be killed if you take him back to Huaraz."

"He is a criminal?"

"No. He is a good man. But some dangerous criminals want to find him. We have to go back now, Carlos. Potatoes are not more important than a man's life."

"He will be safe in Tingo Maria. If he needs help, someone will send him to the church for the night. A priest would not send him away."

"But where can I stay in Pucallpa? I have no money."

"I think the boat captain will feel sad for you and let you stay on the boat tonight."

"And what about tomorrow?"

"Tomorrow will take care of itself. I think Mitch is a smart man. If he waits in the gasoline station, he will find a truck driver who will give him a ride to Pucallpa. It's the only place this road goes to."

"But maybe the boat crew will work late—"

"Your ideas are of no use, Señorita. If we don't unload potatoes on time, we cannot get paid, and if we don't get paid, we cannot pay the farmer for his potatoes, or even buy gasoline for the trip back home. I know you have a very terrible problem, too, but I think Mitch is smart and he will survive somehow."

Tessa turned away from Carlos to hide unstoppable tears. She covered her face with her hands and cried for Mitch, and for her brother's soul, and for her utter helplessness. After a few halting attempts to stop, she finally wiped her eyes with the backs of her hands and turned back to Carlos. He had tied down the tarp rope and walked back to the truck cab. The rain suddenly quickened but she couldn't feel the cold drops against her face and arms. Trancelike, she shuffled back to the cab clutching her mother's crucifix neckless.

***

Mitch paced the road in front of the gasoline station, thumbing for a ride whenever a vehicle passed by. The drivers looked at him but kept going. He wondered if his hitchhiking signal meant something profane or insulting, so he simply put his hand up and made eye contact. The driver of a small sedan stopped but said he was not going to Pucallpa. He tried two other drivers, and got the same answer.

He went into the station building and asked the bored counter clerk how to give the proper signal for hitchhiking. She said she didn't understand what *hitchhiking* meant, and his Spanish wasn't good enough to explain. He pantomimed thumbing for a ride, but when that seemed to trouble her, he pointed to his himself and said "Ride to Pucallpa."

"*Autostopista?*" she asked.

"I don't know… maybe."

"You want to stop automobile?"

"Yes, how can I stop automobile?"

"You cannot. *Policia* will arrest you and want money."

"Then how can I ask for a ride to Pucallpa."

"Ask a driver if he is going there. He will understand."

Mitch went back to the fuel pump area and waited. After what seemed too long, a small white van pulled up. The driver got out and waited for the attendant, trying to ignore Mitch who approached with his best smile.

"*Buenas tardes.* Are you going to Pucallpa?"

"No, gasolina."

"I know, but after you get the gasoline, are you going to Pucallpa?"

"I don't think so."

"All right, thank you."

"What for?"

"I'm being polite—*educado.*"

"Oh. Thank you."

When the attendant arrived, he furtively eyed Mitch while

removing the pump nozzle.

Mitch said "Do you know of anyone going to Pucallpa?"

"No."

"Do trucks often stop here?"

"No."

"Can I wait here in case one stops."

"Only one truck today."

"I know. I was…"

Mitch decided it would further confuse matters if he tried to explain that he had arrived on that truck, so there was nothing more to talk about. A loud buzz from above startled him. He scurried from under the overhang and looked up to see a red-and-white float plane that seemed to be gliding toward the gas station. Wheels had been lowered beneath the floats for a hard-surface landing.

He hollered to the attendant, "Is there an airport near here?"

"Yes."

"Where?"

"Across the river."

"What river?"

"Across the road."

Mitch ran across the road and saw a rushing stream next to it, and a small airport on the other side. The pilot squared up his landing pattern and started a glide toward the runway. Mitch remembered that Tex, the oil camp pilot, usually refueled in Tingo Maria, both to and from the camp. His airplane looked like this one, but what were the chances…

He spotted a bridge about a half-block away, and sprinted to it. When he got to the middle of the bridge, he could see a small building at the other end of the runway. He was panting for air, but kept running as fast as his legs would take him, afraid that the airplane might take off before he got there. By the time he reached the flight line, he was gasping and light-headed.

"Are you okay, bud?"

Mitch recognized the voice. "I'm Mitch, the guy with the boat on the Amazon River. We met at the oil camp."

"Oh, yeah—from Minnesota. What in holy hell are you doing here?"

"I was on my way to Pucallpa, but the truck I was on left without me."

"I'm heading for the oil camp from here, but Pucallpa's not far out of the way."

"I don't have any money to pay you."

"Then I won't ask for any."

"You're a godsent, Tex."

"You might not think so if we get caught in one of these hard rains. Navigating and landing by instruments is dicey business in this area."

A fuel truck pulled up to Tex's airplane and put a step ladder in front of a wing. After topping off that wing tank, the lineman moved the ladder to the other wing. Tex pulled a map out of the airplane and partially unfolded it for Mitch to see.

"I'll more or less follow the road from here to Pucallpa. That way, I might be able to land on it if we had to."

"I hope you can land on switchbacks."

"The road's a lot straighter than the direction you came from."

"How long will it take."

"Less than an hour. After I drop you off, I'll stay within landing distance of the Ucayali River all the way to the Amazon, then fly straight to the oil camp."

"You'd land in the Ucayali? I hear it's a turbulent river."

"It wouldn't be good, but if I crashed in the jungle, it would be really bad. If I survived a river landing, I'd at least have a chance of getting found."

After the fueling was done, Mitch helped Tex push the airplane around to point toward the taxiway. After they got in, Tex ran through his checklist and started the engine. He taxied to the runway and turned northeast during the climb-out.

"I thought you lived in Iquitos, Mitch. If you don't mind me asking, what brings you to these parts?"

"The brief version of that story is that I was looking for someone in Huaraz. The guy was killed by drug runners, and we had to run for our lives."

"*We?*"

"Do you remember that woman who was on my boat?"

"Sure. Cute girl."

"She's on the truck that left without me."

"That wasn't nice."

"She and the drivers thought I was in the back when they left."

"I'm used to bizarre stories in these parts, Mitch, but yours gets a blue ribbon. How will you find her in Pucallpa? It's a pretty big town."

"The truck will be unloading potatoes onto a cargo boat. I'll wait wherever the boats are."

"Then what?"

"We'll try to hitch a boat ride to Iquitos."

"Does she have any money?"

"Unfortunately, no."

"How much do you need? Maybe I can stake you."

"Fifty bucks should buy us passage on something. I'll send

you the money when I get back to Iquitos."

"I don't loan money, Mitch. I'd forget you owe it to me, and so might you. I'll make it a gift. That's a lot simpler."

"Thanks, Tex."

A light rain reduced their visibility, and the sky looked even darker ahead. Tex checked his panel GPS, then added power to climb. They were soon above the low-hanging clouds and under bright sunlight.

After almost an hour, Tex reduced the engine power. They glided blindly through dark clouds with only instruments to guide them. Bumpy turbulence kept Tex busy on the controls until they broke out of the bottom of a cloud, with enough visibility to see a town just ahead.

"Welcome to Pucallpa. We'll be on the ground in a minute or two."

Tex radioed his position on a common advisory frequency, for other aircraft that might be in the vicinity. After making a square pattern over Pucallpa's airport, he lowered the wheels below the floats and glided to a soft landing. He turned off onto a taxiway and taxied to the visitor building, then shut his engine down.

"To keep you oriented, Mitch, we landed toward the northeast. The Ucayali riverfront is east of us. Do you know where that truck is unloading?"

"At a commercial wharf, I guess."

"I saw a lot of boats tied up along a few miles of riverfront. Being at the right spot at the right time sounds iffy to me. But the road into Pucallpa is just south of the runway—why not just wait along the road? You'd recognize the tuck, right?"

"They might have already passed by."

"Okay, let's do the math. How long were you waiting in Tingo Maria before you saw me land?

"An hour or so."

"Add about another hour since we took off. Do you know how long the drive is from Tingo Maria?"

"The driver said about five hours…"

"Hell, they're not even halfway."

Tex pulled a security wallet from under his pants belt and gave Mitch five American ten-dollar bills.

"You're a life saver, Tex. I hope to see you again someday. I want to repay—or let's say *re-gift*—this money to you."

"I'll look you up if I ever get to Iquitos, but I can't count on that happening any time soon. The oil company I'm working for is clearing out of Peru, so after two or three more trips to haul key personnel and critical electronics back to Lima, I'm done. And I'm glad. The rainy season's making it too hairy to fly a small plane like mine through the mountain pass."

"What if you don't get everyone out?"

"The company's sending a couple of boats upriver to complete the shutdown."

"Where will you be working next?"

"I don't know, but there's always work for experienced seaplane pilots who are dumb enough to fly into wild places like this. While I'm waiting for something to come along, I'll shack up with my current girlfriend and squander some money on her. How about you?"

"I wish I knew. Things aren't promising for me in Iquitos."

"Well, good luck, then. I better get going, Mitch. I need to land at the camp before nightfall."

Mitch got out and stood on the airplane tie-down area. He waved at Tex when he sped by on his takeoff run. After gaining some altitude, Tex waved back with a wing waggle.

Mitch strolled along the airport grass to the bridge, and crossed back over the road to Pucallpa. The traffic was light, much of it roofed three-wheel motorcycle trucks with buzzy engines and back ends designed for either passengers or light cargo. The rest of the traffic was made up mostly of two-wheeled motorcycles and small cars.

He looked down the long straight road and felt confident he would be able to see Carlos's truck several blocks away. But according to Tex's calculations, he'd have to wait at least an hour or two. He looked back at the gas station on the next block, and felt the wad of money in his pocket from Tex. He thought about buying a soft drink, but that seemed extravagant compared to the austere life he had been living recently. He decided to wait so he could buy one for Tessa, too, and for Carlos and Tuco. He returned to watching for the truck, even though it wasn't due to arrive yet. He paced back and forth along the road and worried about the next leg of his journey with Tessa. Even if they find a way back to Iquitos, he would then have the police to worry about. When he started to fret about the loss of Paraiso, he wondered how he would earn a living.

He decided to stop worrying about phantom problems and do something productive right now. He went to the gas station and bought a plastic bottle of water. The long drink seemed to un-fog his thinking. He even felt a physical boost. He decided to walk up the road a few blocks, and maybe back, just to kill time.

***

The last leg of the trip was more comfortable for Tessa because the road was straighter. Before this, tight turns to the right always slid her against Carlos, who smelled increasingly gamier as the temperature rose. Now she could rest her head against the window to nod off now and then.

She said, "Carlos, how much longer to Pucallpa?"

He looked at his watch. "I think an hour."

"Do you think I can sleep on the boat tonight?"

"I will tell the boat captain your father is a politician. He might be afraid of trouble if he doesn't help you."

"You can tell him my father is a school teacher. That's the truth."

"School teachers can't cause trouble for boat captains, but politicians can. And that's also the truth."

"What if you tell him my great grandfather was king of the Incas?"

Carlos shot a look at her. "Your family is noble?"

"It was a joke, Carlos. I don't need to sleep tonight, anyway. I'll stay by the boat dock and wait for Mitch."

"There are many docks in Pucallpa. I don't know how he can find the right one."

"I have to believe he will. Where is the cargo boat tied up?"

"Downriver on the north side of the city, almost at the city's end. When we get to Pucallpa, we'll turn off this main road and take a shortcut."

Tessa started seeing billboards advertising a variety of businesses in Pucallpa—hotels, a medical clinic with an image of a happy nurse, a toothy white-jacketed dentist. Traffic thickened and slowed soon after they reached the city limits. Tessa rolled down the window, and the sudden whiff of exhaust reminded her about Mitch. She closed her eyes for a moment to visualize him stranded at Tingo Maria.

Carlos hit the brakes and pitched Tessa forward. He said "A crazy man is standing in the street and blocking traffic. He is waving both arms in the air." He told Tuco to go around him.

"No, wait…it's Mitch!"

Tuco slowly drove into a dirt roadside parking area. As soon as he stopped, Tessa threw the door open and ran to Mitch. He rushed to meet her. and they collided into each other's arms on the side of the road.

"I won't let go of you," she said. "I don't want to lose you again."

He kissed her forehead. "Don't worry. I'm with you from now on. Forever if you like."

She gazed into his eyes, afraid to ask what he meant.

Cars and motorcycle trucks patiently crept around them, but that forced vehicles from the opposite direction to slowdown and squeeze along the road's opposite shoulder. When Mitch saw the jam they created, he took Tessa by the hand and they walked to the front of the truck, where Carlos and Tuco were waiting with happy smiles.

Tessa said, "We discovered you missing about halfway between Tingo Maria and here. Carlos said we didn't have enough time to go back for you, so I was going to wait near the river for you. But you got here *before* us! Did an angel carry you?"

Mitch exhaled a snicker. "Kind of. When I came outside from the gas station in Tingo Maria, the truck was gone. About an hour later, I heard a buzz in the sky and watched an airplane land at an airport across the road. It looked like the plane we saw at the oil camp."

"I remember the American pilot," she said. "His airplane had canoes underneath to land on water."

"They're called floats, and wheels can be lowered beneath them for airport landings. I ran to the airport and it *was* the oil camp airplane."

Mitch pointed toward the other side of the road. "And this is the airport where the pilot took me. He also gave me fifty dollars to find a way back to Iquitos."

"Will there be enough for *pantalones?* My dress is fine for sitting in a truck, but maybe not for a riverboat."

"Sure, you can buy pants we'll still have plenty left to buy food and water for the trip.

After Carlos and Tuco heard Mitch's story, they shook hands with him. Carlos said, "We are happy to see you, Señior Mitch."

Mitch and Tessa got into the back of the truck and Tuco rolled back the tarp. Within a few minutes, they reached the Ucayali riverside and parked near a long dock with four tin-roofed boats nosed into it, each tethered by a single rope from the bow. Carlos told Mitch and Tessa to wait on the shore, then he and Tuco stepped along the dock to board the first boat.

Mitch thought the boat already looked overloaded. He could see the top deck loaded with portable gas generators that were wedged in between waist-high steel barrels of motor oil. Everything was snugly lashed together amidships with ropes, leaving just enough room for a single hammock on each side. He worried that the boat's narrow freeboard— the distance between the water and the top deck—would be dangerous in rough water, especially with this top-heavy loading. He had never piloted a boat down the Ucayali River, but he had seen the whitecaps it churned up when it converged with the Marañon River, forming the Amazon. His concerns were interrupted when Carlos returned with a deckhand following him.

"This man will help us unload the potatoes," Carlos said.

Mitch said, "Did you talk about our passage?"

"Yes, but he said you have to talk to the captain in the morning. There should be no problems, though. I've seen him take passengers before. Be sure to buy hammocks and mosquito netting tonight. When you are underway, you can eat meals with the crew. It might be just potatoes or rice, unless they catch fish."

"What time should we be here?"

"The man said any time before about ten o'clock. The captain sleeps late."

"How long is the trip to Iquitos?"

"About a week for a small cargo boat like this, unless they have to tie up during the night. But the river should be tame and the moon should be bright enough for night travel."

"Where are you staying tonight?"

"I always park my truck here, and we sleep on the tarp in back. We leave when the sun chases away the stars."

Carlos and Tuco carried one gunnysack of potatoes at a time over their shoulders to the boat, and down the companionway, and the deckhand stacked them below. Mitch offered his help, but Carlos waved him off with, "You are a passenger, not a worker."

While the loading continued, Mitch and Tessa walked along the riverfront street. They came to a long park with a beach that no one was using. Mitch took Tessa's hand and she squeezed his, and they strolled down to the silty brown water's edge.

Tessa said, "Did you live on your boat in Iquitos?"

"No, I rent a house that's within walking distance from the river wharf. When we get back, will you be staying at your brother's house?"

"Maybe, if the door key is hidden in the usual place."

"If not, you could stay with me."

She let her hand gradually slip from his. "I don't think we should plan that."

They went to a hotel across the street and asked the owner about his rate in U.S. dollars. The man said ten dollars. Mitch offered three, and pointed out that there probably won't be any more travelers this late in the day. They settled on five dollars for a second-floor room with two single beds.

Tessa said to Mitch "Do you have enough money for another room?"

"Maybe, but we would have separate beds if we stayed in the same room."

"I know…"

"And we need to buy things for the trip."

"I didn't think about that. One room will be all right."

After washing up in the small but clean-looking room, they walked to a shop on the next block, a place where the hotel owner recommended for good quality and low prices. Mitch bought a plain blue tee shirt. Tessa found two pairs of underpants, which she quickly folded, white jeans, and light gray tee shirt with a small tan alpaca printed on the front. The bill came to almost seven dollars. She looked at Mitch for a reaction. and he said they could afford that. They went to a mercado farther down the same street and bought a block of cheese wrapped in waxed paper, and a bag of smoked beef jerky and dried fruits.

"We have almost twenty dollars left," Mitch said. "Let's celebrate our last night in Pucallpa with a restaurant dinner."

Tessa wondered if she could have her own room instead, but she didn't want to spoil his plan. "We'll have a tip-top celebration," she said.

"Let's take our things back to the hotel, and then look for a good place to eat."

At the hotel, Mitch sat in the lobby to let Tessa have the room to herself—to shower, change, and fix her hair. About an hour later, she came down the stairs looking fresh and happy. Mitch's pulse quickened when he saw her, but he tried not to show it. He didn't want her to feel uncomfortable any more about sharing a room with him.

He borrowed a safety razor from the hotel owner, then shaved and showered. The owner recommended a restaurant two blocks away along the river. The restaurant owner was a friend, and always had fresh food and romantic recorded music.

They both had roasted chicken with mashed manioc and corn boiled in lime water. They nursed glasses of white Chilean wine and listened to the soft Peruvian music. When their empty plates were taken by their waiter, Mitch asked Tessa to dance with him.

"I don't know how Americans dance," she said.

"Good, because neither do I."

They held each other lightly at first while Tessa followed Mitch's shuffles one way then the other. He touched her hair with his cheek and brought her a little closer. Her eyes met his, and they let the music wash away painful memories of the last few days. Neither of them wanted to let go when the music stopped, but they returned to their table hand-in-hand, aware of the curious glances from a few other diners.

After they left the restaurant, they strolled along the lighted riverside sidewalk to their hotel room. The trip to Pucallpa had exhausted both of them, and the food and wine settled their last bit of energy.

After getting to the hotel room they tucked in the mosquito netting that overhung their beds, and removed their shoes. They fell asleep within minutes with their clothes still on.

During the night, Mitch woke from Tessa mumbling something incoherently in her sleep. She rolled onto her back and yelled "Estevan!"

Mitch yanked his mosquito netting away, then hers, then gently shook her shoulder. "Tessa, wake up."

She sat straight up with wild eyes.

"It's all right, Tessa. You're with me now. You are safe."

She absently glance around the room, which was barely illuminated by a dim nearby streetlight.

"We're in Pucallpa, in a hotel."

"I forgot at first. I was dreaming. I think it was about something frightening."

Mitch took her hand. "The bad dream is over, darling, so you can have beautiful dreams the rest of the night." She smiled and he kissed the palm of her hand. Then he tucked her mosquito netting back in while she curled up on the bed and immediately fell back to sleep.

***

First morning sunlight startled Mitch awake. He rolled over and looked at Tessa, who was sleeping on her stomach.

"Tessa, get up."

He yanked his mosquito netting free, and then hers while she moaned something half-awake. He stoked the bottom of her foot with a finger and she jerked her leg away, then sat up in bed. "What time is it?"

"I don't know, but we need to get to the boat."

He pulled on his shoes while she untangled her hair with her hands, and then tied her sneakers. Mitch gathered the hammocks and mosquito netting they bought the night before, and picked up the bag of food from the mercado. On their way out, he left the room key on the vacant front counter.

When they got closer to the boat, they saw that Carlos's

truck was gone. Mitch handed the food bag to Tessa when they got to the dock, and she waited while he stepped onto the boat to tie the hammocks.

A man in rumpled brown pants and khaki shirt rolled up sleeves came out of the wheel house.

"What are you doing there?" he said.

"I'm Mitch and that's Tessa on the dock. We came with the potato truck, and we're the passengers going to Iquitos. Are you the captain?"

"Yes. My name is Salvador. *Captain* Salvador. But you are not my passengers. I am waiting for the passengers who paid me yesterday, but you are not those people."

"Didn't Carlos tell you about us?"

"Carlos was gone when I got here. What was he supposed to tell me? If you paid him for passage, he cheated you. He does not choose my passengers."

"Don't you have room for just two more people?"

"No. We are already loaded to capacity."

Mitch stepped to the side of the boat and looked at the waterline. "Maybe over capacity."

"Now you understand."

"Two more people won't change the freeboard much. I can pay something if you make room for us."

"For enough money I could leave a barrel of oil behind. How much will you pay?"

"We have twenty dollars."

Salvador raised his head and forced a sarcastic laugh. "A barrel of oil is worth much more than that."

"Do you know about other boats going to Iquitos?"

"Two, but they already left. And I will leave soon. If those stupid tourists are not here, then I will take you."

Salvador went back to the wheel house and Mitch stepped

off the boat. He took the bag of groceries from Tessa.

She said, "Maybe his other passengers won't show up."

"Even if they don't, I'm not sure we should travel on this boat. It's almost top-heavy enough to sink at the dock. I'm worried about what would happen if we get sideways in rough water, or if he runs aground on a shallow sandbar. Remember the collectivo that sunk the morning I met you in Tamshiyaco? The boat's hull might have been ruptured by something, but it was probably just overloaded like this one."

"How else can we get to Iquitos with twenty dollars? And don't just try to make me feel happy."

"Have I been doing that?"

She smiled. "A few times. But I like it."

A young couple in shorts and sandals, both hauling a stuffed backpack, walked onto the dock and nodded to Mitch and Tessa. The man turned to the boat and shouted something German. Salvador stuck his head out of the wheelhouse door and said "You finally decide to let us leave. Get aboard and let's go!"

While the couple boarded the boat, Salvador said to Mitch "Are you in a hurry to get to Iquitos?"

"No, but we can't stay here long. You know how little money we have. What did you have in mind?"

"You could float to Iquitos on a raft. It will take much longer, but it will be very cheap."

"I don't know how to build a raft."

"Of course, you don't. Only raft builders know how to build safe rafts. When I got to Pucallpa two days ago, I saw a raft almost completed about a kilometer downriver from here."

"I've seen rafts on the Amazon River. They usually carry a family."

"Yes, and for twenty dollars, you and your señorita might become family members." Salvador laughed at his own joke.

Mitch and Tessa walked downriver on the frontage road—first on good asphalt, then asphalt chipped and pocked with potholes big enough to imprison a car wheel. They eventually came to a rough gravel trail, and lastly, rust-colored clay paths ranging from slippery muck to hard-baked surfaces. They reached a raft construction site near the riverbank.

The raft was about twenty feet wide by thirty feet long, consisting of smooth full-length tan logs, each about two feet in diameter. They were neatly lashed together with thick rope. Lighter-colored planks of wood lay crossways, and were tied in place about five feet apart. A pile of woven palm mats had been stacked on one end of the raft, presumably to fit between the crossed planks. Long poles lay on the ground nearby, next to a half-constructed shelter frame.

"*Hola,*" someone called out. Mitch and Tessa turned to see a man striding toward them. His wife was pulling a wood box of tools from the back end of a three-wheeled motorcycle taxi, and then set the box on the ground.

Tessa told the man in Spanish that they were stranded in Pucallpa with almost no money, and they needed to get to Iquitos for the funeral of her brother. She introduced herself and Mitch by first names, and asked if he spoke English.

The man looked at Mitch and said, "Only a little, and very poorly. My name is Eduardo. I am with my wife, Rosa."

Mitched stepped forward and shook Eduardo's hand. "I admire your raft. I am a boat captain on the Amazon River, and I've seen rafts like this many times. I think yours is the most beautiful I've seen."

"You make me feel too important."

Mitch grinned. "And you'll feel even more important if

you take us to Iquitos on your raft."

Eduardo squinted his eyebrows together for a moment. "With my wife and three little children? It will be too crowded."

"I love children," Tessa said. "And I worked at a medical clinic."

"I can read the river and make soundings for sandbars, and I can help with the oars."

"We don't have much food to bring."

"I can give you ten dollars for extra food."

Eduardo looked up, as if contemplating Mitch's proposition. "Ten dollars won't buy much extra food."

"Fifteen dollars then, and I'll help catch fish."

Tessa said, "I can help your wife cook, and she will have another woman to talk to."

"She would like that."

"You see," Mitch said, "we will not be a burden—we will make your life easier and more enjoyable."

"All right, you can come with us," Eduardo said. "But first we have to tack the floor mats into place, build a shelter—big enough for all of us now—and I have to attach the oar poles."

"How long will that take?" Mitch said.

"I think we can finish today, if you help."

"Of course. How will we get the raft in the water?"

"With our hands."

Mitch thought Eduardo was joking, but when he looked around, he saw several thin slide poles ready underneath the raft. "I hope you are stronger than me."

"It looks heavy, but it tricks you. Pick up that balsa log by your foot."

Mitch looked at the two-foot log scrap that had been cut off during construction. He picked it up and raised it over his head with a show-off grin for Tessa before putting it down.

"We will plan to leave tomorrow morning," Eduardo said. "We'll put the shelter together today, and you can stay in it tonight. I see you have mosquito netting. That is good."

Mitch set them on the raft. "Yes, and hammocks."

"The raft wasn't built with hammock poles but you can put them on the floor for sleeping."

"All right. I'm ready to work."

Tessa asked Eduardo how long it will take to get to Iquitos.

"About a month. It will be our last raft trip until next May, when the rainy season ends."

Eduardo positioned the palm floor mats onto the squared cross-beams, while Mitch followed and nailed them into place. Next, Eduardo explained how the steering lock and the shelter would be constructed. They tied pine poles together at the back, making an X design. Into the X, he tied a shelter beam and lashed into place a long steering pole. He told Mitch that the paddle at the end of the steering poles were made from strong mangrove wood. They made steering pole braces on each side for two additional steering oars.

When they were done, the A-frame shelter was about five feet high at the peak. A green tarp was draped over the shelter structure, making it look like a big camping tent that almost covered the back third of the raft. At the very back, an area of about five feet was left uncovered, just enough room for Eduardo to maneuver the long steering oar.

Next, Eduardo lashed the three long oars into place—one on the rear and one on each side about halfway forward. The lashed oars were apparently meant to hang in the water until needed. This was an efficient way to stow the oars because rafts do not move *through* the water, they move *with* the water, and so the dangling oars would not create any drag.

The sun was setting, and Eduardo and Rosa left when it started getting dark. They told Mitch and Tessa that they and their three children would stay that night at the house of Rosa's parents.

The half-full moon gave Tessa enough light to spread the hammocks inside the shelter. Mitch secured their mosquito netting to the shelter's beam and bracing poles, and they slid into their individual makeshift beds.

"Are you tired?" Mitch said.

"A little."

"Are you afraid about living on this raft for a few weeks?"

"No. I feel safe with you."

"Safe even if I decide to climb under your mosquito net?"

She giggled. "I'll feel safe if you just think about it, but please don't try."

After several minutes of silence, Mitch could hear her muffled crying. When she stopped, she said "I keep thinking about my brother. I will never forget those terrible wounds, and then Raul shooting Darla. He let her kill Estevan before he killed her. Estevan was a better person than either of them. And it scares me to think how you and I might also have been killed."

"You are safe now."

"I know, but those memories will leave a scar on my heart."

After more silence passed between them, she said "I will stop thinking about that for now, and just remember us dancing together last night."

***

Early the next morning, Eduardo and Rosa arrived at the raft construction site in separate three-wheeled motorcycle taxis. Eduardo removed plastic crates of provisions and equipment from his taxi, and their three children rode with Rosa in the back of the other taxi. She introduced them to Mitch and Tessa. The oldest was a girl named *Carito*. The second in age was a boy, *Andre*, and the toddler was a girl named *Katia*. Rosa reminded them to be polite because they had guests on this trip.

After Eduardo brought his cargo to the raft site, he said, "Time to see our new home float."

Eduardo tied long ropes to the front and back, then he and Mitch readied themselves to push. The children watched while Tessa and Rosa joined the men. All four adults dug in their footing and pushed and strained until the raft began to move. It eased down the launching poles to the riverbank, and eventually one side of the raft became buoyant. Eduardo told the women to hold the bow and stern ropes, then he and Mitch pushed it the final few feet until it was grabbed by the river. The colossal platform bobbed and tried to follow the current. Rosa wound her rope twice around a tree, and tied it with fast half-hitches. Tessa braced her foothold and clutched her rope as if her life depended on it. Rosa ran to her and showed her how to tie it securely.

***

While Rosa and Tessa stowed crates of food and supplies under the tarp shelter, Eduardo asked Mitch to help him pile nearby rocks about the size of coconuts on the front of the raft. They had been saved as front-end ballast for the trip, but also to sell in Iquitos. The rocks had been rounded over millions of years of tumbling in the river, and people in the stone-free Amazon basin prized them for knife sharpening.

Eduardo brought a steel pan almost three feet wide with a six-inch-high rim and dropped it heavily onto the raft.

"Our cooking pit," he said to Mitch. Both men stacked firewood that Eduardo had hidden in the nearby tall grass. Then Eduardo brought a double-barrel shotgun wrapped in white canvas, explaining that it can be used for hunting and protection.

The timid children tried not to notice when Tessa smiled at them. They huddled close to their mother while she told Tessa how they cook with the fire pit.

"We put fish we catch right on the hot coals," Rosa said. "We'll snare birds and buy meat along the way, and we cook it the same way. We cook everything before insects find it. What we don't eat right away, we dry on a steel grate over hot smoke for at least two days. Smoked meat is safe from bugs and germs."

After the raft was finally loaded, Eduardo stood on the riverbank and dramatically announced, "*Vamos a Iquitos!*" He told Mitch to untie the bow rope and climb aboard with it. Eduardo untied the stern rope and held it tight while he walked along in shallow water until the river's current began tugging at the raft, then Eduardo jumped aboard. The Ucayali River finally took command of the boat and their journey was underway.

Eduardo showed Mitch how to use the oars to steer. He pulled and pushed the long rear steering oar back and forth with twists to coax the raft toward deep water in the middle of the river. Once there, the river's current dictated their speed and direction.

Mitch used a side oar pole to help Eduardo keep the raft in the middle of the river during a bend. Mitch scanned the bank for sandbars that can accumulate at bends in the river, and the Ucayali had far more of them than the wide, lumbering Amazon, or even the tributaries he had navigated.

"You understand the language of rivers," Eduardo said. "And you use the side oar well. If we ever get sideways to the current, the oars are not positioned to work as well. You'll find that steering a bunch of logs is harder than turning a boat."

Mitch laughed and said, "It would help if you put a motor on your logs."

"Oh, that's a good plan. We'll get one at the next village— if they take smoked fish for payment—and if they have a motor, which they won't."

Tessa smiled about the men's bantering, concluding that it's the way men become travel friends, or work companions. She broke the ice with the children by telling them stories, and they kept begging for more. She taught them a few English words, and taught them children's poems, first in Spanish, then in English. They picked up the poems' cadence well before getting all the words right.

She wanted to save some of the stories she remembered for later during the long trip, so she asked Mitch if he had stories that children in the United States like. He told them the Three Pigs story, substituting a jaguar for the wolf. It seemed to frighten them, so he made up a story about three children who lived inside a tree and rode llamas with wings large enough to fly over rainbows and light enough to land on clouds. The children liked that story the best, and the little boy, Andre, ask for another story about those children—then he remembered to add *please, a*n English word that Tessa had taught them. Mitch told them another imaginary tale about the same three children, but this time they found a forest of candy and cakes, with rivers of chocolate soda. Mitch promised another story tomorrow.

The oldest girl, Carito, said, "Why do we have to wait,"

"The story takes a full day to grow in my mind," Mitch said. "I promise we will have a story time like this every afternoon."

When Mitch went to the stern, he saw Eduardo tying the tarp shut in the back, leaving enough room to work the oar.

"That should keep the rain and sun out," Mitch said.

"And when someone needs a *baño,* or wants to bathe, they can find privacy here."

***

After a few days, Mitch spotted a town ahead. He called out to Eduardo, who was asleep in the shelter, hiding from the sweltering midday sun. He came out on his hands and knees and stretched as he stood.

"That is Contamana," Eduardo said. "It will be the last real town we see for several days. Let's try to row our raft to the shore there. Maybe we can buy fruit and bread, and maybe candy for the children."

The three children ran to the front of the raft and watched Mitch and Eduardo work the pole oars, hoping for a chance to get candy. Both girls wore dresses, but little Andre was naked. Rosa brought him a pair of shorts and told him to keep them on.

As they approached a clearing that looked like a canoe landing, the men paddled hard toward a stand of bushy trees. The river's bank caught the raft and Eduardo jumped off with the stern rope. Mitch jumped in with the other line and waded through knee-high water toward the bank. Mitch held the raft back from the relentless current while Eduardo tied his line to a tree, then he tied Mitch's to a different tree. Tessa stood and watch, afraid the men might be found by piranhas—a remote danger, but a fresh memory.

There was a slab-wood hut in Contamana that served as its general store, with very little to sell. Eduardo bought two bottles of beer and a handful of wrapped Brazilian hard candies. Rosa and Tessa inspected rolls of printed cotton cloth, and talked about which pattern would make the most beautiful dress. They left with fresh bananas, oranges, and figs, all rolled into large banana leaves. Rosa added coconut-sized lemons to squeeze into the tan river water they boiled for drinking. Eduardo bought a single filtered cigarette and offered to share it with Mitch, but Mitch said he didn't smoke tobacco.

"Do you smoke anything?" Eduardo asked.

"I smoke fish," Mitch said, but then he had to explain his joke. By the time Eduardo understood, it wasn't funny anymore.

Life aboard the raft settled into a few daily patterns. For breakfast, the women cooked whatever fish had been caught in the submerged nets and funnel trap overnight. Lunch was usually "travel soup," made from dehydrated vegetable, and toasted flatbread smeared with a hint of precious canned butter. Eduardo secured slip-looped snare wires in the rear among small berry branches he had found in Contamana, hoping to attract and trap birds. Any large enough to eat were immediately gutted, skinned, and set on still-hot coals in the firepit, to be ready for the next meal. The innards were tossed into the fish trap as bait.

Story time was always right after supper, and Mitch would make up whimsical tales with happy endings to give the children something positive to sleep with.

Edward and Mitch took turns watching for possible sandbars during the night. Mitch made a sounding line with thin rope tied to a small oval stone from the rockpile. He tied a knot about every foot and secured the free end to the oar post. If in doubt about the river's depth, he would drop the rope into the water to measure its depth. But these precautions were born of habit, of years boating up and down the Amazon River. Mitch knew sandbars would have to be very shallow to ground these buoyant balsa logs. And it would be easy to push the raft free with oar poles if that did happen. Still, although irrational, using the sounding line when in doubt soothed his need for vigilance.

***

On their fourteenth night—as noted by the number of tiny notches Eduardo sliced into his oar pole each day—it was Mitch's turn to take the first watch. When everyone was bedded down inside the shelter after dark, he sat on the floor just behind the rockpile and leaned against an oar pole. The river was wider and unhurried on this stretch. An almost imperceptible breeze from the mountains would sometimes gust just enough to ripple the plastic-coated shelter tarp. He stood up every half-hour or so, and if the raft had started to drift sideways, he would use an oar to coax the bow back in line. He remembered that Eduardo said keeping the bow forward would give the maximum control authority to the oars. It also made it easier to see where they were heading. Aside from those practical reasons, it satisfied Mitch's sense of order—if you see a hulled boat meandering sideways downriver, it could mean it's in trouble.

The moon was full and clear bright stars blinked across the black sky, all the way to the forest's canopy, which gradually got higher as they moved downriver. Fireflies flickered above the grassy riverbank. As usual, the night air was almost as hot and humid as during the day. Mitch felt a sudden cooling draft on the back of his neck. He spun around and caught Tessa blowing on him. She stepped back with a teasing grin.

"I surprised you, didn't I."

"You often surprise me, my dear."

Tessa sat next to him. "What does it mean to be your dear?"

"It means you are important to me."

"Like a friend?"

"Yes, but more like a lover."

"Then you are my dear."

After a bit of self-conscious silence, he said, "Did you have trouble sleeping?"

"The moonlight is very bright."

"Maybe you can sleep better with me."

Tessa sat on the woven mat floor a few inches from him. He put his arm around her waist and nudged her closer.

"We can pretend we're on a camping trip," he said.

"When I was a child, I read a magazine story about American girls who camped together. They scouted for buffalos. It sounded very dangerous to me."

"I think they just sell cookies now."

After considering that, she said "Do you like to camp?"

"I've never been camping, but I'd like to try it with you."

"I'll be sad when our raft camping trip ends. I feel peace here, with you. And the children are sweet. They love you for your magical stories. They knew about llamas, but now they think some can fly."

Mitch touched a finger over her lower lip. She turned to him and their kiss was as unhurried as the night. While they sat next to each other, Mitch tightened his arm around her, and she rested her head on his shoulder while they listened to the nocturnal jungle creatures yelp, screech, and chirp. Tessa lay down on the floor mat and rested her head on her arm.

Mitch soon heard her sleepy, peaceful breathing.

He quietly reoriented the raft with an oar while Tessa was still curled up on the floor. Her eyes eased open, and she watched him without moving. When he sat down, her eyes drooped and she fell back to sleep.

***

After the next morning's fish-and-bread breakfast, Mitch used the charred end of a firepit stick to draw a hopscotch pattern on the raft floor. He wasn't sure about the rules of hopscotch, but he improvised a series of single and double squares, then hopped and skipped over them to demonstrate the game. After watching this exotic dance, Carito and Andre begged to try it. The toddler, Katia, started to cry from this sudden burst of mayhem and hid behind her mother.

This game became the children's main activity all week. They soon showed up Mitch's skills with one-foot hops and backward skips. One day Carito twirled around on each square as she skipped across the hopscotch squares. Little Katia eventually worked up enough courage to toddle from one end to the other on her own, ending with a big smile, and an applause from everyone else. The next week, Mitch showed the children how to jump-rope, both solo and with twirlers on each end. Eduardo and Rosa even tried, but immediately became entangled in the rope. The two oldest children howled with laughter, and Katia tried jumping without the rope, but couldn't get off the ground.

The children's favorite part of the day was when Mitch told them bedtime stories. He made up a story of a family that traveled all over the world on a cloud, and each night he added episodes that ran parallel to the life they were all living, complete with friendly talking birds and stars that sparkled with changing colors. The cloud family went to exotic places, like lakes made of ice instead of water, and where cold white flakes fell from the sky, and you could either catch them with your tongue or form them into hard balls to play with. Eduardo absently worked his oar while enjoying the story, and Rosa and Tessa listened while they washed supper dishes in a plastic bucket.

Mitch and Tessa always slept next to each other, but under separate mosquito nets, even when sleeping outside in the open when rain didn't threaten. There were too many eyes and ears aboard for anything more than an occasional surreptitious kiss. One evening, Tessa told him she was starting to feel uncomfortable about their close sleeping arrangement. They were not married—not even engaged—and Eduardo and Rosa might consider it improper with their children aboard. But when Mitch brought these concerns up with Eduardo and Rosa, they agreed to be like *acompañantes*—chaperones— and would say something if the children became too curious.

One night, Tessa seemed quieter than usual.

Mitch said "How are you feeling?"

"Oh, I'm fine." After a few minutes, she said "Today I washed myself with the bucket behind the shelter, and Carito came and watched me while I got dressed. I asked her if she would like to wash, and she said no, but she had a question."

Mitch said, "Can you tell me what it was?"

"She wanted to know if it's easier to be an adult than a child. I told her no, but things that give you joy or trouble are different. I didn't know what else to tell her. I am not her mother, so I had to be careful."

"I think your answer was good advice. Carito is lucky to have you for a friend."

"The children are lucky to have you for a friend, too. You

teach them exciting games and tell beautiful stories from your heart."

Mitch thought about that for a moment. "It makes me happy to see children have a better childhood than I had."

He could soon tell by her easy breathing that she had drifted into a peaceful sleep.

***

A few days later, after lunch, the adults sat around the firepit while the children lounged inside the shelter with their story books.

Eduardo said "Have you noticed the river moving faster?"

Mitch said "No, I didn't notice. How can you tell?"

"Each day I choose a tree and count the number of seconds it takes us to pass it. I time the passing from the front of the raft to the back. Our speed has almost doubled since we left Pucallpa. We have never traveled downriver this fast."

"The rains must be unusually heavy in the mountains," Tessa said. "This means we'll get to Iquitos sooner."

Eduardo nodded. "And that will be good, but could also be dangerous. All that rain means the Ucayali River will become dangerously fast when it finally converges with the Marañon River. If we get through their angry struggle safely, the two rivers will blend into a single peaceful river, the Amazon."

Mitch said "I got too close to the confluence of these rivers with my boat once. I remember the roar of clashing whitecap waves. I would never risk trying to get through that mess with a boat like mine."

"It is safer for rafts because balsa wood cannot sink. But the raft could be flipped over, or break apart."

Tessa said, "What if someone falls off?"

"We'll tie each of us to an end log," Eduardo said. "If the

raft breaks apart, we will have something to keep us above the water and we'll stay together. Rosa and I are glad you are here to help the children."

Tessa said, "How long before we get to the confluence?"

"In a few hours we will arrive at the village of Genaro Herrera, where we will stop to buy fresh food and water. After that, the Marañon River will be about two days away, and then we will be about five days from Iquitos."

***

When they reached Genaro Herrera, Mitch and Tessa jumped off the raft into shallow water with tiedown lines, while Eduardo waggled the far-side oar to force the raft sideways onto the shore. After tying each rope to different trees, Mitch and Tessa helped Rosa get the children down off the raft.

The children ran around the village's landing area in their sandals, then ran up and down the dirt trail that went from the landing to the village. Carlito and Andre played tag, and little Katia tried to keep up. While the adults walked up the hill, the children begged their parents to buy more candies and a bottle of Inca Kola to share. When they arrived at the village's general store, the man attending it said he didn't have either of the children's requested items. Mitch used his last two dollars to buy a few colorful cartoon magazines and a tin of crisp Brazilian cookies.

***

The next day, the children bickered with each other more than usual, as if acting out the adults' quiet tension. Clouds had descended from the mountains, and it rained hard during midday. They huddled together inside the shelter and ate slices of canned beef and bread they had bought in

Genaro Herrera.

Eduardo turned to Rosa with a serious look. "We'll be busy tomorrow."

She just nodded, knowing her husband didn't want the children to worry. Their family had floated through the confluence many times before, but always earlier in the year. Before leaving Pucallpa on this trip, Rosa had questioned Eduardo's decision to make this last trip. But she would not question the decision now. There is no room on a raft for regrets or blame.

Rosa smiled at the children. "The water ride will be more fun this year. We'll tie ourselves together and pretend we are floating on a bouncy cloud, just like in Mister Mitch's stories."

Katia was too young to understand, but Andre clapped his hands with excitement. Carito frowned at her mother and said, "We always just hold onto ropes when the rivers mix. Only father is tied because he stands to paddle us through the waves."

Tessa said, "I think your parents are doing this for me, Carito. I cannot swim, and I have been worried that I might fall off the raft."

"I will hold your hand," Carito said. "The danger doesn't last very long."

Tessa kissed her head. "Thank you, but I would be afraid of pulling you off unless we were both tied to a log."

***

Later, during the oppressive midday heat, when the equatorial sun's full molten measure pours strait down from overhead, the adults lounged together near the bow while the children read their new cartoon magazines inside the shelter.

Eduardo said "If we don't make the confluence during

daylight tomorrow, we'll tie up for the night. I hope we don't have to do that, though. I don't know if there are hostile tribes in this area. Tessa, do you know?"

"I don't know this area at all. The Yagua Indians near Tamshiyaco are very friendly unless strangers scare them. I've always heard that Jivaro headhunters live far up the Amazon, but I don't know about the Ucayali River."

Night came before reaching the Marañon, so they had to tie up before it became too dark. Eduardo and Mitch took turns watching the jungle, with Eduardo's loaded shotgun at hand.

***

Before untying the next morning, Eduardo and Mitch sorted through the ropes, and Eduardo separated them into hasty coils.

Eduardo stood and scanned the group. "We'll tie a rope across the floor from one oar pole to the other. Rosa and the two older children can hold onto it while we work the oars, and Rosa can hold onto Katia. Tessa, can you help Rosa with the other two children?"

"Yes, of course."

"We will all be tied to the same end balsa log, just in case the raft breaks apart. Mitch, you and I will allow enough slack in our safety ropes to work the oars. We'll have to work hard and fast, my friend. If we get sideways, we could lose some control of the raft. Going backward would take away all control. When we reach the Marañon River, it will hit us from the left. I will work the stern oar, and Mitch, you can paddle the left-side oar to keep us pointing downriver."

"What if we flip upside down?" Mitch asked.

"I don't think the rivers are wild enough for that yet, but

even if they are, we would only be in danger of rolling over for a few minutes. Just in case, we'll keep our safety ropes long enough to avoid getting trapped underneath the raft if it flips. But to answer your question, we'd be in God's hands."

Tessa said, "Can I paddle the other oar to help Mitch?

Eduardo said, "Paddling from the other side won't help very much. Helping Rosa with the children is more important."

"Even if I can't swim?"

"Neither can Rosa and the children, but you will all be tied to the same log. The log cannot sink, so you won't need to swim."

Early in the afternoon, something caught Eduardo's attention, and he hurried to the front of the raft.

"Do you hear that?" he said to Mitch.

Mitch stood and cupped his ears. "It sounds like a storm."

"It is a storm—but not from the sky. Rosa, Tessa, tie the children now. Mitch, tie yourself to the oar pole. We must hurry!"

Eduardo quickly rolled up most of their supplies in blankets and then tied the bundle. He secured the fire pit by lashing it to one of the raft logs. Rosa and Tessa gathered the tethered children next to them and they all sat and clutched the overhead safety rope—except Katia, who was snuggly tied to Rosa.

They all waited without a word between them. The rush of water began to rumble. Mitch could smell mist from unseen roiling water. He looked at Tessa, and her tense expression melted into a confident smile for him. He could see by the children's worried looks that they knew some kind of danger lie ahead, dangerous enough to scare their parents. Mitch readied his oar in the water. Rosa reminded the children to grasp the overhead rope.

"Here we go!" Eduardo said. He pumped his oar in and out of the water, pushing back and forth to correct the heading. As if fighting off invaders, the Marañon slammed into their left side, making the raft bob up and down from the river's angry power. Whitecapped waves spit foamy mist into the air like hellish steam. The raft plunged headlong into the turbulent chaos, then the bow shot up out of the water as if gasping for air. A hideous roar thundered loud enough to muffle Eduardo's frantic yells from the back, "Row harder now, faster!" Mitch could barely hear the children's screams. When he glanced back at Eduardo, he noticed everyone's faces wet from river spray. Rosa had one arm and a leg around the rope while clinging to Katia. The Marañon's superior power slung the raft sideways, even while Mitch paddled furiously to force the front of the raft to the right. In the middle of the dueling currents, the raft lurched sideways and cross-currents began to buck the raft back and forth out of control. Water swooshed up over the raft and slid Tessa, Rosa, and the children to the other side. They clawed and crawled back to the middle while Katia screamed with fear. Carita and Andre stared at Mitch with terrified eyes. When he looked back, Eduardo was gone.

Mitch couldn't let go of his oar—he was in the middle of a fight he had to win if the others were to survive. When the raft was finally jettisoned past the raging rapids and onto calm water, Mitch untied himself and ran to the stern. He took a long, grateful breath when he saw Eduardo struggling to stand.

"Eduardo, take my hand."

"I slipped and hit my head on the rail. How are the others?"

Tessa came and clutched Mitch's arm with both hands, as

if holding onto him.

"Everyone is fine," Mitch said to Eduardo. "Just a little wet."

All three of them released an emotional laugh, just short of tears.

Mitch said, "I don't think we lost anything, either."

Tessa asked Eduardo if his vision was normal, and he said it was. As soon as she saw him stand without help, she went to help Rosa. Andre was worried that their cartoon magazines got wet, and Rosa said if they were, the sun would dry them, and promised they would be even funnier then.

When Tessa looked up, she saw something shiny downriver, near the left shore. She used her hand to shield the sun while the raft floated sideways down the peaceful Amazon without anyone working the oars. She pointed the object out to Mitch, and he said "It looks like one of the oil barrels we saw on Salvador's boat in Pucallpa."

Tessa kept her eyes on the barrel as they glided toward it. "How could just one roll off? They were all tied together."

"Let's take a look," Mitch said, and he started aligning the raft's heading with rigorous oar strokes, while edging closer to the riverbank.

Tessa took the other oar and paddled in the opposite direction to help straighten them out.

Mitch said "How did you learn to steer a raft."

"From watching you. And sometimes canoes are paddled the same way."

"You've paddled canoes?"

"Estevan taught me. He made a dugout canoe when he was a teenager."

While Eduardo helped paddle from the stern, Rosa unwrapped the wet blankets and spread them on top of the shelter tarp to dry. She tied a long rope from the shelter beam to the front of the raft, and draped wet clothes over it.

They could see that the oil barrel was beached sideways on a sandbar. When the sand resisted the raft's progress, Mitch jumped off with the bow rope in hand. He waded through soupy sand that tried to swallow his feet, but it became firmer as he got closer to the barrel.

Tessa pulled off her sneakers and jumped onto the sandbar.

"Is the barrel empty?"

Mitch tried to roll it back and forth, but the weight held it fast in the sand.

"I think it's full."

Eduardo tied the raft to a tree and joined them. The three children stood together spellbound as they watched this exciting mystery unfold.

"It's too heavy for us to lift," Mitch said.

Tessa said, "Maybe if both of us…"

"It's probably heavier than both of us."

"It's too valuable to leave behind," Eduardo said. "Let's get a rope around it and oars under it. If you and I can push it up from underneath, Rosa and Tessa can pull the rope from the raft."

Carito said she would help pull. Not to be outdone, Andre said he would pull, too.

Mitch tied a stevedore's knot around the middle, then he and Eduardo tipped the barrel over two oar poles that Eduardo had leaned against the raft's edge. Tessa joined Rosa on the raft and they pulled on the rope while Eduardo and Mitch push from below. Carito and Andre grabbed the loose end of the rope and pulled as hard as they could. When the barrel got to the edge of the raft, Mitch and Eduardo got underneath and pushed with every muscle in their bodies until it rolled onboard. Rosa and Tessa grabbed it so it wouldn't roll off the other side into deeper water. After Mitch climbed back onto the raft, the four adults pushed the barrel upright on the count of three. From that position, they could slightly tilt it and roll it on its rim to the center of the raft.

After inspecting the barrel, Mitch pointed out scratch marks and a small dent in the top rim, but there was no evidence of leaking.

Tessa said, "Why didn't it sink?"

"I don't know, "Mitch said, "but maybe because oil is lighter than water. That's why oil floats on water when it spills. This barrel might have slipped out of the cargo rope when Salvador's boat lost control in the rapids. It must have sunk, otherwise Salvador would never leave this valuable cargo behind. According to maritime law, Eduardo, I think you can claim salvage rights."

"Who would buy this much oil from me?"

"Oil is used by car and boat repair shops, and for ship engines. I think you could sell it for a good price."

***

It drizzled off and on the next three nights, giving some cool relief from the heat, but leaving steamy humidity behind. Eduardo and Mitch took turns piloting the raft, which was much easier on the gentle, relatively straight, Amazon River than on the swift Ucayali.

The Amazon River widened more each day, and they kept the raft close to the left bank instead of the middle, ready to beach it when they reached Iquitos.

The fourth night brought a hard, cool rain that kept everyone huddled inside the shelter. Rosa wrapped Katia with a blanket and she fell asleep while raindrops pattered against the plastic tarp.

Eduardo said, "I think we will reach Iquitos tomorrow morning. Tonight, I will open the bottle of beer I've saved, and we'll share it to celebrate."

Mitch said, "Where do you stay in Iquitos?"

"Our nights will still be on the raft until we go back to Pucallpa on a collectivo."

"I can't imagine going through that confluence on a collectivo," Mitch said.

"The passenger boats are very long and the propellers give them more control. The biggest danger is top-heavy overloading, so we are careful about the boat we choose."

Tessa asked, "When will you return?"

"As soon as we sell the raft and stones—and the barrel of oil."

"Rosa said, "I always bring herbal remedies and I trade them for commercial medicines at a pharmacy we know. Then I will sell the commercial medicines in Pucallpa."

Tessa said, "Will it take long to sell your raft?"

"No, not long," Eduardo said. "There are always people waiting to buy rafts from Pucallpa. They build little houses on them and tie them to other rafts in Iquitos's floating neighborhood. It's a cheap way to live in Iquitos. They don't have to pay taxes or bribes."

"That neighborhood is one giant raft," Mitch said. "I've seen those people stepping from one raft to the other to get to the riverbank."

Rosa said to Tessa. "What are your plans in Iquitos?"

"I don't know." She glanced at Mitch. "I can't go back to Tamshiyaco because of trouble with my father. I was hoping to go to Lima for nursing school, but I don't think that is possible now. Maybe I can get a job at the Iquitos hospital. I used to help out at the clinic in Tamshiyaco."

Eduardo turned to Mitch. "Will you return to trading with the oil workers?"

"My plans have changed, too. I lost my boat for not paying off the police chief, and the oil camp is closing. I think my only way to avoid being arrested is to sign on as an ocean ship's deckhand—if there are any docked in Iquitos."

"How long would you be at sea?" Eduardo asked.

"I don't know. Maybe a long time."

Tessa listened while staring at the floor. The rain suddenly stopped, and she left the shelter and walked to the front of the raft.

Mitch joined her and touched her back with his open hand, and she turned to him in tears.

"I keep losing people in my life, and now you are leaving me too. Why can't you work in Iquitos? You could drive boats or fix them, or something. You're smart. You can do anything."

"But if I'm caught, I could spend the rest of my life in prison. I have some money in the bank, but not enough to last long. And I promised half of it to Luis. Before I leave, I will give the other half to you. Maybe it will be enough to enroll in nursing—"

"I don't want your money, Mitch, and I don't want to be a nurse anymore. Maybe I can work with you on a ship. I know how to cook."

"A cargo ship is no place for a woman. I couldn't protect you."

***

As the sun sank below the treetop skyline, the four adults

shared Eduardo's bottle of warm beer in tin cups. Instead of feeling festive, the celebration fizzled along glumly while the raft drifted, with each of them sorting through their own thoughts. When night fell, the deck was still damp from rain, so everyone rolled into their blanket inside the shelter, except whoever's turn it was to keep a lonely watch under the vanilla half-moon.

***

Eduardo was on watch when Iquitos first came into view. It was a few miles downriver from the bend they were drifting around. Weak pre-dawn street lights made glowing halos in the haze above low buildings, and a few lighted households were already preparing for the day. Eduardo knelt on one knee in front of the shelter and shook Rosa's leg. She sat up blinking, then stepped around the sleepers to join him at the front of the raft. Mitch came next, and then Tessa. The four of them chewed beef jerky and dried fruit slices while the children slept, and watched Iquitos grow sharper as they drifted ever-closer.

After eating, Tessa and the men pushed and pulled on the oars to force the raft closer to the shoreline. They aimed for a stretch of riverfront with just a few boats tied to nearby trees. Eduardo said this would be a good place to beach the raft and tie it up. He said that whoever buys the raft will hire a boat to pull it to their chosen location.

When the sun rose to its mid-morning place in the sky, Eduardo gave Mitch a few Peruvian soles, worth about one dollar, for taxi fare to the bank. Tessa left with him and while on their way, they watched for police officers, ready to duck below the taxi's windows if they saw one. When they got to the bank, the teller, a fortyish pudgy woman, recognized

Mitch as a regular customer. She read his withdrawal slip, then counted out a stack of soles, a little more than two hundred dollars' worth.

Before they left the bank, he tried to give some of the money to Tessa, but she shook her head no.

"What will you do without money?"

"I'll stay at my brother's house for now, then look for a job. I know where he hid a door key, and where he hid some money inside."

"Someone might be watching for you. Not just a policeman, but maybe another assassin looking for Rafael's sister."

"I don't care."

"You say that to punish me."

"I say that to be honest, Mitch, not to hurt you. I don't want to leave you, but if I must, then I must take care of myself until you return. Goodbye." She started to cross the street, then stopped and looked back. "Please don't worry about me. Take care of yourself."

Mitch watched her jog across the street and disappear around a corner. He sprinted after her and grabbed her arm when he caught up. She spun around with tears streaming down her cheeks. "It hurt me to leave you just now, Mitch. I wish I hadn't, done it like that. I know you have to hide, but if you ask me to wait for you, I will wait forever if I have to."

They wrapped their arms around each other, and Tessa cried into his shoulder.

"Instead of just asking you to wait for me, I'm asking you to marry me when I return to Iquitos. I can't promise you anything but more trouble, Tessa, but I will always love you."

"Mitch...that's all I want."

Chapter 23

Mitch and Tessa went to Luis's house, and Mitch knocked on the door. Luis opened it and beamed.

"Mitch! Tessa! Come in!"

Luis turned and yelled "Gardenia, come and see a miracle."

Mitch said, "Getting back here might have been a miracle, Luis, but it was a very difficult miracle."

Everyone found a chair, except their two sons, who sat on the floor. Gardenia brought a tray of glasses and a pitcher of lemon water with a fresh chunk of ice floating in it. Mitch told them about Rafael's death and Darla's betrayal. Tessa explained how they fled from Huaraz in a potato truck, then down the Ucayali and Amazon rivers on a raft. Fantastical tales are common in this part of the world—some are at least partially true, some not at all—but Luis and his family were mesmerized by the bizarre adventures of Mitch and Tessa in exotic places they had heard of, but had never seen.

Mitch said "Most of our business money is still in the bank, Luis. I withdrew about a hundred dollars' worth for each of us before coming here. I added your name to the bank account, so you can withdraw more money whenever you need it."

"We have enough money for now," Luis said. "I have been

piloting boats to take tourists to a couple of nearby jungle camps. I just greet tourists at the airport, and take them directly to a thatched-roof longboat. After a few days in a luxurious camp, they return home without knowing anything about Iquitos or the real jungle. But I don't think they care."

"Does this job pay well?"

"Yes, and almost everyone tips me when they leave, especially the Americans. If you and I had a boat as big as Paraiso, we could deliver tourists to all the jungle camps around here and upriver. We would be rich."

"I have to leave Iquitos for a while, Luis, but first, Tessa and I have an announcement to make. I asked her to marry me this morning, and she accepted."

Gardenia clapped her hands. "Such wonderful news!

Luis said, "Congratulations to both of you. When is your wedding?"

"We haven't had time to talk about that. All this happened just a few minutes ago."

"You might not have to leave Iquitos, now," Luis said. "We have a new temporary police chief, and maybe you can buy Paraiso back from him."

"What happened to Chief Santos?"

"Three weeks ago, when he had his usual morning coffee at the downtown café, he discovered that someone added battery acid to his coffee."

"How did he discover that?" Tessa said.

"From choking to death. Until he can be replaced, a government lawyer from Lima was sent to manage the police department. A policeman I know told me that the lawyer complains all day about the heat, and he makes the officers work too hard, and he doesn't allow bribes. They hope he goes back to Lima soon."

Tessa turned to Mitch. "Maybe you have enough money in the bank to buy your boat back from this lawyer. He can't take it to Lima."

"I shouldn't have to pay for something I should rightly own."

"I know, Mitch, but rightly or not, you don't own it anymore." Pounding at the door startled Tessa and she bolted out of her chair.

Luis hurried to a front window and peeked out. "Police," he whispered. "Quickly, hide in the kitchen." Mitch and Tessa followed Gardenia into the kitchen.

When Luis opened the door, two police officers glared at him. One said "We have been sent by the acting chief of police to bring in a woman named Tessa Cortina. Do you know where she is?"

"Why does the police chief want her?"

"He didn't tell us, but it must be serious. Is she here?"

"No. I think she's in Lima."

Gardenia listened while she quietly helped Mitch and Tessa step up onto a kitchen chair and climb out the kitchen window. When they were out, she accidently bumped the chair against the table when putting it back.

One of the policemen hollered at Luis, "Who is back there? Answer me, or we'll arrest all of you!"

Luis said, "I don't know—"

They pushed him aside and stormed into the kitchen. Gardenia stared at them with wide eyes when she saw them pull their guns from their holsters. She backed out of the way when they ran to the open window. One of them hollered to his partner, "Let's go around to the back—I saw them running down the next street!"

The officers ran out the front door with Luis trying to keep up. "Don't shoot them," he shouted. "They are harmless."

Two officers had been watching the back of the house. One of them ran after Mitch and tackled him, then held him down while the other officer started to run after Tessa.

Tessa stopped and turned. "Leave him alone! I'm Tessa Cortina, the sister of Rafael. I'm the one you want. I will go with you, but first let him go free."

Mitch stood and said, "No, I'm Mitchel Winslow. I'm the one you want. Not her."

The officer who tackled him said, "We know about you, Winslow, but no one wants you now. Our temporary chief will explain everything to Señorita Cortina at our headquarters."

Mitch said, "Then I want to go with her."

"All right, but don't make me chase either of you anymore. I don't get paid enough for that."

Chapter 24

When they arrived at police headquarters, one of the officers told Mitch and Tessa to sit on a bench near the entrance. The officer stood guard while the other one tapped on the chief's office door, then went in to his office.

Mitch said to her, "I think this is about Rafael—I mean, Estevan. I'll tell them you had nothing to do with his organization."

Tessa said, "They cannot punish my brother now, so I think they want to punish me."

"I'm a witness to what happened, Tessa."

"They will doubt your honesty, and they won't want to believe me."

"Then I'll find a good lawyer. Someone who knows the judges around here."

The officer who went into the chief's office came out and ushered Tessa and Mitch into the office, then left and closed the door behind him.

A short balding man in a crisp open-collar white business shirt hand-motioned for each of them to take a chair in front of his desk.

"My name is Alberto Diaz. Are you Señorita Cortina?"

"Yes, and please tell me why I am here."

"Of course, but first I'd like to know who you brought along."

"I'm Mitch Winslow."

"And, Mister Winslow, what is your relationship with Miss Cortina?"

"I'm her fiancé."

Tessa peeked a smile at him.

"Congratulations to both of you. Now, Tessa—if I may address you informally—first of all, you are here because of a legal issue with a certain vessel."

"I'm the one you want," Mitch said. "That is, or *was,* my boat. I take full responsibility—"

"Please, Mitch, let me finish. It is no longer legally your boat. The former police chief had lawfully confiscated it."

"That was a setup," Mitch said.

"Perhaps you can get a good lawyer and sue the city of Iquitos, but wait until we're finished here. Chief Santos had sold the boat to Rafael Domingo, who is deceased. We received his remains yesterday from a morgue in Huaraz, with instructions to contact you regarding funeral instructions. Did you know about this, Tessa?"

"Rafael was my brother and I know he died."

"My condolences to you."

"Thank you."

"A local funeral home will help you make burial arrangements."

"All right."

"Did you know that your brother took legal title to the boat in question, both in his name and equally in your name?"

"No…"

"Well, congratulations again. You are now sole owner of a boat. Title to his house was also in both your names, so ownership reverts to you. That means you are now the sole remaining owner. Your next visit should be to the local bank, because I've been told they have documentation that made you co-owner, and now sole owner, of his accounts. I suggest you move your money to a secret account in a Caribbean bank before someone makes a claim against you."

"Like who?" Mitch asked.

Diaz stood. "Like the Peruvian government, for past income taxes. That advice is my marriage present. You may go now, and I wish both of you well. At least you won't start your lives together in poverty."

Chapter 25

The next day, Tessa asked Mitch to request her father's permission to marry her. Even though his answer would be predictably positive, observing that traditional respect would help heal any lingering strife between Tessa and her father—and lessen any misgivings about his future son-in-law.

The wedding took place three months later, a respectable amount of time according to Tessa's father, and because it took that long to reserve a marriage date at the Catholic church in Iquitos.

During that engagement period, Luis contracted with four more remote jungle camps to greet and transport tourists to the all-inclusive camps aboard Paraiso. Tessa and Mitch split the profits with him. This arrangement freed Mitch enough to negotiate the purchase of a local collectivo company, which included two aging double-deck passenger boats. He and Tessa planned to restore the boats and increase passenger safety with careful maintenance, thorough crew training, limiting the number of passengers, and carrying enough floating throw rings to rescue all passengers.

When Mitch had first inspected Paraiso after leaving the police chief's office, it appeared that no one had used it since he tied it up at the Nanay River. He found the luminescent mushroom that the night hunter chief had given him, still sitting where he had left it above the instrument panel. After they bought the collectivo business, he broke the mushroom into three pieces, leaving one where it was on Paraiso's instrument panel, and wrapped the other two in clear plastic to mount aboard each of their new vessels' instrument panels.

***

One day, Mitch used his new satellite phone to call his sheriff deputy friend in northern Minnesota. The deputy said the district attorney had dropped the investigation against him. The shotgun pellets could not be traced to the gun that fired them, and the expended shell casing was never found. Although Mitch had an obvious motive, the district attorney didn't have enough evidence to build a convincing case.

***

The day before the wedding, Luis took Paraiso to Tamshiyaco to pick up Tessa's father. Her father stayed with her and Mitch that night in the grand riverside house that, unknown to him, once belonged to his son, Estevan. Mitch and Tessa, of course, slept in separate bedrooms that night. Until they could hear her father peacefully snoring.

The local tailor who made Tessa's wedding dress, also made a suit for Mitch and for Luis, who was Mitch's best man. Invited guests showed up randomly throughout the ceremony—such non-punctuality being customary and perfectly acceptable, and even expected, in Peru.

The reception party was at Marcel DuPreise's *Restaurante del Selva*. Marcel had a large party canopy erected outside to accommodate an expected overflow crowd. Unbeknown to her father, Tessa had paid for most of the extravagant, expensive reception dinner.

Even Marcel wore a tight-fitting suit for the occasion that night. He closely orchestrated the cooks, bartenders, and dining room crew, but took time to bring two pisco sour cocktails and sit briefly with Mitch while Tessa danced with her father.

Marcel said, "Your bride is beautiful tonight."

"Yes, in many ways."

"Will you be returning with her to the United States, now that you are free to?"

"There's no longer anything to return to, Marcel. Like with you, everything I want is right here."

THE END

Please visit JamesLuger.com to preview my first suspense-romance novel, "Lost in Dalat."

While there, you can sign up for advanced notices of forthcoming books.

-- JL